Normally the True Queen Shaia, hidden within her young daughter, Princess Marjia, kept up with the affairs of state. But today she was absent.

Wizenbeak went into the grand bedroom and found Lady Djilas sitting on the bed holding Princess Marjia's hand. Marjia looked somehow . . . different. "Our little Marjia had a bad nightmare last night," the lady in waiting said.

Something is a whole lot worse than that, the wizard thought. "What sort of dream was it?"

Then, suddenly, Marjia blurted it out. "I don't remember anything since the day we escaped from the palace!"

That was the moment when Shaia's spirit entered her body, Wizenbeak thought unhappily. Shaia gone?

"It could be a sorcerous attack of some kind," Lady Djilas said.

"I want my Mommy," Marjia said.

This whiny kid is my beloved wife, Wizenbeak thought resignedly. "Well, Marjia darling, we have some good news and some bad news. The good news is that you are Queen of Guhland. The bad news is that your mother is dead, your father is dead, your brother is dead, and I am your husband."

By Alexis A. Gilliland
Published by Ballantine Books:

WIZENBEAK
THE SHADOW SHAIA
LORD OF THE TROLL-BATS

THE END OF THE EMPIRE

LORD OF THE TROLL-BATS

Alexis A. Gilliland

A Del Rey Book
BALLANTINE BOOKS • NEW YORK

A Del Rey Book
Published by Ballantine Books

Library of Congress Catalog Card Number: 91-93147

ISBN 0-345-37467-3

Manufactured in the United States of America

First Edition: May 1992

I'D LIKE TO DEDICATE THIS BOOK TO LESTER DEL REY.
YOUR EDITOR!? I THOUGHT YOU WANTED TO POUR HOT LEAD IN HIS SHOES!
LORD OF THE TROLL-BATS
AV 91

What Has Gone Before

CIVIL war in Guhland had become inevitable when the old king died. Prince Kahun, Prince Gatsack, and their youthful stepmother, Shaia, called the Witch-Queen, acting on behalf of her minor son, Prince Dervian, were implacable enemies.

In the months before the death of King Grathnys, Dr. Wizenbeak, a mountebank, troll-bat husbandman, water-wizard, and minor-league agent for Prince Gatsack's faction, was sent into the northern wastelands to found a colony. En route, he rescued an accused witch from burning, and, recognizing Jankura's natural talent, made her his apprentice.

On the death of Grathnys, Prince Kahun seized the throne of Guhland, directing a mob against the Royal Palace which tore Shaia into unrecognizable pieces. Before the mob killed her, however, Shaia had arranged to send her children to safety and cast a spell so that when she died her spirit would enter the body of her daughter, Marjia. After defeating Prince Gatsack in a winter campaign, Prince Kahun made himself first king and then patriarch of the Syncretist Church. As king-patriarch, he rewarded the witchfinder faction that had supported him by unleashing them on the people of Guhland.

Himself condemned as a witch, Wizenbeak had already begun resistance against the witchfinders when Dervian and Marjia appeared upon his doorstep. Disguising Jankura as the missing Queen Shaia, Wizenbeak raised the standard of rebellion. Fighting with mercenaries rejoining their queen, half-trained volunteers, and a few good troll-bats, Wizenbeak defeated the successively larger armies sent against him until

Kahun was killed, and Jankura, still posing as Shaia, was placed on the throne of Guhland. Archdeacon Gorabani, a voice of moderation in the Church, became the new patriarch.

As Regent for Prince Dervian, Jankura was immediately confronted with invasion from abroad and treason at home. As a reward for his past success, Wizenbeak was promoted to archdeacon and put in command of the Tarelian Order, the mighty arm of the Church Militant. He continued to display his unlooked-for genius as a general, defeating the invaders in a brilliant campaign. Meanwhile, doing what was politically necessary, Jankura crushed a minor but dangerous conspiracy of witchfinders. Patriarch Gorabani, humiliated and outraged at her tactics, abandoned moderation to organize a coup d'état with the full support of the Church.

The coup failed, but Prince Dervian was killed, ending the Regency. Jankura, exposed as a pretender, stood with the Royal Army surrounding the Tarelian Order, which is defending Patriarch Gorabani. Princess Marjia discovered the only way out: *first* Wizenbeak must make himself patriarch, and *then*, having proven himself worthy, he must marry her in order to make himself king-patriarch of Guhland. Civil war was thus averted, and Jankura was enabled to step down, as Gorabani chose prison over martyrdom.

Offstage

On the other side of the mountains, a crisis has been building in troll-bat society. Dragons they were used to, dragons were easy, troll-bats had coevolved with dragons. Humans, however, were a recent, withing the last millennium, acquisition, and the far more useful humans were also far more difficult. The question of whether human livestock is sentient or not has split the trives of troll-bats into warring factions. The practice of breeding humans for stupidity and docility had been ignored by the laissez-faire troll-bats of Goldentrive, who prospered mightily in consequence. As a result, Goldentrive now finds itself estranged from its traditional allies and threatened with extermination by its bitter enemies. The only escape is a long-forgotten path under the mountains.

1

Man Is Born to Trouble . . .

GORABANI, the clerisiarch . . . the former clerisiarch who had so recently been patriarch of the Syncretist Church, sat in the gloom of his cell, telling his beads with a notable lack of concentration. It was not a bad cell, he reflected bitterly, eight by eight feet, with a tiny slit for a window set higher than he could reach to admit a modicum of fresh air and sunlight. A few pallid rays shone through for an hour or two each day, barely enough illumination to read those few scrolls his gaolers had grudgingly permitted him. Freshly whitewashed in his honor though it had been, the cell remained dark and still smelled of must and cold stone. And even if he weren't shackled to the wall, it was still a prison.

A key rattled in the lock, and his door swung slowly inward. It wasn't mealtime; perhaps they were going to bring him the candle he had asked for. Three men entered his cell. The first, wearing the simple black robes of a lay brother, he recognized as his old friend and ally, Archdeacon Darussis. Behind him were two guards, the larger one plumpish, the smaller one wiry and angular.

"There he is," the larger guard said.

The archdeacon nodded and smiled without warmth. His face was more lined than the former patriarch remembered, and his eyes remained hidden in shadow. "Doctor Gorabani, I presume?"

Oh? "We've met already, Doctor Darussis. What can I do for you?"

The smaller of the two guards hit the larger one from behind, catching him under the arms and lowering him silently to the floor.

"Change clothes with our friend here, your Holiness," the pudgy clerisiarch replied grimly. "We're breaking you out of this place."

Swiftly Gorabani slipped on the guard's uniform as the other two put his own garments onto the unconscious man and lifted him onto the hard wooden cot.

Darussis took out a vial of clear liquid and looked at it for a moment. "I feel bad about this," he said. "Yukje here refused to take our money, going to all that trouble because he was loyal to our cause." He opened Yukje's mouth and emptied the vial into it. The man coughed, swallowed, and died.

The archdeacon folded the dead fingers around the empty vial and adjusted the rough wool blanket over the body. Feeling around in his pouch, he then removed a wide-mouth jar and carefully worked lose the cork stopper. Setting the open jar down on the blanket, Darussis produced a small parchment envelope, from which he emptied a reddish powder into the jar. He then stirred the hissing, bubbling mixture with a pair of wooden sticks for a few seconds until the foam crested and broke. It smells like new-mown hay, Gorabani thought. How could such nasty stuff seem so agreeable? When it was sufficiently viscous, the archdeacon poured it over the dead face of the guard and began reciting a mantra as he worked the stuff into approximately the shape he wanted with the wooden sticks. Presently Darussis switched both sticks into his left hand and ran his right hand over Gorabani's face.

After the mantra's third or fourth iteration, the jelly began to assume Gorabani's likeness, the high cheekbones and beaked nose appearing first, then the more subtle lines of character. The changes became progressively less noticeable, and after the eleventh iteration Darussis was satisfied. He spoke the phrase which set the mask, wiped off the sticks with a rag, and dropped the rag in the jar, along with the parchment envelope. Then he restoppered the jar and put it in his pouch. "This will give us time to shake clear of pursuit, your Holiness," he said, dropping the sticks beside the jar. "At least it betters the odds. Now let's go. It were a shame to waste the gift which Yukje bought for us so dearly."

"Where are we going?"

"Out," the guard said. "If we get clear, when we get clear, we'll tell you anything you want to know." He had a mediplano accent one could cut with a knife. "Sir."

Gorabani nodded. As they closed the cell door behind them, the guard plucked at his sleeve. "Lock the door, sir," he said softly. "The keys are on your belt."

"To be sure," the former patriarch agreed, holding up the iron ring with a score of keys jingling from it.

Which one? he wondered. Then he remembered—not which key—but the solution to the general problem. He didn't even have to recite the mantra as a mnemonic to recall the spell. He just ran one long forefinger over the keys and selected the one that felt tacky. Clerisiarchs of the Syncretist Church were not supposed to practice magic, but they were obliged to understand it, a fructifying paradox not always honored in the pressure of day-to-day existence.

The key turned in the lock, the bolt shot home with satisfying smoothness, and the three men walked down the corridor to freedom.

"You're too soft to be any sort of king," Queen Marjia said. "Way too soft. You ought to stop fooling around and have Gorabani killed."

Wizenbeak looked up from his cluttered desk. "My dear," he said. "I didn't hear you come in."

She pulled up a chair and sat down, a graceless, flouncing move that reflected the age and training of her prepubescent body rather than the steely spirit within. "My dear." She sneered, mocking his manner of speech. "My *dear*! Why I married you, I'll never know!"

This was a reprise of an old argument. They both knew why she had married him, but he already knew better than to remind her that it had been her idea. Or even that it might have been the best that could have been done in the circumstances immediately following his rather unceremonious elevation to the patriarchy. He changed the subject. "What has Gorabani done now?"

"Nothing. He just is." Marjia shook her pretty blond head in a gesture that would have expressed grimness in her mother, who had been known as the Witch-Queen, but came across as mere petulance in her. "One of these days that son of a bitch is going to escape, and when he does, half of Guhland is going to be ready to kick off the civil war again."

"Play differently, lose differently," the king-patriarch said, adjusting the black velvet cap of maintenance on his head. "With Gorabani under lock and key, the opposition can't move. Kill him, they'd select someone else who'd make us all sorts of trouble running around loose. Besides . . ." he fell silent.

She made a face. On her mother it would have been a scowl, but she was too plump and smooth for it to be much of anything. "Besides, you promised, didn't you?"

"What? Not to take the life?" He shrugged. "It's true. A king ought not to break his promises just because it's convenient. Or because his wife is starting at shadows."

Marjia chose to ignore the wizard's jibe and turned her attention to his desk. "What's this garbage you're working on?"

"The usual. Matters of consequence. Affairs of state. What kings do when they aren't strutting about on parade."

His queen picked up one of the scrolls and read off the title. *"Brujao's Commentary on Saint Posalanji's Order for the Regulation Of Troll-Bats?"* She shook her blond head. "Are you still wasting time trying to rationalize the laws on troll-bats?"

Wizenbeak sat back in his chair and folded his hands across his lean midriff. "Why not?" he asked. "The Syncretist Church has one set of regulations, the state of Guhland has another, both of which are rotten with exemptions."

A draft fluttered the candle flames, stirring the shadows around the room into uneasy motion. "Well, sure, for the glass industry." Using the raw materials provided by their master, troll-bats made mother-of-glass. Mother-of-glass was a water-soluble powder, the solution of which dried naturally to a glass, or it could be made to form a gel which became a glass upon steaming. "A lot of money there."

"And a different set for the medical profession, darling. A lot of money there, too."

Marjia put the scroll back on his desk. "What about the charlatans, mountebanks, and bush wizards like yourself? What of them?"

"Well, what about them?" He pushed his emerald spectacles

back on his nose. "Speaking from personal experience, the money isn't there. So we regulate the hell out of the poor bastards, but they work with troll-bats because it's a living."

A slow exhalation of breath. "When I was a girl, you know, I studied Brujao. And later I learned Ursprach so I could read Saint Posalanji in the original. You know what I found? Her original text had been altered back in antiquity." She rested her chin on one hand. "You could see where words or paragraphs had been scraped off the parchment and a different hand had written in something stupid."

"How did you get in to see the original?" The archives were kept by monks, and women were strictly forbidden.

She giggled, an incongruous sound. "That was a long time ago in another country, and besides, the wench is dead."

"You don't think we ought to do something?" Wizenbeak asked, pulling at his mustache. "Hell, when I was a kid, I cleaned out my dad's hutches for him. All my life I've worked around troll-bats, and now I—" He blinked and shifted to the royal we. "As king-patriarch, we have a chance to put a hand to that crazy patchwork of laws and make something rational out of it."

"No." Marjia sat pondering the matter for a moment. "Well, maybe. If you want to study the matter, it couldn't hurt, I suppose." She sat back in her chair, swinging one leg that didn't quite reach the floor. "The issue will never go away, you know."

"Hunh? What are you telling us?"

"It's like a pendulum, you understand? The Orthodox came in with a very strict attitude on sex and troll-bats. Over time they loosened up—sex because people are people, troll-bats because the little monsters are so damned useful. Naturally, the people who *could* took advantage of the ones who couldn't or didn't know how, so that Syncretism was born out of ignorance and fear. And wouldn't you know, right off the mark they were very, very strict on troll-bats. And the people who used them."

"Sex, too, of course," the wizard added. "It comes with the territory."

Marjia nodded in agreement. "Sublimation of the sexual urge gives you both the energy and the inclination to beat on people. Or burn them. Time passed, and Syncretism loosened up eventually, but there wasn't room for a new church, so we had the 'reforms' of Mambrino and his needle, and witch burning was back with a vengeance."

"And Mambrino tried to wipe out the troll-bats, only he failed."

"Or he failed first. Eventually the Syncretists loosened up *again*. So when my stepson, the ever-so-pious Prince Kahun, started moving against me, the first thing he tried was magic. Well, hell, I was better at it than he was."

"Right, right," the wizard said. "That was about the time I got involved with palace politics."

"So when magic didn't work, the natural way for Kahun to go was to denounce me as the 'Witch-Queen' and dust off Mambrino's abandoned 'reforms' to bring me down."

"Only it wasn't time yet," Wizenbeak said, "and when he loosed the witchfinders on the land, he sparked a rebellion, burning too many people for the wrong reasons."

Marjia smiled and kicked her foot. "Which we won, kind of. At least we're here and he isn't. Do you see now why working over the troll-bat laws is a dumb idea?"

"All right, this was something I knew but didn't really appreciate. The way you put it, troll-bats are what have been driving the whole of our history."

Queen Marjia pulled her legs onto the chair and looked at him over her knees. "Absolutely. The Church clamps down on the little monsters as hard as they can, compounding troll-bats with sexual morality, and then things slowly loosen up until the next time. Sweet reason has very little to do with it. Hey, you want to leave your mark on Guhland, stick to something noncontroversial, like land reform."

If humans had had trouble with the integration of troll-bats into their civilization, the reverse was also true. On the other side of the mountains that marked the end of the world on the maps of Guhland, the Honorable Kachkas of some of the several trives of troll-bats that inhabited that part of the world gathered together to discuss the resolution of issues touching on that most useful and aggravating domestic animal, the human.

"What ought to be done about Goldentrive?" The question was couched in a code relying heavily on olfactory cues, great chords of aromatic fragrance pungent with historic resonance, rich with allusive association.

There was a stirring among the assembled troll-bats. Trouble had been expected and trouble had arrived. "They are the flesh of our flesh, our own beloved kin," was the response, a choral restatement of conventional wisdom missing many of its accustomed voices. "Why should we do anything?"

"Goldentrive has become impudent," a reply came, tinged with the cinnamon of hidden envy and the new-mown grass of apprehension. "They no longer defer to the greater wisdom of Sisulia Trive. They spurn the advice of our Honorable Kachkas and rely on their own strength to resolve disputes."

The assembly repeated the last two sentences with variations, concluding with a rhetorical flourish, "Our beloved kinder no longer defer to their parents, Sisulia Trive. They spurn our Honorable Kachkas. Can this grief be long endured? Must these insults go unredressed?"

"Momentous questions, truly," a new voice said, a quartet rather than a chorus, sharply focused and redolent with an alien suite of odors. "The dragons of Hashma Trive have been engaged with Goldentrive, your so-illustrious sept, for these many long months. Goldentrive, making a virtue of a necessity, has restructured their order of battle to use fewer of their young males by granting greater autonomy to their animals."

The protest was purely formal, almost a whisper, repeated for emphasis. "Animals cannot behave autonomously. Animals cannot act autonomously. Animals cannot fight autonomously."

"Dragons cannot," Hashma agreed, "but we have, of course, domesticated other animals in the historical past which remain dangerously close to their feral roots."

"Animals cannot fight autonomously!" The protest was stronger now, a denial of unwanted reality.

"Wild animals survive without our intervention," the Hashma quartet replied with the faintest touch of resinous asperity. "Dragons, domesticated from the beginning of recorded time, cannot survive without the most demanding husbandry. But humans, as is well known, become feral all too easily."

The assembly stirred, and the voice, the collective voice, a small chorus of Goldentrive's Honorable Kachkas, laughed sarcastically. The actual sensory expression was three kinds of musk superimposed on blooming heather underlain with a hint of carrion. "The embassy of Hashma Trive surely seeks to excuse the lamentable performance of their arms by claiming that Goldentrive has used ferals against them. Absurd! Totally ridiculous! War cannot be waged by wild animals. War requires discipline of the highest order."

"Yet your young males are not controlling their animals on the field of battle." This from an unexpectedly large number of the Honorable Kachkas of Sisulia Trive. "Not even the dragons."

"This is a matter of training," the cool reply came. "We have for so long been accustomed to directing our dragons in the most minute detail, it has become the conventional wisdom that every animal should be led the same way. Humans are smarter than dragons."

There was a general laugh among the assembled troll-bats. To be smarter than a dragon was the opposite of high praise. "How, then, do you train your war animals?"

"How do you train any animal?" was the reply. "You teach them to do what they can at your command. For a dragon, direction and speed; strike with the tail or strike with the head; bite to hold or bite to slash. Commands so simple even a human can give them!"

"As you see," the Hashma quartet said. "Under the press of battle, Goldentrive has granted its animals an unprecedented degree of autonomy. A Hashma dragon flies into battle with its pair of human archers, each under control of a young male warrior to order and direct performance, a young male to direct the dragon and a senior male warrior in overall command. How are the dragons of Goldentrive led into battle?"

"Much the same as yours, Honorable Kachkas. Two human archers, one of whom is charged with directing the dragon, a senior male warrior to command." The fungal aroma of the assembly's dissatisfaction was palpable, and Goldentrive felt obliged to expand its answer. "Often a young male goes with them to be trained in the arts of war."

"Autonomy think you, Honorable Kachkas? Our kith of Hashma Trive, who have borne us little love in the past, has claimed it to be so." Sisulia Trive pondered the question for a moment. "Perhaps a commission should be formed to look into the question of autonomy."

"A worthy suggestion," a sextet snapped, cutting themselves out of Goldentrive's main group. "An honorable suggestion. Our beloved parents maintain the strictest neutrality between their own kinder and the distant kith of Hashma Trive in a war that ought to be shared by all. And when the Hashma embassy comes before this assembly to complain that they aren't winning, the Honorable Kachkas of Sisulia propose a commission to see if they approve of the way Goldentrive wages war."

"Giving autonomy to animals is a serious charge, Goldentrive. Ferality, as you must surely understand, could undermine our civilization."

"If we were not fighting for our lives, we might display more sympathy for your theories of animal husbandry," the sextet replied, and then, bringing in the whole chorus of Goldentrive, "What about arranging a truce, which was the pretext which brought us to this place?"

"No truce," Hashma declared coldly. "No truce, no truce, no truce with those who would destroy us." The suite of odors in "us" suggested that Hashma Trive and the troll-bat civilization were equally threatened.

The assembled troll-bats debated the question of a commission at interminable length, at last deciding to appoint one. However, as a concession to Goldentrive, the Honorable Kachkas of Sisulia Trive agreed once again to deliver forty dragons which had long since been paid for.

2

. . . As the Sparks Fly Upward

THE short, wiry guard who had earlier introduced himself as Edsvart Olmsby and asked for Gorabani's blessing brought in breakfast from the canal boat's tiny galley. Now dressed as an unemployed mercenary, he unfolded the dark wood table from the white-painted wall and set a pot of coffee on it, with flatbread and hard cheese on a wooden platter. Pulling mugs and tableware out of a cupboard, he then went topside to chat with the deckhands and generally keep an eye on things. They were among friends, but it was best to be watchful.

"Well, I've told you the basic story three or four times already," Darussis said, filling his cup. "The drama of what happened after you got taken out of the picture, so to speak. If I knew what you were looking for, I could give you a better picture, focus in on the important details."

"If we knew which details were important," Gorabani conceded, "you could tell me one time only, and I'd have it right. Everything I needed to know, all laid out for me." He sighed. Rehashing the details was a harmless enough way to pass the time. "The wedding, now. Did you hear any gossip?"

The archdeacon took a sip of coffee and made a wry face; boatmen liked it brewed strong, yes, indeed. "The royal wedding? You want the gossip on a royal wedding? Oh, come on." Gazing out the open door, he watched a line of newly leafed willow trees slip past the canal boat as the shore drifted away. Gorabani prompted him.

"Oh, yes. The royal wedding. After his brilliant military so-called career Patriarch Wizenbeak married Princess Marjia to secure his claim to the throne of Guhland. Dignity is called for, right? At the ceremony, the story was that he'd stuffed his codpiece with a hard salami and you could smell the garlic nine rows back."

There was a sigh. "Very funny, Darussis," the other said, filling his own cup. "Your first problem is that you talk only to your friends, and all your friends hate old Wizenbeak like poison. Your second problem is that you repeat yourself unmercifully. You keep telling me about that damn salami, and they smell the garlic farther back each time. What did you hear about Marjia?"

"Dirty jokes," he said sullenly. "She's what, thirteen? Talk about your May and December marriages. That's what people talk about, anyway."

The boat turned as the canal changed direction, faithfully following the line of least resistance around a rocky hill the river had cut through, as Gorabani shaded his eyes against the glare of the morning sunlight bouncing off the water. "So you heard nothing. What about the coronation?"

The archdeacon sliced off a piece of cheese with his knife and ate it. "A big show, but tasteless. Marjia was featured to emphasize the legitimacy of a certain useless wizard. Did you hear the one about the salad chef and Marjia's—" He checked himself. "I expect I told you already."

Gorabani nodded and picked up a piece of flatbread. "And Marjia's hairdresser? Yes, yes. It was funny the first time." He took a bite of the bread and chewed it reflectively. "There might be a pattern in this, a trinity, forming the points of the nabla if we could only see it." He broke the bread in three pieces. "Wizenbeak, the mountebank risen far above his station. Princess Marjia, whom you and your friends discount totally." He held up the third piece of bread and looked at it. "And someone else."

"You wish to count Marjia as significant?" Darussis smiled politely and shook his head, dismissing the idea. "She's nothing. A child. A girl child at that. A pawn to be pushed about the board by any strong hand that can reach her."

"Ah, indeed. After . . ." The former patriarch hesitated. The thought of the Saint Posalanji's Day assassination, which he had ordered, stirred up a cloud of self-justifying apologies in his mind. It had come so close and broken so badly . . . He scowled as he recited the mantra for calmness, and then, as that mantra was beginning to bite, he recited the synergistic form of the mantra for clarity of thought.

As they took hold, he began to focus on what was important today, not on what he had done in the past, or should have done, but on Princess Marjia. Was she the key to the present? Perhaps. It would depend on what she had done, on what she had been in the past. "After her brother, King Dervian, was slain, the princess wound up with Wizenbeak." He nibbled at the third piece of bread and took a sip of coffee. "What strong hand pushed her into his grasp?"

The other rested chin in hand and scowled. There had been several reports from eyewitnesses, and on that point they agreed about what had happened. The hysterical little girl, suddenly released from the threat of instant death, had run directly to the wizard, leaping into his arms, in fact. Then there had been a brief conference, after which the regent and her generals had gone off, leaving Wizenbeak holding the princess. In hindsight, it was an appalling mistake for the regent to have made, especially after the death of Dervian. The pudgy archdeacon shook his head.

"Nobody, your Holiness. In the confusion of the Saint Posalanji, it just happened."

"Maybe, maybe not." Gorabani took another sip of coffee. That country girl pretending to be the Witch-Queen, the regent for the youthful King Dervian, might very well have been too shaken to consider long-term strategy. And one of her generals—it would have been the older one, Genzari—had been wounded in her defense. Say he was in shock. But *someone* in the regent's party would have asked for custody of the princess. He was sure of it; she was their key to the future. Only in the confusion of the moment, the regent's people had been told no, and they had taken no for an answer. Wizenbeak? Never. Shaken as they were, if the wizard had said he wasn't giving the princess back to them, the flag would have gone up right then. So that left . . . Marjia herself.

"It could have been happenstance," Gorabani said at last, holding his mug of coffee in both hands. But the location of Princess Marjia had been critical to Wizenbeak's becoming first patriarch and then king. Clearly it seemed as if Marjia herself had chosen where she wanted to be. This would have been a heavy load for a thirteen-year-old child to carry. So the question was: Why did Marjia choose Wizenbeak? A father figure, perhaps? After the fact it was evident that she had chosen wisely, brilliantly even, BUT. She was thirteen, and he was lean and old and ugly, not a young girl's beau ideal by any manner of means. Never mind power politics; at thirteen she ought to have shunned him utterly. Gorabani's eyes caught the sunlight dancing on the wooden paneling, and he repeated the mantra for clarity of thought.

Outside, a fish jumped in the canal, making a splash. The reflected sunlight on the wall danced as the ripples moved through the water and a memory surfaced effortlessly in the clerisiarch's mind.

"The results were ambiguous," he said softly.

Darussis raised his eyebrows in polite inquiry. "Oh?"

"Long ago, when Prince Kahun took the throne. Remember how the mob sacked the Royal Palace and Queen Shaia was killed, and her body was mutilated beyond recognition?" The pudgy archdeacon nodded. "We tried various spells to verify that Shaia was indeed dead. The answers were basically yes and no."

"I remember," said the other, who had done much of the work, "but what has that to do with anything?"

"That maybe, perhaps, the Witch-Queen lives on in the body of her daughter," was the answer.

The archdeacon pursed his lips. Mowpater's spell to slip the fist of death was a classic, known to every serious student of the art. The only drawback was that to try it, you had to commit yourself to dying . . . and there had never been a confirmed success.

"Think about it," Gorabani continued. "After the sack of the palace, the only people of consequence who escaped were the children, Prince Dervian and Princess Marjia. They turn up in the north, and lo, Wizenbeak leads the rebellion against King Kahun." The former patriarch finished his coffee and put the cup down. "Dervian gets installed as king, just as his mother would have wanted."

There was a pause. "What about the country girl, the Shadow Shaia?"

"Jankura? That would have been her name, yes. A nice touch, that, confusing the issue no end. We were deceived and struck at the pretend Shadow Shaia instead of the real one, even when we *knew* that she was an impostor." Gorabani folded his arms and sat back against the bulkhead. "So go back to the Saint Posalanji. Princess Marjia runs to Wizenbeak, but who is the strong hand that decides Marjia is going to stay with the old fool? The steely spirit of Queen Shaia."

Archdeacon Darussis looked thoughtful. He had never been able to get an unambiguous reading on the death of Shaia, and nobody could definitely say that Mowpater's spell *didn't* work. As a working hypothesis this might have some slight promise. "That could be worth our consideration," he conceded. "Princess Marjia is nothing, but if she is somehow animated by her mother's spirit . . ." The sentence trailed off into silence.

"Think about it, then. Wizenbeak does her bidding, and bang! I'm out as patriarch. What choice did I have? The next day Patriarch Wizenbeak meets with our little pretender and her generals and tells them he's going to marry Marjia and make himself king-patriarch, and bang! The Shadow Shaia is out, too. By then she was in even worse shape than I had been. No choice for her, either."

"You still think Wizenbeak is part of a triad?"

"Yes, absolutely! Triads are magical! Wizenbeak and Princess Marjia and, ah . . ." He hesitated. "Someone."

"The spirit of Queen Shaia?" Darussis prompted.

"No, no. By now Shaia figures to be pretty much at one with her daughter. My choice for the third member of that triad would have to be the country girl . . . what's her name, Jankura. The one who was pretending to be the queen. Whatever the hell became of her, anyway?"

A shrug. "She dropped out of sight right after surrendering the Royal Army."

"Interesting," Gorabani said. "Very interesting. Find out what happened to her."

Darussis opened his diptych and made a note in the soft wax with his stylus.

* * *

Alerted by his archer's warning, the Bythanna commander quickly spotted the three Hashma dragons two thousand feet below them, undulating toward the Goldentrive positions on Thornbush Ridge. "Hey, great!" he said. "Yosie, keep altitude until we get the sun lined up behind us." His driver nodded her close-cropped blond head. "Julia, I see those three enemy worms below. Are there any more?"

"Yes, actually," his archer replied. "Leading and below them are another three."

Six to four, Bythanastros mused, but we'll take the first shot and come out heading into our own territory.

"Good thinking," Julia said, catching his articulated thought. "It holds just as well at nine to four, too."

She spotted another three, thought the troll-bat. Oh, hell. Pulling himself together, he formally addressed the warrior under his command, a well-born young troll-bat from the Arvesthanas group who was leading the second of their two pairs of dragons. A touch of wild honey with overtones of woodspice conveyed authority with experience. The command itself was articulated in Ursprach, the human speech-analog, both because he wanted the humans to understand it and because it could be agreeably unambiguous. "Arvesthanas, we both go for the point worm on the top three. After that, hit for the same group with me. Understand?" The reply was a whiff of grass smoke, hot, acrid, and eager. The younger troll-bat had received trive-training, but this was his first battle experience in real life.

Then they had the sun at their backs, and without waiting for any further orders, Yosie kicked the lead dragon into a dive. The dragon on Bythanastros' right, charged with keeping hostile worms off his tail, followed at once. On his left Arvesthanas, startled at the speed of their reaction or perhaps at the lack of orders, led his pair into the fray a half second later.

Julia's first shaft hit the forward Hashma archer in the center of the back; her second embedded itself in the side of the dragon just above the middle pair of wings. They swept downward toward the trio of dragons on the right. Bythanastros looked back as an arrow whistled past his ears and saw his support dragon slam its head against the side of the attacking Hashma dragon, hitting the rear archer with its tail as it went past. The archer was knocked from her seat, but the lifeline saved her from falling.

Good, Bythanastros thought. That will slow up the whole crew and maybe spoil her aim for a while. Then they were upon the enemy below. A Hashma dragon lunged for them, jaws agape, and Yosie, holding her mount under control with her legs, thrust at the oncoming head with the butt of her spear. The spear caught between the leathery lip and the pale pinkish gum line, and they swerved as the thrust of the enemy worm pushed them out of the way of its bite. Julia loosed a shaft at the lead archer but aimed low, her shaft grazing the slick scaly side of his dragon and glancing off to skewer the Hashma warrior that had been sitting on her target's shoulder. The deflected arrow tumbled end over end with the shocked and dying troll-bat near the middle of the shaft.

Then they were over Thornbush Ridge, the four of them spiraling slowly above Goldentrive territory as they gained altitude. The nine Hashma dragons had formed into a defensive circle, wasting their arrows by loosing them at the entrenched enemy from a great height. They made no effort to engage the smaller number of dragons that had kept them from launching an effective attack and, after a while, drifted back across the valley.

"Not too shabby," Julia said after they had resumed altitude. "I counted two empty saddles, and one of the rear archers wasn't shooting, just hanging on."

"Bythanastros!" It was young Arvesthanas, boiling with sixteen scents of humiliation and rage. "I had a perfect chance at the lead dragon's throat, absolutely perfect, and when I gave the command, my animal, Rose, acknowledged it and refused to obey! She must be punished! She must be made to obey her lawful master! I demand that the full measure of the law be invoked upon her!"

The older troll-bat winced. The smell of lemon flowers and ginger conveyed satisfaction with the outcome and impatience with the complaint. "That would have been at the initial attack, at the start of the action?"

"That's right," Rose said, speaking without formal permission. "Young Hotspur wanted to engage dragon to dragon, just like in the early days of the war." The scent of musk conveyed impatience with a fool; humans had very little grasp of nuance, but occasionally one would make an unexpectedly strong point. "I ignored the juvenile half-wit and carried out the attack as you ordered it."

Technically, Arvesthanas has the right of it, Bythanastros thought grimly as he scanned the horizon for signs of enemy activity. Nevertheless. He paused and shook his ears. Perhaps we can persuade him of the error of his ways? The pungent aroma of dragon dung expressed displeasure and impatience. "Why should I punish YOUR animal for obeying MY orders? Your imbecile strategy would have had you fighting two against three while I continued on down to engage two against six."

The rage expressed by fat dripping on hot coals was almost palpable. "I would have been fighting two against two almost immediately! If my animal had obeyed me!"

"Sure you would, Hotspur." The underlying smell of urine and vinegar was a deliberate attempt to cool the argument. The nose belied the words heard by the ear, conveying an intellectual insult rather than a visceral one. "No doubt you would have taken out a second dragon by sheer virtuosity and run off the third so as to come back to the barns covered with glory. Meanwhile, down below, what happens to *me*? I get chewed up and spit out, and my sideworm as well. Two against six is not the smart way to go."

"That isn't the point," Arvesthanas shrilled, spilling fat on the fire of his rage to flash up into greasy evil-smelling smoke. "The *point* is that I gave a direct command and my animal refused to obey!"

"The point," Julia said easily, with the barest hint of vanilla asperity, "is that Bythanastros is in command here. I obey him, Yosie obeys him, and you are *supposed* to obey him. When you did not, Rose, who understood what the plan was a whole lot better than a certain junior warrior, chose to follow Bythanastros' orders and not yours. What's wrong with that?"

"What's wrong with that!?" Arvesthanas sputtered, losing control, "Warriors do not debate with their animals! Warriors are to be obeyed without question!"

"As the senior warrior is obeyed by his subordinates," the older troll-bat said as a medley of odors diminished into nothing, an unmistakable warning that the argument had gone far enough. "Look at the results. We went four against nine, inflicting casualties while suffering none. *And* we kept the nine from harassing our forces on the ground. Not a bad day's work, I'd say.''

''Ha! Casualties, you say? Garbage! I would have inflicted casualties! I would have chewed them up and spit them out! And you side with the animal instead of your own kinsman? I shall appeal this insult to the council and to the trive, you may rely upon it!''

Bythanastros twitched his ears in irritation, disregarding the multifarious and redolent annoyance of his subordinate. Arvesthanas had learned too many things that weren't so in his training and couldn't shake loose from them in the face of reality. Nevertheless, he made one last attempt. ''Get your nose clear, Hotspur! We, this group right here, are supposed to be flying a dozen worms at full strength. The reason we're only flying four is that's all we have that are fit for service. Goldentrive can't *get* any more, you understand? We can't go for that decisive action of yours if it means taking losses we can't replace.''

''Dragon dung!'' the young warrior shrilled. He was furious but back in control, articulating his thought in Ursprach without more than the barest hint of olfactory insolence. ''You fight like a fat old Kachka! You back animals against people! And *then* you whine that the miserable results you get justify your wretched, cowardly actions! To hell with the council; this is going back to the trive!''

''Complain and be damned,'' Bythanastros said. ''I will not have a subordinate that refuses to obey orders.''

''When we're done with you, you won't *have* any subordinates,'' was the response. ''The Athanastros sextet will see to it!''

3

The Art of Mastering Domestic Infelicity

THE capital of Guhland was the walled city of Cymdulock, and the high ground dominating that city was occupied by a pair of castles which, over time, had been built, expanded, and refitted into a complex fortress called the Citadel. In peaceful times the dynasties ruling Guhland, the House of Grathnys and before them the House of Khotanje, had constructed various comfortable and capacious palaces within the city itself. In times of trouble, however, they had repaired to the Citadel.

Under King-Patriarch Wizenbeak, the Royal Palace that had been the seat of the House of Grathnys was being rebuilt and restored to its former glory. Absent any immediate address, and feeling less than totally secure in the thrones which he had so recently seized, the new master of Guhland followed ancient tradition to make his domicile within the Citadel.

The logs in the tall marble fireplace had burned down to embers. King-Patriarch Wizenbeak sat at the end of the dark wood table, laying out the cards by the light of a pair of large tapers impaled on gilt-bronze candlesticks. A stack of diptychs, color-coded with red ends and yellow sides sat at his elbow, royally ignored.

In the privacy of the Royal Suite he wore by choice a residue of his profession, the green and white striped shirt that came below his knees, signifying a water-wizard, then the black velvet cap of maintenance, worked with gold thread and seed pearls, a black wizard's robe cut of finer stuff than any wizard could afford, though the numerous pockets were lumpy with props and paraphernalia. Even in the Royal Suite, however, he could not escape the insignia of office thrust upon him by eager hands. The robe bore elaborately worked patches displaying "WR," for Wizenbeak Rex, in scarlet and gold: right breast, left breast, and on the center of the back. The shirt bore a wide tape of white silk heavily worked with gold thread to simulate the great chain of office he wore as patriarch of the Syncretist Church.

For formal occasions, and whenever the king-patriarch left his quarters the occasion was formal, a variety of the most imposing costumes hung in several wardrobes crowded into the room. Each wardrobe displayed a large banner, appropriate to the specialty contained therein.

There was a knock on the door by the near side of the fireplace, and upon the king-patriarch's response, a guard opened the top half. "Your handler of troll-bats, sir."

"Send him in," the wizard said, smoothing his beard.

"Janko" Jankura entered, made a perfunctory obeisance, and, after the door closed behind her, sat down at the table. Tall she was and lean enough to pass easily for a man, wearing as she now did the black robes of a lay preacher in the Syncretist Church, with her head shaved in a tonsure, the dark hair making a shadow under her fair skin. Echoing the shadow on her pate, skillfully applied makeup suggested a closely shaved beard on her face.

"How long am I going to have to wear this ridiculous outfit?" she asked.

The wizard shrugged. "As long as it takes for your enemies to forget and forgive. How are we progressing with Mischka and Branka?"

She rocked her hand, palm down. "Pretty good, as long as I can hold their attention." A deep sigh. "Mischka understands maybe forty or fifty words . . . that is, he acknowledges understanding those words." Jankura opened her diptych and pushed it across the table. "That's the list. Branka—" She pulled at her nose and frowned.

"Branka's the brighter of the two," Wizenbeak observed thoughtfully.

"That may be the trouble. He understands all sorts of stuff he has no business knowing about and won't obey the simplest instructions. I can see why nobody ever did much work with sober troll-bats, though. How do you motivate the little bastards if they won't work their little tails off for that shot of kimjii root?''

''If you aren't making mother-of-glass, sober is the way to go. You can't use a tranquilized troll-bat for healing.'' He checked himself. ''At least you shouldn't.''

''They do, though,'' Jankura said. It was one of the things that gave country healers an uncertain reputation. ''Sometimes when I give a command, I have the feeling that Branka would like to argue with me about it, only he can't talk, so he just plays stupid.''

The wizard looked at her over the top of his emerald spectacles. ''You've given me an idea,'' he said. He studied her diptych, counting the words Mischka admitted to knowing. ''Forty-seven words here. Why don't you reduce them to hand signals? That way, you can signal to the troll-bats, and they . . . maybe . . . can signal you back.''

She looked dubious but made a note with her stylus and put the diptych back in her robe. ''I'll give it a try,'' she said. ''The other thing . . .'' There was a knock on the door, and the guard announced the queen.

''Come in,'' the king-patriarch said, squaring his cards and setting the deck before him. Queen Marjia swept into the room, a plumpish young lady in her early teens, blond hair carefully coiffed.

''Where's Duke Viluji?'' she snapped. ''I told the son of a bitch I needed to see him here!''

''Patience, darling,'' the wizard said, catching her eye over his spectacles. Perhaps if she had more presence, she would be a little less peremptory, he thought, and then remembered the Queen Shaia of old. Or perhaps not. In those days Shaia had been downright imperious. And then, just as she was about to break into the pause he had imposed on the conversation, ''Viluji will arrive directly, I have no doubt. We are discussing the matter nearest his heart, 'land reform,' the polite euphemism for distributing churchly real estate into secular hands.''

She made a face, sat down at the table, and sorted through the stack of diptychs. ''Didn't you do *anything* with these? I told you it was urgent to get started on the goddamned program!''

''They can wait,'' he said easily, pushing his glasses back on his long nose.

"Don't you listen to me? Don't you EVER listen to me? You old fool, hold off on land reform, you alienate your supporters, OUR supporters, and encourage our enemies! This stack represents the whole of the mediplano, and you haven't touched it!"

"A little patience, darling," Wizenbeak said. "We have a full plate with the land reforms in the central counties. Try to do it all at once and nothing will get done anywhere."

Jankura got up and poked at the fire with an iron poker. "Overreaching will kill you," she said, moving a charred log into the coals. "Better to break one stick at a time than struggle with the entire bundle."

Marjia ignored her. "If a great ill is to be done, your King-Patriarchship, it should be done all at once and put behind you!"

The wizard gathered up his cards and put them in one of the pockets of his robe. "That's the theory," he agreed, "but it isn't the only theory. The fact is, I think we *are* overreaching somewhat doing land reform through all the central counties. Once that's behind us, in a year or two, *then* we can move on to the mediplano."

Queen Marjia shook her head. "You wanted to go county by county. That's being kind to your dog by cutting his tail off an inch at a time!"

"On that issue you were right, darling, and I went with what you wanted. Now?" He ran his fingers through his whiskers, pulling at his mustache. "Now I think you're pushing it."

"It's bad statecraft, you old fool!"

Wizenbeak sat back in his chair and recited the mantra for serenity. I really will have to make an appointment to play with Mischka and Branka one of these days, he thought. A change in aggravation is almost as good as a vacation. He let his breath out slowly. "Bad statecraft? That depends on how you look at it."

"How do *you* look at it?" Jankura asked, while Marjia sat in grim-faced silence.

"Giving out the lands of the Church is a favor to your friends," he replied, "at least the secular ones. The rapacious Duke Viluji comes to mind for some reason. As a rule, such favors should be doled out slowly, so as to bind those friends to your bosom for as long as possible."

A knock on the door announced Duke Viluji.

"Talk of the devil," the wizard said quietly, and then "Send him in."

The guard admitted Viluji, a rough-faced little man who looked like a jockey. Jankura stood up, a gesture of respect; the other two remained seated. "Sorry I'm late, your Majesties," the duke said deferentially. "Terribly sorry."

Sit down, Viluji," Wizenbeak said, sourly.

"Thank you, sir." He slid his chair up to the table and glanced at the stack of diptychs with red ends and yellow sides. "Have you decided what to do with the Church lands in the mediplano?"

An informal truce having been arranged between Hashma Trive and Sisulia Trive, a representative group from Goldentrive, the Athanastros sextet, arrived at the Bythanna Group dragon barns around noon. As befitted their station, they were borne on the backs of nine sleek courier dragons, green and gold and built for speed. When the dragons had been properly housed, the troll-bats flew in a swarm to the central flue behind the barn, first the Honorable Kachkas from Goldentrive in a compact mass, with the members of the Bythanna Group trailing behind like an untidy plume of smoke.

The Honorable Kachkas themselves were six female troll-bats of advanced age and considerable girth who had been integrated into Goldentrive as a group after Goldentrive had absorbed Athanastrive many years earlier. As a result of seniority and natural ability they wielded considerable power, doing much to set the agenda which Goldentrive followed. They were also capable of acting autonomously, as they were now doing. With them traveled several other Honorable Kachkas in various supporting roles and their entourage, older females aspiring to be admitted to the trive and younger males to handle the animals. Their expressed scent was formal, judicial neutrality expressed as stored amaranth with woody highlights, suggesting a barn, clean and empty, ready for use.

In striking contrast, the Bythanna Group was a loosely integrated gaggle of perhaps two hundred. It was mostly juvenile, preponderantly male, and held to some sort of order by a few dozen breeding pairs still actively involved with their young and the senior warriors. While they had been fighting Goldentrive's war for some time and were less deferential than a more sedentary population might have been, they remained a collection of individuals rather than a coherent force.

Where the representatives of Sisulia Trive conveyed authority and a certain regal presence, the daughter group lacked the coherence to convey anything. Where the sextet and its entourage were organized and sharply focused, the troll-bats constituting the Bythanna Group were dispersed, inattentive, and even disinterested. Together they gathered at the central flue, the sextet occupying the traditional seat of authority at the top of the pendant.

There were three flues behind the dragon barns, inverted funnels of a glasslike substance that was supported by a network of ropes that were hung from a pole perhaps one hundred feet tall. All three flues were set against the south side of a low ridge, their edges gracefully scalloped and carefully positioned, two feet off the ground where the ropes were tethered to the pegs, three or four inches at the lowest point between. Each flue covered about ten acres, and in the throat of each flue the pendant was attached to the support pole.

The flues were simple machines created by the troll-bats in order to fly their dragons with greater ease and comfort. What they did was provide the webbed hands of troll-bats with a massive rush of air directed upward. The troll-bats, in turn, provided a major part of that impetus to their dragons, flying them at a great, if limited distance. How the troll-bats did this was not known, and although the learned Brujao and others had speculated at great length on the matter, it remained black magic.

How the flues worked was simple physics. The sun warmed the air on the ground, which was trapped by the inverted funnel. As the warm air rose, it was driven toward the center, and at the center, the pendant constricted the throat of the flue so that it was there the warm air reached its maximum velocity. The troll-bats in the pendant reached out their little webbed hands to draw kinetic energy from the rushing air. They could handle other kinds of energy, but moving air was what they liked best, and it was this energy that was transferred to the dragons to keep them aloft. A rule of thumb was that on a clear day, it took two acres to fly one dragon.

"Oh, our dearest cousins, we bring you greetings from the heart of Goldentrive." The opening speech was elegant and formal, containing many flowery phrases, with herbal and floral scents as well, all carefully nuanced and calibrated. It went on and on, in slow spirals rehearsing the familiar litany of ancient complaints. Outside the flue, at a respectful distance, sat the human audience, mostly warriors directly involved with the outcome.

Lean, sinewy, and blond, Yosie and Rose rested at ease on the side of the ridge with their archery coach, the crippled male troll-bat Oskvas. The humans were three-quarters sisters, having been conceived in the same year by the same father to mothers who had also been conceived in the same year and who were consequently half sisters. "We've heard all this," Yosie said. "When are they going to cut to the heart of the matter?"

The troll-bat flicked an ear. "This *is* the heart of the matter," he replied. "What is it you want?"

"What's going to happen to our group leader?" Rose asked. "That snotty little Athanastros kay-det comes in and tries to get us all killed with his ignorance. Then he makes a big deal out of nothing."

"Athanastros." The articulated thought was tinged with vinegar and redolent of dragon dung. "The group, not their cadet, the brash and callow Arvesthanas, is what is important here." There was a pause as hindclaws scratched at scruffy fur. "You humans. Always worried about the individual."

Rose shrugged. "Train one, train the group doesn't work. Our group leader, Bythanastros, is really good, all right?"

"The noble Bythanastros wouldn't be in so much trouble otherwise, one expects."

"What?" Julia sat up.

"Well, of course," Oskvas said. "He tried to organize Bythanna Group into a trive a few years back. You'd know that if you were paying any attention."

"I didn't. I don't." Yosie looked thoughtful. "So what happened?"

"Goldentrive moves people around, you know," the troll-bat said. "There were maybe six prospects we were working with as a sort of core group, a pair of triads. The females, four of them, were pretty sharp.'' He stopped. This isn't really the business of humans.

''Gossip is gossip,'' Yosie's response came. ''What happened?''

''Oh, once Goldentrive found out that Bythanna was serious about shaping up into a trive, two of the females were promoted and two of them were transferred to another group. Their replacements . . .'' He produced the most delicate suggestion of dragon dung. ''What were we talking about?''

''Bythanastros,'' Rose said, wandering back into the conversation. ''And sharing his experience.''

''Oh, yes. You think the other males aren't picking up on what he tries to put across?''

''Well, sure, Oskvas! When Bythanastros goes back and shares his experiences, there are maybe two or three males out of what—thirty?—that perform up to his level. None of the rest are interested in what he wants to tell them, except the ones already doing it.''

''They learn it.'' Even I have learned it.

''Well, sure, they learn it, but they don't understand what they know. They have a situation, they have to think about what to do instead of just doing.''

There was an amused whiff of citron. ''You, the animal, think you have a troll-bat trained?''

''Sure,'' Yosie said. ''When you trained us to draw the bow, what you told us was that the animal and the trainer were each part of the system. And the reason that you were such a good animal trainer was that you didn't like people.''

The troll-bat flexed his deformed wing, and there was a hint of autumn heather mixed with wild rue. ''Ah, Yosie, that wasn't what I said, not at all what I said.'' He shifted out of Ursprach into the unarticulated discourse of troll-bats. We have existed in a state of tension, the trive and I, for some time. Since Bythanastros gave up—not his fault, of course—on the Bythanna Group . . . He fell silent. ''Why am I telling you this?''

Gossip is gossip, Yosie thought. ''Go on with your story.''

Very well, frivolous female human. ''Goldentrive, or *any* established trive, actually, discourages males from trying to rise above their station. They made an example of me as a warning to Bythanastros.''

"What did they do?" Yosie asked.

"Enough. Enough so that I am an isolani, mutely listening to the discourse of my betters, who much prefer my silence. As my contribution to the group, I train animals, like you."

"Whatever," Yosie said. There was a stir in the assembled troll-bats. "What are they doing now?"

"Taking testimony from the Athanastros cadet. Sisulia Trive seems shocked that there would be four dragons and eight humans patroling with only two troll-bats."

"They knew that already," Rose said, shifting her weight. "That must be why they sent the little son of a bitch down, so that they'd have official testimony to chew over. Maybe some of those other old biddies are observers, witnesses to make sure the story is reported straight."

"Goldentrive is in trouble," Yosie remarked suddenly. "You can smell it if you reach for it. Something burning, but faint, almost out of reach."

"A remarkably astute observation," the troll-bat said with a touch of genial spice. "One wouldn't have expected it from a human. Sisulia Trive and Hashma Trive are seeking to force Goldentrive back into compliance with our cultural norms."

"What do you mean?"

A flurry of scratching. Perhaps one shouldn't tell animals about what will befall them. The knowledge might encourage ferality.

"Come on, Oskvas," Yosie said softly. "How can animals have knowledge about anything?"

The troll-bat smelled embarrassed. "The deal which Goldentrive will be making is the best they can do."

"They want to reduce animal autonomy," Rose said. "Human autonomy, anyway; the dragons are hopeless. Sisulia has been pushing it for years, and it looks as if they may finally get it." She ran her finger very lightly over the little animal's head fur. "Then whom will you have to talk to, old friend?"

4

In Which Matters Slowly Become Undone

THE youthful queen of Guhland looked across the table first at Viluji and then at her husband. Jankura sat at her elbow, ready to take notes. I have too little control here, Marjia thought bitterly. Still, things are looking up. Maybe we can work our way out of this mess, after all. Maybe. "We have decided not to touch the Church lands in the mediplano for the time being," she said. "May one presume to remind a nobleman so much more experienced than I that patience is a virtue?"

"Let us be frank," Duke Viluji said, clasping his hands together. "I did not support your pathetically feeble claim to the throne of Guhland in the interests of truth and justice. You were committed to land reform, and it is my wish to reform as much Syncretist real estate as quickly as possible. This . . . this policy is caution carried to the point of cowardice."

Wizenbeak pushed his emerald glasses back up his nose. "We have a lot to be afraid of, Viluji," he said coldly. "Gorabani escaped recently and will make us no end of trouble. In the mediplano, Duke Bhumraji has been hiring mercenaries. In Cymdulock, under this very nose, plots against us spring up like mushrooms after a long rain. However . . ." The king-patriarch fixed the little man with a cold stare as he mentally reviewed the book on him, an intimidation tactic he had picked up from a county magistrate many years before.

Duke Viluji fidgeted; in spite of his manifest weaknesses, the old bastard was a formidable presence. "What is it, your Majesty?" he asked, uneasy in spite of knowing he held the stronger position.

"Ah, Viluji. You are one of the sort whose hunger grows with the eating. We don't know if you are more dangerous fed or hungry."

"Meaning?"

"Meaning that you'll get a slice of that melon when we cut it."

Viluji slammed his hand on the table, making the shadows from the candles dance. "Then cut it now, for God's sake!"

Wizenbeak pulled at his mustache, hiding a smile behind his hand. "You really should cultivate the virtue of patience," he said, "even if it was Marjia here that recommended it. We *are* cutting it, but such a big melon takes time."

Duke Viluji shook his head. "You are involved in an endless dance with lawyers over the most trivial points of theology and law when you have the power to say 'Do it!' and see that it is done. Why don't you do it?"

"You have danced with enough lawyers to know that it is necessary," the king-patriarch replied, holding his gaze steady. So. The good duke wants to force things to go the way he wants them to go. Perhaps it is time to call his bluff. *If* he is bluffing. But what if he isn't? Then *maybe* I'm better off breaking with him sooner, but I think the crafty little bastard is bluffing. When in doubt, run your mouth without giving anything away. "Perhaps you wonder why we are working so diligently to return to the heirs the property of Orthodox landowners whom the Syncretist Church burned as witches?"

The thin mouth twitched, halfway between a grimace and a smile. "Your Majesty's love of justice is well known."

"Flattery will get you nowhere." Nor sarcasm, either, you little bastard, Wizenbeak thought. "The fact is, I am . . . we are King of Guhland and also patriarch of the Syncretist Church, holding neither position very securely. So we move cautiously."

"When you move at all."

"Patience, little man. Once we have returned the wrongfully seized Orthodox real estate to the Orthodox heirs, we then indemnify the 'innocent' Syncretists who gave it up with Church real estate. In the process, all the legal problems, which concern me as king, and all the theological problems, which concern me as patriarch, will have been solved."

The little duke smiled mirthlessly. "*Theological* problems, your Majesty? What garbage! We are talking about real estate and real politics here."

"Theology," Wizenbeak said. "In real political terms, a large part of the military force at my disposal is the Tarelian Order, of which we are the master. The Tarelians are *also* the mighty arm of the Church Militant, so I am obliged to maintain their good opinion." He gave a sigh. "Which involves a greater sensitivity to theological issues than some of us might find convenient."

Viluji gave a shrug and a pull of the nose, dismissing the problem as trivial. "Why mess around, then? Why not give the Church lands to the Orthodox directly?"

"We had considered that," Marjia said. "It has the virtue of simplicity and the vice of setting Guhland up for a holy war in the not too distant future. Think about it: Church lands in the hands of the Orthodox would be a permanent source of aggravation, a cause to be embraced by every true believer. Put the same lands in the hands of the Syncretist faithful—" she smiled sweetly "—and the problem disappears."

"At least it shrinks down somewhat," Wizenbeak remarked. "Those seeking revenge for justice inflicted on them will always find grist for their mills. Somewhere."

"Your Majestic Holiness' professed concern for justice is touching." Viluji scowled. "You might weigh it against the needs of your supporters."

"Our predecessor, King-Patriarch Kahun, may he rest in peace, did not love justice, though what he did was very popular in some circles. You can see where it got him," Wizenbeak replied, rubbing his eyes with thumb and forefinger; it had been a long day, and the accumulation of stress and fatigue was making itself felt, the more so since the mantras for clarity of thought were incompatible with the mantras relieving headache. "Our intention is to cut the seamless web of Church land tenure as reparation for the evil which was done in the name of the Church."

"So you intend to open a little hole, a nice, tidy little hole, working ever so carefully with pinking shears when you ought to cut boldly with your sword?"

The king-patriarch nodded. "Exactly so. The Church needs

to make penance for the evil it did. Repentance is a thing which the Tarelians understand and will tolerate.''

''That's property that your dukes won't be getting!''

I can't shake Viluji loose, can I? Which means I've got to call him, bluff or no bluff, Wizenbeak thought grimly. The little bastard gives me no choice. ''So it is,'' he said, looking over his emerald spectacles. ''If you don't want to wait for what we'll give you, get the hell out of the government!''

There was an almost inaudible squeak from the queen. Her magic had convinced her that the duke was in deadly earnest. That there was no choice but to accommodate him.

Duke Viluji sighed and composed his hands for prayer. ''The Syncretist Church owns the better half of Guhland,'' he said after consulting his calculus of self-interest. ''I am sure that in the end you will have no difficulty satisfying your loyal supporters.''

So my magic misses again, Marjia thought grimly, completely oblivious to Wizenbeak's elation at having faced down the duke. I've slipped badly.

The tall glass windows overlooked a cutting garden that filled the vases in the chateau with flowers in season. The garden was bordered with a tall brick wall built less for defense than for privacy, a secondary function being to provide support for climbing roses. City living, Gorabani thought. In the absence of danger, comfort takes precedence over safety, comfort and luxury. He rubbed his face with a black-gloved hand. Well, for the moment my safety depends on secrecy. The strongest tower would avail me nothing.

A servant entered with a shallow cut-glass bowl filled with yellow and purple pansies, which he set on the dressing table opposite the bed. ''The gentlemen from the mediplano have gathered downstairs, your Holiness,'' he said. ''May I advise the company when you intend to have audience with them?''

Gorabani shrugged. ''I'll see them at once. Announce me as Clerisiarch Gorabani, NOT as 'his Holiness,' you understand?''

''Yes, sir,'' was the reply, but face and body language expressed clear disapproval.

Gathered at the dining room table downstairs were Archdeacon Darussis and the gentlemen from the mediplano; Edsvart Olmsby and his half brother, Guilliam Lascajao, the bastard and third son of Duke Lascajao; Archdeacon Bhumraji, the youngest brother of Duke Bhumraji, with two retainers, a strategist and an accountant; and the nephew of Duke Yssemer and his fencing master.

Archdeacon Bhumraji took Gorabani's hand and kissed his ring, which was a silver skull with ruby eyes, having no religious significance at all. "Your Holiness," he said worshipfully, "give us your blessing."

Gorabani responded automatically, making the sign of the nabla and saying "Bless you, my son." Then he took the tall chair at the head of the table and looked at his audience. "Be seated, gentlemen." When they had arranged themselves around the table, he took out his diptych and opened it.

"This was not my first order of business," he said, "but it seems we must address it. We . . . I, rather, do not choose to act as a pretender to the patriarchy."

"Your Holiness *is* the patriarch," Bhumraji protested. "The pretender is surely that mountebank Wizenbeak."

Gorabani composed his black-gloved hands in an attitude of prayer. "That may be true, perhaps, but it is beside the point. If I set myself up as the rival patriarch, it will split the Church."

"With all due respect," Darussis said, "you are too cautious in this matter. I have found very little sympathy for Wizenbeak among the people."

The former patriarch laughed. "Ah, Darussis. When was the last time you talked to one of them? More to the point, if I were to raise myself up as the patriarchal rival to King-Patriarch Wizenbeak, I would have to oppose his policies, most notably his proclaimed policy of indemnifying the Orthodox community with Church real estate."

"You do, I hope, oppose this pernicious policy?" Archdeacon Bhumraji asked.

"Yes. Unequivocally. However, there are large sections of the country where burning the Orthodox as witches to seize their land is not kindly regarded."

"And large portions where it is, your Holiness," Olmsby said. "Especially including the mediplano."

"Thank you, Edsvart; you establish my point. A schism along those lines would benefit neither Guhland nor the Church."

"Well, look, your Holiness," Olmsby protested, "as good Syncretists, how can we rise against the patriarch?"

"Read your history," Bhumraji said. "The mediplano has done so repeatedly. Still, having our own patriarch in times of trouble would be a great consolation. Will your Holiness not at least consider the possibility?"

Gorabani rubbed his aquiline nose with one finger and looked thoughtful. "It would depend," he said at last. "This may be one of those cases where the threat will serve more efficiently than its execution."

"The threat will have to do," Bhumraji said. "What are we going to execute?"

"Civil unrest, of course," the former patriarch replied. "In Cymdulock, where the Orthodox prospered and are proportionately hated, we will organize resistance to the rape and pillage of the Church. In Rosano we will seek to raise a revolt."

"They haven't rebuilt the city wall in Rosano," Darussis said, "and by all accounts they aren't going to. That will make it hard to sell the revolt to anybody that matters."

"The men of property, you mean?" Gorabani composed his hands in an attitude of prayer. "Perhaps. Nevertheless, to keep Rosano from rising will tie up a major part of the Royal Army. When Wizenbeak is thus weakened and immobilized, your masters will rise in the mediplano with more force than he can bring against you."

"Then what?" Yssemer's nephew asked. "The odds look good, but Wizenbeak has risen to power against the odds."

"We force him to make a painful choice," Gorabani said. "If he suppresses the people in the central counties, then he does not have an adequate force to win decisively in the mediplano. If he moves decisively in the mediplano, the central counties rise up behind him."

"Either way he loses," Bhumraji said. "But what if the war in the mediplano goes on?"

"He loses then, too," Edsvart Olmsby said. "He needs the quick victory to hold his throne."

Bhumraji scowled. "Maybe," he said at last. "What else are we doing?"

Gorabani glanced at his diptych. "We will continue to work for the confusion of our enemies. Diplomatically, we may be able to turn one of the dukes supporting his cause, possibly young Bedirny. Magic,'' he said. ''Well, any use of magic is somewhat problematic. If anything turns up, we'll use it. Now, then, who will be doing what?'' The meeting shifted from strategy to tactics as the details of the revolt worked themselves out.

That evening Darussis received a message as he was dining with Gorabani. ''Well,'' he said softly, ''magically, something *has* turned up.''

The tall clerisiarch refilled his glass with white wine. ''What have you got?''

''The three points of the nabla, just as you suggested. Jankura is with them, disguised as a monk.''

''In the Royal Household? With access?''

''In the Citadel, in the Royal Suite, handling the troll-bats the wizard uses.'' Darussis giggled. ''I mean that the king-patriarch uses when he stoops to wizardry.''

Gorabani took a sip of wine and sat back in his chair. ''Indeed,'' he murmured. ''The three of them together, eh? Wizenbeak, and Jankura, who WAS the Shadow Shaia, and Queen Marjia, who IS the Shadow Shaia. What do you think?''

''Queen Marjia is such a precocious little girl, too,'' the pudgy archdeacon said. ''By some accounts a very forceful young lady. By others a pushy obnoxious little bitch.''

The former patriarch picked up a napkin and blotted his lips to hide his smile. ''Either description fits the little darling's mother, Queen Shaia of blessed memory.''

''Huh, huh, huh. Aren't *we* getting charitable in our old age.''

''Ah, Darussis. It would appear that Mowpater's Forty-Second Spell actually works.'' The tall clerisiarch mopped up the last of the cream sauce on his plate with a piece of bread and ate it. ''A pity we can't ride up to the Citadel and ask for confirmation.''

''What are you going to do?''

Composing his black-gloved hands, Gorabani bowed his head for a moment of silent prayer. ''At the proper time I shall break the spell. There must be a dozen ways, at least, to undo that crazy, complicated thing.'' He sighed. ''You know, as an attempt to slip the fist of death, it had a kind of weird beauty. As a spell you have to live with, the fragile thread that binds your soul to the body of another, it's just awful.''

"Indeed," the pudgy archdeacon said, who had a professional appreciation of awful spells. "When, in your estimation, is the proper time?"

"When Wizenbeak prepares to march against the mediplano, as he surely must, *that* will be the proper moment." He raised his drink. "Confusion to our enemies!" the former patriarch said, draining his glass in the solemn toast.

Darussis tasted his wine and looked skeptical. "What will pushing Shaia off this mortal coil accomplish, even if you can do it?"

"It will settle an old account," Gorabani replied at once. Then he saw what the archdeacon was driving at. I don't know, actually, he thought. What *would* it accomplish?

"With Shaia? Come on, she's unfinished business, sure. And if she's really there—and for all your fancy inferences, I seriously doubt it—let's root her out. But our main problem is Wizenbeak, and this will hardly touch him."

The other twisted the silver skull ring on his black-gloved finger. "We do what we can. The king-patriarch must depend on Shaia to some extent, for advice, for counsel, as a sounding board. Things that Princess, or even Queen Marjia couldn't provide." Then he smiled. "It must surely increase the possibility that the opposition will make mistakes, and for that reason alone it is worth doing."

5

Mutiny and Sedition

KING-PATRIARCH Wizenbeak sat on the throne of Guhland, surrounded by courtiers, wondering if there might not be a better way to conduct the business of state. Duke Viluji caught his eye and received the nod, slipping through the press to stand at the king's elbow.

"Two things, your Majesty," he said with professional deference, "which may, perhaps, be somewhat related. In the mediplano Duke Bhumraji has rejected your extremely generous offer of reconciliation. While he has not yet raised the banner of outright rebellion, this would appear to be only a matter of time."

Wizenbeak nodded. It was bad news but hardly unexpected. "We shall deal with it in good time," he growled. "Your second?"

"There is an appeal to a couple of death sentences coming up," the little duke said. "Guilliam Lascajao and Edsvart Olmsby, the defendants, are the third son of the duke and an acknowledged natural son. We can't hope to split him off from the rebellion Bhumraji is raising if we kill his children."

Something nobody tells you about being king, the wizard thought, is that your courtiers keep bringing you dung on silver trays, and your job is to smile and eat it. "Shouldn't this have gone before one of those worthies I appointed to the King's Bench the other day?"

"They declined to hear it," Viluji replied with a shrug. "Some hair-splitting argument about jurisdiction or something equally inane."

It was perfectly reasonable. If affairs of state were going to weigh into the outcome, let the king do it his own stupid self. "Well, then, I suppose we'll have to hear the case, won't we?"

"You should understand these are high-spirited young boys," Viluji said. "They didn't intend any harm, and I strongly recommend that they be shown clemency."

Wizenbeak nodded his head and pushed his glasses back on his nose. Viluji sounded like counsel for the defense. "You know my indisposition to take the life," he said softly. "If I can spare them, I will. What else is there?"

"Reasons of state," Viluji said. "The boys are the third and natural sons—"

"Of Duke Lascajao. With whom we hope to remain neutral in our coming altercation with Duke Bhumraji. You said that already. Why don't I hear of the matter directly."

"Very good, your Majestic Holiness. On the assumption that you might wish to do that very thing, I had the bailiffs bring them before the King's Bench, down the hall. When will their cases be heard?"

"Immediately," the king-patriarch said, rising from his throne with a certain lack of eagerness.

There were two groups of men waiting before the King's Bench. The defendants, a pair of strongly built young men in their early twenties, were manacled and wore the black robes of graduate students, the basic black robe of the lay preacher, with purfling, a colored tape sewn along the edge to denote the field of study. The taller of the pair wore red for theology; the shorter wore yellow for law. Beside them were several police officers and Count Gelenian, Cymdulock's chief of police. The other group consisted of a pair of expensively dressed lawyers and their entourage. Rank, the wizard thought, has its privileges. Certainly they impressed Viluji.

"Let's hear it," he said, taking his place on the dark wooden bench behind the dark wooden desk. When nobody moved, he gestured for Count Gelenian to approach.

"Your Majesty," Gelenian said, bowing. He followed the court protocol, which he had evidently been rehearsing, and finally launched into the case for the prosecution. "As your Majesty knows, there has been considerable opposition to your policy of returning the 'witchlands' to the proper heirs. This opposition has taken several forms, including threats to the heirs and to the faithful citizens who have accepted the alternate property offered them."

"Oh, really," one of the elegantly dressed lawyers said. "The opposition issued threats, did they?"

Wizenbeak looked at him. "Can you deny it, sir?"

"The matter is irrelevant, if not totally frivolous, your Majesty. What we have here is a ruthless frame-up by incompetent, brutal, and stupid men who are grossly jealous of their intellectual and moral superiors!"

"Your mastery of irrelevance is impressive. Continue, Count Gelenian."

"We had more threats the past few weeks than we could handle, sir. And some of them were put into execution. There have been seven or eight cases where the victim had been threatened after moving into a house awarded by the court and was subsequently burned out. We questioned a number of the men known to have issued such threats, and they gave us names."

"Torture," the lawyer said. "The interrogation was brutal and excessively cruel."

"We followed regular police procedure," Gelenian agreed. "Up to now we haven't had any complaints. Eventually we got a break. One of the small fry killed a rival in a fight over some woman, and we told him we'd hang him if he didn't cooperate."

"Entrapment, your Majesty! The man admits it! Simple justice demands that this case be dismissed out of hand."

"If the learned counsel will permit, I'd like to hear what happened," Wizenbeak said. "You will serve your client better by displaying a little courtesy."

"Our informant, Gusji Darkeyes, who made his living pimping in the university district, told us that a little bonfire had been planned in the Foxhall neighborhood." He consulted his diptych, "The evening of the fourteenth, at the Durriken house, on Third Street nearest the new F & T Canal. We staked the place out, and about ten that night a canal boat passed by and a half dozen young men jumped onto the towpath. They carried bundles of faggots, which they piled at the front door and under the front porch, and when they struck fire to light them, Sergeant Chahar here blew his whistle and his men moved to apprehend the arsonists."

Chahar nodded. He had a bandage across his forehead and his left arm in a sling. "There were five of them," he said. "Three ran north on the towpath, and two ran south. There were four of us, and we ran after the larger group, blowing our whistles to summon help. At Fifth Street a pair of constables appeared to head them off, and two of the three drew steel to fight their way out." He jerked his head at the defendants. "The taller brother was one of them. They killed one of the constables, Officer Hamjin, five years with the force, and wounded me before they were disarmed."

"There seems to be false testimony here," one of the lawyers said. "The chief of police says 'half a dozen,' the arresting officer says 'five.' How do you account for this discrepancy, Sergeant?"

"Our informant, Gusji, got off the barge with them. He acted as lookout for the others, and he didn't run away."

"We are satisfied," the king-patriarch said. "How did you disarm them?"

"With jittes." He touched the jitte in his belt, a wooden club about two feet long, sheathed in steel, with a steel hook to engage an enemy sword. "It was all over in less time than it takes to tell it. More officers came up, and we took them in. The two that had swords, they wouldn't say anything, but the third guy told us where we could find the ones that ran south, and that's where we found Master Edsvart here, and his friend, hiding in the back of a cellar tavern."

"It was dark," the lawyer said, "and the identification is uncertain, and in any event, the city would be a better place to live with fewer of these brutal cossacks patrolling the streets, enforcing—" He checked himself. He had been about to say "an evil and unjust law" to the king who had written it, not a truly smart move regardless of the facts of the case. "—this most unpopular law."

"Gusji Darkeyes had given us their names," Count Gelenian said. "All five of them."

Wizenbeak motioned Viluji over to the bench. "This is open-and-shut murder of a police officer," he said. "We can't let these men off."

Viluji looked concerned. "Hanging them will have the most awful consequences, sir."

Right, the king-patriarch thought, pulling at his whiskers, and not hanging them will have some awful consequences, too. Reaching for time, he asked, "What happened to the other three?"

Gelenian consulted his notes. "Mors Phadel, a second-year student at Saint Ehu's, was hanged. Sfranji Hadar, also a second-year student at Saint Ehu's, was hanged. Albanas of Rosano, an unemployed mercenary, testified against his comrades and got five years for arson and attempted arson."

"And what are these two young noblemen doing when they aren't burning honest folk out of their houses?"

"Guilliam, the older, is taking his doctorate in theology at Saint Ehu's College," the lawyer replied, "where he is also an assistant lecturer. Edsvart, his half brother, is studying law at Saint Brujan's."

The king-patriarch again summoned Duke Viluji to the bench. "So. These two young noblemen have put their lives at risk to oppose our policy of returning Orthodox property. Which is also the rock on which land reform rests. Advise me, Viluji."

The little duke consulted his calculus of self-interest. "Do what you think is right," he said at last. "If Bhumraji and Yssemer rise against us, Lascajao always figured to follow."

"Hold them as hostages against their father's good behavior?"

"A third son and a bastard? No. That would look as if your Majesty was grasping at straws."

It would look as if I were afraid, the wizard thought sadly. And the police deserve better.

"Let them speak for themselves," he said at last. "The two of you, studying theology and law, took the law into your own hands. Your sword killed one police officer and wounded a second. Why shouldn't you hang for it?"

Guilliam, the taller of the two, stepped forward. "The law," he said softly. "Your law. We should obey the law of the Lord of the Troll-Bats? I say NEVER!"

Edsvart, the bastard, raised his manacled hands where he stood. "We are in the right, and history will judge us honorable men! Kill us if you will; we will be avenged!"

Wizenbeak looked over his glasses at their lawyer. "And you, sir, do you share their passion for martyrdom?"

The lawyer shook his head. "No, your Majesty. But they *will* be avenged. That a rebellion is brewing in the west is common knowledge, and Duke Lascajao, their father, torn in his loyalties, had sought to steer clear of it, remaining true to your Majesty in the hopes of winning your heart and mind to the cause of righteousness."

"To hang these poor boys," the second lawyer said, "would be worse than a crime, your Majesty; it would be a blunder! Enough blood has been shed to avenge the loss of one brutal policeman; more can hardly be required. And reasons of state must also be weighed in the balance here; kill these children and they will be avenged many times over. What father could endure such an insult, nay, such an *injury*? What father could resist avenging the murder of his children, did it lie in his power to do so? This case bears directly upon your Majesty's policy in the mediplano."

"There are political arguments against their execution," the king-patriarch conceded. "Should we then take them as hostages to hang if their father rises in arms against us?"

It was a hard question. The two lawyers looked at each other. "This is something beyond the boundaries of the court, your Majesty," the first said at last. "We could not properly venture to advise you on how to conduct the affairs of state."

"However," the second said, "taking them hostage would serve their interests as well as your own."

"Sometimes it is not easy to know one's interest, counselor. When in doubt, one seeks to be just." Wizenbeak sat back on his bench, resting his hands on his knees. "You, Guilliam. You have studied theology. Do you imagine that you know what is the will of God?"

"God hates you," the young man replied coolly. "I am but His instrument."

"A wholly responsive answer," Wizenbeak murmured, "impressing us with your sincerity. And you, Edsvart, who would have dedicated your life to seeking justice. What have you to say for yourself before I pass sentence?"

"The Syncretist Church is nourished by the blood of martyrs," was the reply. "I do not seek martyrdom, but I do not shun it, either. In the conflict between God and the Lord of the Troll-Bats, God cannot lose."

The king-patriarch beckoned Viluji and Count Braley to the

side of the throne. "So much for realpolitik, Duke Viluji. Braley, you've been saying we have to deal with Duke Bhumraji. It's about to happen. Yes or no?"

"Well, yes," his strategist said, "but . . ."

"Good. We'll discuss your 'buts' in council."

"We now pronounce sentence," Wizenbeak said, recalling the mantra for calmness. "Guilliam Lascajao, for the crime of killing a policeman, I sentence you to death by hanging."

There was a stir in the court. He heard a slight intake of breath from Duke Viluji. The chief of police, Count Gelenian, looked satisfied rather than pleased. Sergeant Chahar nodded in mute approval. The defense lawyers drew in their breath, preparatory to hissing.

"Edsvart Olmsby, for the crime of killing a policeman, I sentence you, also, to death by hanging." Wizenbeak sighed and sat back in his chair. "Sentence in each instance to be carried out tomorrow at dawn. In consideration of your father's rank and noble sensitivity, hanging, a lower-class mode of execution, is to be changed to the more honorable decapitation."

He shook his head and pushed his glasses back on his nose. The young idiots! They gave him no choice. They as much as admitted being guilty of high treason, an offense calling for shocking and truly unenlightened penalties. "Take them away." The lawyers came up, protesting and complaining. He let them run on until they began to repeat themselves and then dismissed them. If one killed someone, no matter the reason, one ought to listen to the complaints of the relatives and the whining of the lawyers. Otherwise killing would be too easy.

Oskvas flexed his crippled hand. Their concern was touching, if animals could be said to express concern. "I'll be all right. Listening to the trive and talking to humans, training them for work that must be done, this is my life. There will be changes, sure, but they won't touch me; they won't touch any of us."

Yosie shifted her leather belt to ease the weight of the saber on her hip and scratched under her armor of glass-reinforced dragonskin. Dragonskin, the cast-off hide of growing dragons, was a light, porous leather which was made into armor by saturating it with a solution of mother-of-glass and then steaming it until the glass set. To ensure flexibility, a resist was applied to form a pattern of glass hexagons. Two layers gave mobility and protection sufficient for fighting in the air. Infantry used three or sometimes four layers. She looked across at Rose, her three-quarters sister. "What sort of changes?"

"What the war is about," Oskvas said incautiously, "is the theory and practice of animal husbandry. For nearly a century Hashma Trive has practiced a rigorous selection in the choice of the . . . what do you call them? I know the order of their names on the list, but the word, your word, escapes me. King-gods? The male that is selected at your annual games and fathers all the children for the next year."

Yosie supplied the term. "God-kings," she said. "The games demonstrate fitness, strength, divinity. The festival afterward celebrates the sacrificial death of the old and the selection of the new to ensure life's continuity. But you knew that."

Oskvas scratched at his scruffy fur. Just when you imagine you understand animals, they surprise you. "I have watched you kill the old god-king, yes. But what is it you mean by 'sacrificial'?"

"It is part of the bargain," Rose said. "The word 'sacrifice' is rooted in the word 'sacred,' that which is holy, honored, held in reverence. Sacrifice is the offering made to the sacred, to the gods, that they may smile on our endeavor."

Perhaps we have said too much, the crippled troll-bat thought, doubt welling up in a cloud of cold, wet fungal odors from the floor of an autumnal forest.

"Perhaps you have," Rose said gently, picking him from her shoulder and cradling him against her heart. The two women stepped through the canvas flap of a long rectangular tent into one of the smaller human barns. "Here we are."

Even though the canvas was translucent, the room was dark, but the troll-bat could pick out perhaps fifty women by their individual scents. A little concentration showed him thirty women wearing arms and armor, most of whom he had trained in the use of the bow, and another dozen, grandmothers, long past childbearing age, which the group kept alive for reasons connected to the long maturation period of human infants.

One of the grandmothers stood up and came over. Straight she was, and wiry, her leathery hide sporting a variety of scars that suggested an ancient familiarity with weapons. She wore a scarlet headband to keep her shoulder-length hair in place and a brownish kamcha jacket, a wool garment knit large and shrunk to size in very hot water. Across her body was slung a leather pouch, and over the pouch a blanket roll, held in place with neatly tied tapes, while about her waist she wore a tooled leather belt with a loincloth. Her legs were bare, and on her feet were sandals of woven straw.

"Good afternoon, Oskvas, I am Heatherfields-Hsven. You may call me Heather if you wish. My daughter, Yosie, tells me that you'll be giving us an account of the trival conference this afternoon."

The salt spray of apprehension tinged with ozone and seaweed washed over him. Hsven was the year she was conceived, the year of her personal god-king. Which meant . . . the troll-bat searched through his memory . . . she was incredibly old for a human, maybe forty or forty-one years. I don't know if I should.

"Come on, now," Yosie's mother said gently. "What did they talk about?"

"Goldentrive is making negotiations to end the war, which we cannot win," Oskvas said cautiously. "Probably Hashma Trive will insist that some limits be put on the autonomy you now enjoy, but talk still goes on. Nothing is settled yet."

Heather generated the disturbing scent of kimjii flower. "Hashma Trive has had a heavy hand on the selection of the Hashma humans' god-king for more than a century. Sisulia Trive, off and on, for nineteen years out of the last thirty. Goldentrive, pulled together out of bits and pieces, never. Are you surprised that we remember these things?"

"A little," the troll-bat conceded. "They touch on your interest, to be sure, but without the trive to remember for you, how can an individual bind time before they were ever born?"

Rose stoked his fur and smiled, projecting the suite of aromas from a flowering meadow. "They manage," she said.

"We manage," Yosie's mother agreed, letting the narcotic fragrance of Kimjii fade into a soft terpene undertone. "You want to know why big, strong Hashma Trive couldn't beat Goldentrive on the field of battle?"

The paint thinner was better, Oskvas thought, almost pleasant. "Why?"

"Animal husbandry," the old woman said. "Hashma dumbed down their humans to the point where they are next to useless. They'll do what you troll-bats tell them, just like the dragons, but for fighting they aren't worth much."

"Feral humans aren't worth much, either!"

"A matter of opinion, little troll-bat." Terpenes shifted to musk which was now edged with something else that was pleasant and distracting at the same time. "We have been holding, when by the numbers we ought to have been crushed. And by 'we' I do not mean troll-bats, though Bythanna Group has fought valiantly! I mean us, Goldentrive's humans, who are not feral, as your own experience will testify."

"We have trained many of you," Oskvas agreed, "and you show good discipline. Nevertheless, the potential for ferality is there."

The old woman laughed, and musk shifted momentarily to lilacs and avricod nectar. "War is for animals," she said. "Wild, fierce, passionate animals. A human *needs* the potential for ferality; otherwise they're worthless."

"Ferality is a two-edged sword," the smoke-tinged concession came. "Useful but dangerous to the user."

Sisulia Trive, our beloved mother, leaves us to fight "her" battle, the reply came from Heather, unarticulated in the troll-bat fashion. The smell of kimjii flower was back, and a slow smoldering resinous smell that she hadn't used before. "What is the deal Hashma wants to make?"

"Hashma wants Goldentrive to use god-kings selected from Hashma's humans," Oskvas blurted, astonished to hear what was coming out of his mouth. "Everything will be the same for you as before, until the festival at the end of the year."

"Will Goldentrive accept?"

The little troll-bat had been apprehensive; now he was terrified. Goldentrive was stalling for time as long as the truce held, but they would accede to Hashma's demands in the end. He had to get out of this den of ferals to warn the trive of the danger! He laid his good hand on Rose's heart and delivered the *coup de coeur* that killed by fibrillation.

To his astonishment there was a little blue spark that stunned and dazed him. He lay in Rose's hand, consciousness fading in a swirling mixture of coriander and woodsmoke, and the last thing he heard was Heather saying: "Goldentrive will accept. Now what?"

The Privy Council Chamber had few other virtues than being close to the king-patriarch's quarters. Rough-hewn stone walls, flagstone floors, a pair of massive oaken doors studded with iron bolts, and narrow windows set near the top of the twenty-foot ceiling hinted at its turbulent history. To accommodate the room's latest function, the walls had been whitewashed, the high narrow windows had been glazed, a rug had been laid on the floor, and a rectangular dining room table with eight chairs had been placed on the rug.

King-Patriarch Wizenbeak sat at the head of the table in his high-backed chair, Queen Marjia at his right, his strategist, Count Braley, and Lasco Genzari, the general of the Royal Army, on his left, the other seats being empty. Count Braley was a master swordsman, perhaps as a consequence of being so handsome as to appear effeminate. Genzari was in his midforties, the personification of dignity, with closely cropped gray hair and a neatly trimmed mustache. The cut he had endured on Saint Posalanji's Day was healing but did yet not permit martial exercises.

"You shouldn't execute those nice Lascajao boys," Marjia said. "The policeman was a commoner."

"Those nice Lascajao boys were engaged in high treason."

Lasco Genzari looked up. "I don't understand your Majesty's thinking," he said politely. "We've been working all spring on the premise that we could split Duke Lascajao off from Bhumraji and quash the rebellion bloodlessly. And then you decapitate his two sons, and the whole policy is out the window."

The king-patriarch sat back in his chair and fiddled with his chains of office. How can I tell him that it wasn't right to let those two young nobles go free when their less privileged followers had already been hung? That's no way to run a country, doing the right thing and shaping unrelated policies to fit your actions. "What is it you want to know?" he said at last. "Why I ordered the executions or why I abandoned the policy?"

"Both, actually. You could have taken the lads as hostages for the good conduct of their father, the duke. Why didn't you?"

"Because I don't approve of killing hostages," Wizenbeak

said. Which was entirely true. "And because your policy of splitting Lascajao off from Bhumraji . . ." He shook his head. "My policy. I embraced it. I'd hoped it would work, but when Lascajao's sons are in Cymdulock playing at high treason, no. The sweet reasonableness of Duke Lascajao is a deceit, a sham. Misdirection practiced by our enemies to buy time while they prepare for war."

"You could be mistaken," Queen Marjia protested. "The sons might not reflect the thinking of the father."

"That argument is too subtle," the wizard replied sadly. "With one son I might have considered it. But you heard those young men before the King's Bench. Fanatics, both of them."

"The realities of politics," Count Braley said, "might lead the duke to bend where his sons would not, they not having his great responsibilities."

Wizenbeak pondered the matter. In fact, Duke Lascajao *had* demonstrated considerable tactical flexibility. On the other hand . . . "Those boys are two apples that did not fall far from the tree," he said with finality. "It might even be true, my rationalization. To believe that Duke Lascajao would act otherwise is wishful thinking."

"He might, sir."

"So he might, Genzari, but it isn't the way to bet. When can we be ready to march?"

The general of the Royal Army sighed and considered the question. "Supplies must be gathered, horses shod, all of the usual impedimenta gathered together. Given our present state of readiness, it should take three or four days, but you'll be lucky to get out of Cymdulock in a week."

"Announce four days. Try for four days. We'll take the week if we have to." Wizenbeak pushed his emerald spectacles back on his nose and opened his diptych. "What forces will we take?"

"Play differently, lose differently," Genzari said, fingering his carefully trimmed mustache. "It looks as if the executions will bring the rebellion in the mediplano to a head before *anybody* is ready. The question is, How do we respond to the situation we have created with such a show of confidence?"

"Go to the mediplano and put down the rebellion," Count Braley said, smiling.

"Easy enough to say," Genzari agreed. "Pull the Royal Army

out of Rosano, and the local fanatics will have a backfire for that rebellion going in five minutes. The same, to a lesser extent, here in Cymdulock. Your Majestic Holiness has taken power with very little time for consolidation.''

Wizenbeak nodded in rueful agreement. ''Time we didn't have. We still don't, for that matter. We *will* have to go into the mediplano,'' he said, wiping his spectacles off with a handkerchief, ''eventually. The only question is, Do we go when we choose or when Duke Bhumraji chooses?''

''We go now,'' Count Braley said, ''with what we can spare. The problems of command, having one army under three independent dukes, will do a lot to offset their advantage in numbers.''

''You intend to split their forces by maneuver so as to defeat them piecemeal?'' Marjia asked.

''Basically, yes,'' Count Braley replied, whose carefully considered strategy was to dance around until the enemy made a fatal mistake.

The youthful queen looked doubtful. ''How long will it take you?''

''That will depend on the gods of war,'' he said. ''The forces we can deploy to the mediplano are the Tarelian Order and about half the cavalry in the Royal Army. The rest is needed to keep the peace in the central counties.''

''The Tarelians and cavalry, eh?'' The king-patriarch sat back in his tall chair and scratched the end of his nose with his stylus. ''Was it you who told me that Duke Bhumraji's army is four-fifths mercenaries?''

''That would be lower now,'' Genzari said. ''I understand that the duke is passing some of his hired swords along to Yssemer and Lascajao.''

Wizenbeak laughed. ''Our own beloved Duke Viluji was in such a sweat to get his hands on the Church lands in the mediplano. I wonder what the Church offered those three dukes to revolt.''

Marjia pulled a sour face and shrugged. ''If they win, you'll find out.''

''Unthinkable that those broad lands should escape the clutches of some damned duke,'' the king-patriarch said. ''At least it must be unthinkable to our dukes. Count Braley.''

"Yes, sir?"

"We have a second string to our bow." He outlined his plan to them.

"That's crazy," Marjia said, "but it might work."

Lasco Genzari looked thoughtful. "It might work even though it *is* crazy."

"It is a delight to serve your Majestic Holiness," Count Braley said, laughing. "That plan of yours is crazy enough so that it *will* work!"

In the tent, Rose contemplated the unconscious troll-bat in her hand. She had felt his panic and to some extent understood it. To act without direction, without the authority of the trive, was unthinkable. "I don't know, Heather," she said at last. "What can we do?"

"Hashma Trive is bound and determined to rearrange our lives for us," Heather said. "If you are going to do anything about it, you have two choices: You can ask for permission, or you can ask for forgiveness."

"Should we be doing something?" one of the archers asked.

"Hashma Trive is going to take the games away from humans and give us a god-king selected by troll-bats, Melissa. What do you think?"

"Is that really true, Heather? They wouldn't take away the games, would they?"

The older women laughed. "You'd have what Hashma's humans have, darling, a nice little party at the year's end. Nothing sacred, just animal husbandry with the cooperation of the animals. You get right down to it, that's what this war is all about."

"Ask forgiveness," Yosie said.

The response from the archers and drivers was scattered and uncertain. "What? What do you mean? Forgiveness for what?"

Heather answered them. "Forgiveness for acting in our own interest. Forgiveness for defending the sacred nature of the games. Will you act? Will you defend?"

"No," Melissa said, "that is pure ferality. We should ask Goldentrive's permission or at least consult with Bythanastros."

"Bythanastros doesn't speak for the Bythanna Group, and even the group isn't free to do anything," the old woman said. "And Goldentrive? Goldentrive is caught between a rock and a hard place.'' Then she smiled. ''You don't want ferality? Rose, hold the little bastard up. When we get back, we'll tell the trive that Oskvas here made us do it!''

That provoked a general laugh. ''Do what?'' someone asked.

Heather looked around at her audience. They were drivers, archers, and old hands like herself. This was about as elite a group of humans as one was likely to find. If you can't persuade these people, she told herself, you can't persuade anyone. They're listening for you to say something. SAY SOMETHING! She cleared her throat. Her mouth was dry. ''Night raid'' was all that came out.

''No good,'' Melissa said. ''Even if there was enough time to load chaff and straw into the flues, even if the Bythanna Group was willing to go along, they couldn't lift us off without permission from Goldentrive.''

Melissa is a fool, Heather thought grimly, and the stirring of anger loosened her tongue. ''A night raid doesn't have to be riding dragons,'' she said. ''Think about it. If we start walking right now, we can reach the Hashma barns before midnight.''

''What'll you do when you get there?'' one of the older women asked. ''Without troll-bats drawing lift from the flues, the dragons are going to be real sluggish to handle.''

''Put the torch to them,'' Heather said. ''Barns, grain storage, chaff stacks, everything. With all the confusion, we'll slip out real easy and get back in time for breakfast.''

For a few minutes everyone was talking. Then Melissa shouted for silence. ''All right, all right,'' she said as they quieted down. ''We can do it. The question is, Do we want to?''

''No!'' Heather said. ''The question is, What *else* can we do?'' She looked around the tent, meeting every eye. ''The answer is nothing! Now, are we going?''

''Honor the games!'' Yosie shouted, raising her fist. It was the shout that announced the sacrifice of the previous year's god-king, and the audience gave it back to her. ''Honor the games!''

''We're going,'' Melissa said. ''What will we do when we get back?''

Heather shrugged. It was a fair question and one she couldn't answer. ''Ask forgiveness,'' she replied. ''It's got to be better than asking permission.''

When spring approached summer in the north, the sun did

not sink far below the horizon and the night sky provided enough light to walk in the woods. Heather led her small force down the beaten path to Thornbush Ridge. They were disciplined and quiet and easily evaded the sentries posted on both sides of the battle line. Then there was the long approach to the Hashma barns, uphill most of the way. Good, Heather thought. They'd be retreating on the downslope.

As they came up to the edge of the barnyard, a sentry stopped them, a eunuch with a short sword and a spear. "Good evening, girls," he said. "Out for a little stroll?"

"Something of the sort," Heather replied as Melissa slipped behind the sentry and cut his throat.

Then they fanned out into the shadows, and when Heather thought they had had enough time, she chittered like a dragon hatchling. She saw one or two sparks as fires were struck and then nothing. By the time the alarm was sounded, her people had begun coming back, and by the time they were all there, the barnyard was swarming with troll-bats and Hashma humans, trying to fight the fire, trying to save some of the dragons from the barns, and trying to get organized.

"Should we pick off a few?" Rose asked. Shooting targets against the firelight would be easy.

Heather shook her head. "We've done enough for one night, I think. Let's go home and have breakfast."

6

Things Start to Break

THE former patriarch stood by the south wall in the little cutting garden, studying how the rosebushes had been trained to climb the trellises. "As you see, Darussis, the gardener and his plants are at odds with each other. The plant wishes to grow in all directions, while the gardener wishes it to grow only here, in the plane along the wall. When the plant, poor thing, ignorant of the gardener's design, follows its nature and grows wherever it can, the gardener does not lecture, does not rebuke, does not in fact say anything, but takes his pruning shears and cuts the plant to conform with the plan he has in mind."

The smaller clerisiarch folded his arms and studied the rosebush for a moment, trying to follow the turn the conversation had taken. "What does that mean? If the Church is the gardener and the faithful are rosebushes, then we ought to prune them on a regular basis?"

"One of your few weaknesses, old friend," Gorabani sighed, "is that tendency to read a text or a poetic image so literally that the sense is mislaid if not lost completely."

Darussis shrugged and cut a yellow rosebud with his pocket knife. "I liked it better when we were shearing sheep," he said, slipping the rosebud into the lapel of his black robe. "Pruning rosebushes? What sort of allegorical allusion am I supposed to find in that?"

A servant approached them discreetly, carrying a neatly tied stack of wooden chips on a silver salver. "These messages just arrived, your Holiness. The messenger urged me to bring them to your attention at once."

Gorabani gave a perfunctory acknowledgment and opened the stack of chips. "So," he said after the servant had withdrawn, "the army of King-Patriarch Wizenbeak is marching for the mediplano tomorrow morning."

"What sort of force is he taking?"

The former patriarch studied the chips. "The Tarelians, of course. And cavalry. The units are listed with their commanders and supposed numbers." He gave a sigh. "Some of our strategists might make more sense out of this than I can, but he appears to be advancing into the mediplano with a force significantly smaller than that of our three dukes."

"Ah. You mean he *didn't* take the whole Royal Army so that the central counties could rise?"

"Evidently not, Darussis. Someone, Genzari, perhaps—" The tall clerisiarch paused. "Lasco Genzari, you know, has the unspectacular virtue of steadiness. We must hope that his masters continue to be unlucky. He, or it might have been another, must have understood our strategy and acted to oppose it."

The smaller clerisiarch smiled politely. "The strategists can work it out, your Holiness. In the meantime, old Wizenbeak has traded a strategic problem for a tactical one. Let us hope that Bhumraji can take him."

"He killed Lascajao's sons and moved at once," the other mused. "Maybe Duke Yssemer . . . ?"

"Who can say? Wizards have been known to make interesting mistakes now and then. I am sure our strategists, at least, will be interested in the boring details contained in those little wooden chips."

"Yes, yes," Gorabani said, handing over the stack. "Let us pass the information along in the pious hope that it will prove useful."

"What about the queen?"

Gorabani rubbed his chin with a black-gloved hand. "What about her? I can't prime the mirror until after sundown, but everything else is in readiness. After dinner?"

The little clerisiarch took a moment to smell the roses. "After dinner will be fine," he said softly.

That evening Darussis looked over what Gorabani had laid out on the table, in front of the carefully prepared triptych mirror. The full mantraset, or spell, was written on a parchment scroll that was held in place with a bronze incense burner at one end and a silver candlestick at the other. Carefully embedded in the spell were the tokens of identity, a small lock of Marjia's blond hair, held in place with red sealing wax, and nail clippings from her mother, Queen Shaia, embedded in black sealing wax. Connecting black and red sealing wax was an intricately drawn line, looping back and forth, and written above the line was the counterspell that would break Mowpater's Forty-Second.

"That's all?" he asked doubtfully. "No black cocks, no blood spattering, no nothing?"

Gorabani shrugged. He had had the same reaction himself, but this was the full mantraset, all that was indicated. "The effect is subtle, so nothing spectacular is called for."

"What do I do?"

"Read the line in the left-hand mirror and light the candle. Read it again, the same line, in the right-hand mirror and light the incense. Read it a third time in the center mirror, and that's it. I'd do it myself, but after priming the mirror I can't use it, I can only watch."

"Very well," the little archdeacon said. "Watch the mirror and tell me if the spell bites." He read off the mantraset in the mirrors, lighting candle and incense as he was instructed.

"It's biting," Gorabani exclaimed after the third repetition. "It's biting! Look! Look quickly!"

The left-hand mirror reflected the letters of the spell in red fire, and the line along which they were written glowed like a hot wire and faded into nothingness. The right-hand mirror reflected the letters in green fire, and the line along which they were written liquefied, separating itself into individual droplets, shiny little balls that didn't wet the paper as they rolled off the edge. Finally, in the center mirror, the letters glowed yellow and the line began to smoke where it touched the black wax. Then a tiny spot of bright yellow flame appeared and moved slowly toward the red wax; where it passed, the line was completely gone. When it reached the red wax, smoke engulfed all three mirrors in roiling gray clouds, and when the smoke cleared after a few moments, the mirrors were just mirrors again, reflecting the unaffected parchment.

Having completed the spell, Gorabani removed his black

gloves from his pocket and put them slowly back on. "Wizenbeak was going to march on the mediplano tomorrow, was he? I'll bet *this* delays him for a day or two!"

"I expect it will," Darussis agreed. "And I expect that we can at last mark paid to the Witch-Queen."

The tent was surrounded by a rope cordon which marked the boundary beyond which the prisoners were not allowed to pass. On the third day a eunuch brought in two caged troll-bats, the animal trainer called Oskvas, and the commander of dragons, Bythanastros.

"Goldentrive wants you to leave them in the cages," he said as he lashed the cages to the corner pole of the tent.

"Why are they being brought in here?" Yosie asked.

"I have no idea," the guard replied as he left. "Good luck, warriors."

Heather sat herself cross-legged before the two troll-bats, generating a whiff of leather with overtones of ginger by way of greeting. So why are the two of you being thrown in with the animals?

Oskvas twitched one ear, his hunched posture enhancing the sense of fungal depression he conveyed.

"You really stirred things up with that barn burning," Bythanastros said. "Hashma Trive insists that it was a deliberate violation of the truce for which the Bythanna Group if not Goldentrive must be held responsible." The little troll-bat shifted to aromaticizing. Sisulia Trive is split on the issue, part agreeing with Hashma Trive and part arguing that it was dreaded human ferality. Goldentrive . . .

What about Goldentrive? Heather prompted after a long pause.

"Goldentrive argues that while their animals may have acted autonomously, it was an act of war. That's your fault, you know. Feral animals are supposed to kill and run."

"I know," she said. "Then the trive gets out the posse to hunt them down. It really whips the blood, that hunt."

Bythanastros scratched a couple of times and shook his ears. It does, he agreed, an acrolein smell suggesting something of remembered excitement. Then he shifted to human speech. "You didn't run, you came back instead, and you said, 'We did this for Goldentrive,' and that shook a lot of the Honorable Kachkas, at least in Goldentrive. And when you said, 'We submit ourselves to Goldentrive's judgment,' and *did*, that really shook them."

"What about Sisulia Trive?"

There was a derisive whiff of cooked cabbage and garlic. Those old fools? They don't want to hear it. The easiest case to deal with is some sort of low-level violation of the truce. The issue of human ferality touches on how you are bred, on how your god-kings are selected, all the animal husbandry issues at the root of the war. It makes rational discussion impossible, would you believe?

"Ah," Heather said. "That's why you're here, then. You and Oskvas are thrown in with us to pretend that it was you troll-bats who violated the truce?"

"That's about right," Oskvas said resignedly. "It may be the last thing we can do for the trive, confessing that we were the ones that led you on the barn burning. Tell us about it sometime so we can give convincing testimony."

"We're going to go up as a group, and the troll-bats take the rap?" Melissa asked. "Sounds good to me."

"Hashma Trive lost nineteen dragons in the fire," Bythanastros said, "not to mention all that other stuff. Hashma wants damages, they want compensation, they want strategic indemnity." He sighed. "Goldentrive is halfway willing to apologize. In the meantime we're playing to Sisulia Trive in the hope that they come down on our side for once."

"Well, then," Heatherfields-Hsven said. "Maybe we can cut a deal."

"What sort of a deal?"

"You need our cooperation, right? But you don't need all fifty of us, just me and two or three others, the so-called leaders of the pack whom you enticed into breaking the truce."

Doubt expressed itself as long-dead fish.

Leather and ginger came back at the caged troll-bat, sarcasm enhanced by musk and hot oil. Poor old Bythanastros. Let the rest go, and I will cooperate with you. Otherwise, you and your trival politics can go to hell!

The warrior troll-bat shook his ears. "Oskvas?"

Nothing. Then a sour "Do whatever you damn well please."

"No help." Bythanastros sighed. "Pick two others, then, and I'll ask to have the rest released."

Heatherfields-Hsven stood up and turned to her audience. "You heard," she said. "I need a couple of volunteers for whatever the hell it is that's coming up."

"What if they don't let us go?" Melissande-Armani asked, otherwise known as Melissa.

"Then we don't cooperate, and you haven't lost a thing by volunteering. One more?"

"I'll go," Yosefina-Kortats said, otherwise known as Yosie.

"Fine, daughter. Bythanastros, call in the proposition to Goldentrive and see if you can get the troops off the hook."

After one final meeting with his generals, ensuring a smooth solution of the innumerable details involved in moving an army, Wizenbeak held court for several hours, sorting through the innumerable details involved in leaving a country to run itself for an uncertain period. He then retired to the Royal Suite to work on his correspondence. He was not surprised at Marjia's absence from court; she was an astute observer, but children, even queens, were supposed to be seen and not heard, and that she found boring. He did miss her when working in his study.

Normally the True Shaia hidden within Marjia kept up with the affairs of state via the written word flowing across his desk. She read faster than he did, and she thought faster than he did, and her background enabled her to understand at once things that he was able to work out only with great difficulty. As a courtesy she let him read everything first, or perhaps it was intolerable waiting for him to finish something she wanted to talk about, but he was still pressed to keep up with her. Without her, the process was smooth, and serene, and very slow.

Leaving a stack of color-coded diptychs on his secretary's desk, he at last went down into the small dining room. There he found his own place set, but none other.

"What *is* this, Hobs," he growled at his chamberlain. "We aren't eating alone, are we? Where is her Majesty's dinner?"

"In the kitchen, your Royal Holiness," Hobs replied. "Her Majesty the queen said she wasn't up to eating today."

"Nothing?"

"No, sir. Not lunch, nor dinner, neither. Lady Djilas took a tray up to the bedroom, and it was sent back."

Wizenbeak went into the grand bedroom and found Lady Djilas sitting on the bed, holding Princess Marjia's hand. Marjia looked somehow . . . The wizard hesitated. The face was the same, the body was the same, but she was wearing them differently; he hardly knew her. A chill wind stirred in his bones, rustling his viscera like so many dead leaves.

"Our little Marjia had a bad nightmare last night," the lady-in-waiting said, looking up at him. "She found it very upsetting."

Something is a whole lot worse than that, the wizard thought, fighting a sense of panic. "Ah, yes. Would you ask Brother Janko to come in, please?"

When Jankura entered, Branka, curious, or maybe hoping for a little play, climbed out of Jankura's robe, followed by Mischka. Wizenbeak stroked Branka's ears, took Mischka, who had been Marjia's own personal troll-bat for a short time, and extended the little animal toward her. There had been some degree of bonding with both of them. Now there was no sign of recognition, not from Mischka, who enjoyed playing with the little girl, and not from Marjia, who liked working with troll-bats in general and with Mischka in particular. The wizard felt the hairs rising on the back of his neck. Something is wrong, seriously, terribly, horribly wrong, he thought as he handed the troll-bats back to Jankura.

"How upsetting was it?" his mouth said. "The dream, I mean?"

"She was very upset," Lady Djilas said. "Weeping, crying like I have never seen her . . ."

"Let her Majesty answer," the wizard told her. "What sort of dream was it?"

"I don't remember." Then, suddenly, she blurted it out. "I don't remember anything since the day we escaped from the palace."

Oh, shit, Wizenbeak thought. "What's the last thing you do remember, then?"

"I was in the sedan chair with my brother, and they set the chair down, and then I was here." There was an unmistakable whine in Marjia's voice and in her intonation; her phrasing was not in the least like her mother's.

That was the moment when Shaia's spirit entered her body, Wizenbeak thought, unhappily. Shaia gone?! He needed to consult her badly . . . and, an almost unadmitted afterthought, he missed her!

"The queen was feeling queasy all morning," Lady Djilas volunteered. "She declined to take lunch, and in midafternoon she complained of a severe headache. Her flow—" She hesitated, then pushed on. "—her menstrual flow began. It was her first period, often a difficult time for a woman, and I thought that was what it was. I fixed her a pad of soft cloth, and . . ." She hesitated, sorting out the day's events. "She said she thought she'd take a nap. Only she didn't. When she lay down on the bed, she had a kind of fit."

"What happened? I mean, what did she do?"

"She thrashed around, and when I held her, she began to cry. I thought I was hurting her, but when I let go, she grabbed hold of me." She pushed the green silk sleeves of her dress back above her elbow, showing fresh finger bruises.

"Right." The wizard sighed. "Did she say anything?"

"For a few minutes it was as if she was having a conversation with herself, but one-sided, none of the questions, only the answers. Talking very fast. She sounded . . ." Lady Djilas paused, trying to remember. "She went from panicky, before she started talking, to distraught, to resigned."

"I don't remember," the little girl whined.

"We're here to help you," Wizenbeak replied, wondering if that was exactly true. "Lady Djilas, do you remember anything she said at that point?"

"She said, 'I made a difference, I did!' and she repeated it two or three times. She said, 'It wasn't in vain!' The last thing she said was a man's name." She hesitated again, not because she didn't remember but because saying the name might get somebody into bad trouble.

"Was it Zeldones?" Wizenbeak asked as a direct question.

"Yes, sir." If the man knows the name, don't lie and don't evade. You don't need a stranger's troubles on your plate, Lady Djilas thought.

Wizenbeak gave a sigh. "He died on Saint Posalanji's Day,

but he was the one who led the royal children to safety when the mob stormed the Royal Palace. She might have had a crush on him."

"Was he the tall officer taking the sedan chair to the Citadel?" Marjia asked.

"That's him," the wizard said. "Was there anything else?"

"After she said 'Zeldones,' Marjia rolled off the bed and cracked her head on the floor. Hard. She was out long enough for me to lift her eyelids, to see that her eyes had rolled up, but not long enough for me to summon help. She woke up right away, just like she is now."

Now what do we do? Wizenbeak wondered.

"It could be an attack sorcerous of some kind," Lady Djilas suggested. "That staff of magic users you have might be able to do something."

"Maybe," the wizard said doubtfully, contemplating the collection of charlatans and incompetents he had inherited from the previous administration. "Mostly they work warding off spells and other mischief as assigned. They wouldn't admit that anything got by them. *Could* get by them. On the other hand . . ."

There was a long pause. "On the other hand?" Jankura prompted at last.

"There are ways to recall lost memory," he said, professing a confidence he did not feel. "In days gone by we, ourselves, have used a few of the more gentle." As a traveling mountebank he had sometimes hypnotized members of the audience, playing various tricks with their memories.

"I want my mommy," Marjia said.

This whiny kid is my beloved wife, Wizenbeak thought resignedly. "Lady Djilas. Did you tell her anything about what she didn't remember?"

A shake of the head.

Right, the wizard thought. We need to approach the little darling with maximum sensitivity to spare her delicate feelings. Only how to begin?

"Well, Marjia darling," he began after the hoped-for inspiration did not arrive, "we have good news and we have bad news. The good news is, you are queen of Guhland." He waited a second to let that sink in. "The bad news is, your mother is dead, your father is dead, your brother is dead, and I am your husband."

It took them half an hour to calm her down.

7

Searching for Counterspells

THERE wasn't any time. The army marched at dawn, and what was he going to do with his suddenly disoriented child bride? Lock her in a tower for safekeeping? Not actually a bad idea, but after a moment's reflection he dismissed it out of hand.

"Well, kid," he said at last, "do you want to see if we can get your memory back?"

"Will it hurt?" she asked doubtfully.

"No, no. Either you remember or you don't. Lady Djilas, her Majesty will not require your services for . . . well, until morning, anyway."

"I'd like to help if I could, your Majesty."

She likes Marjia, he thought, which has to be worth something. Working with the mind could be disconcerting, like trying to make one's way through a maze of mirrors that offered the most unexpected vistas. The fact of the matter is I'll be trying to figure out what I'm doing as I go along. You, you'd be there. A powerful distraction even if you could resist kibitzing an old hacker groping for a solution. "Thank you, darling," he said gently, "but I can't imagine what you might be doing."

"Aren't two heads better than one?" Marjia asked.

"That's what Brother Janko is here for," the king-patriarch said. "And if we need more heads, he has the troll-bats."

Lady Djilas paused at the door. "You're sure you don't want me to summon the Council of Wizards, your Majesty?"

Wizenbeak thought again of the collection of charlatans and incompetents he had inherited and sighed. "Thank you, no."

"Now what?" the queen of Guhland said when the door had closed. Wizenbeak sat her on the chaise longue and pulled up a straight chair for himself. From a pocket he produced a small gold pendant on a fine gold chain. The lamp on the end table made it glow redly as he let it dangle at eye level.

"The pendant," he said, pitching his voice low and speaking softly, "the pendant is gold, inlaid with enamel, making a *tau* nabla, the most potent of magical forms. Watch the pendant. Watch the pendant." Twisting the chain, he made the pendant spin slowly, slowly in the lamplight, and he slowed his speech to match the spin. Marjia went into a light trance after a few minutes, the first stage.

She made herself comfortable on the chaise longue, carefully kicking off her shoes as her mother had always insisted she do before putting her feet on the furniture.

"Can you hear me, Marjia?"

A long sigh. "I can hear you, master."

"The last day you can remember before you found yourself here, you were riding in a sedan chair with your brother. Can you remember?"

"Yes. We were going uphill. We had a blanket because it was so cold."

"Go on."

"They put the sedan chair down."

"Go on."

"And I was here in this bedroom."

A blank, the wizard thought, not terribly surprised. He took out his diptych and scribbled notes to himself in the wax. The notes led to questions, and the questions led to further notes. Having remembered a theory, he worked his way down the list of questions it suggested.

An hour later he was no further along.

Wizenbeak looked at Jankura, who had been watching the procedure from the foot of Marjia's bed. "Ah, me. There are three levels that I know how to use. The first one just drew a blank." The troll-bat on her shoulder stared back at him, curious but impassive.

"Well," Jankura said, "try the second one, then."

The second level involved putting the subject into as deep a sleep as possible. It was slow, patient work, but there were tests that could establish how far along they were, and in the end Marjia was well and truly on the second level.

He had her describe her brother and the blanket and the inside of the sedan chair in minute and stupefying detail. But when they put the sedan chair down, it was a direct cut to the bedroom.

A blank on two? the wizard asked himself, looking at the troll-bat.

Wizenbeak shook his head. "Not yet, Mischka, darling. Shaia, can you hear me?" Nothing. "Shaia, can you hear me?" Nothing. "Shaia, can you hear me?"

"Shaia isn't there," the little girl said in a distant voice.

"I need to talk to your mother," the wizard said. "I need to talk to Shaia very badly. Will you help me talk to her? Will you help me talk to her, please?"

There was a long pause. He repeated the request and repeated it again.

"I want to help you," the little girl's voice said faintly, "but Shaia can't remember to talk. She isn't there, and she can't remember." The wizard felt a cold wind blowing through his bones. This wasn't going to work, but he didn't want to quit.

He tried the lines that had seemed most promising on the first level: Shaia leading her daughter into Mowpater's Forty-Second Spell, Shaia's emotions that Marjia must also have felt, and trying to get Marjia to remember what her body had done. Nothing.

He looked at his troll-bats. "Well, then. What about the third level?" A black cloud of panic welled up inside him, fear of failure swirling around remembered caveats about the process itself.

"We've never used the third level," Branka said.

"And it isn't a good idea when we're so tired, either," Mischka said. "Not tonight."

"That's reasonable enough," the wizard said, and then looked over his glasses at Jankura, who was leaning against the bedpost, her eyes closed, one troll-bat in her lap and the other nested in the crook of her arm. Talking to the little monsters was bad enough, but when they started talking back to you, it was time to call it a day. He put Marjia into her nightgown and tucked her into bed.

Now what? It had just gotten a whole lot later than he liked to think about. He made an effort to concentrate on the mantras to restore memory, and they marched past his weary gaze, blurring a little at the edges.

"Hunh," he grunted, and pushed his glasses up on his forehead. "Utterly useless, every bloody one of them." There had been an idea earlier. Had he made a note of it? The wizard opened his diptych and looked over his notes. There it was, printed along the right-hand side. "Marjia?"

"Yes, master?"

"When I count to three, you will go to sleep and wake up in the morning. You understand?"

"Yes, master."

He tilted the diptych so the light would make the printed letters show more clearly. "While you are asleep, I want you to try to dream about all the things your eyes saw, your ears heard, and your body felt during the time . . ." He had been about to say "the time you can't remember," which wouldn't do. ". . . from when the sedan chair was put down until this morning. Will you do that?"

A pause. "I'll try, Master Wizenbeak," the small voice said doubtfully.

"Do your best, Marjia. When you wake up, on this one special time you will be able to remember your dreams. You will be able to remember your dreams as clearly as if they had really happened."

"I'll be able to remember my dreams?"

"This one time, this one special time. Yes. Now it's time to go to sleep. One, two, three!"

The little girl was asleep instantly.

The wizard walked to the end of the bed and touched Jankura lightly on the shoulder. Her eyes opened at once. "Will she remember?"

"I hope so. Probably, yes." He was too tired to yawn, and the sky was already lightening. He would have liked to go to bed and stay there. But if he went to bed for the two or three hours he had, he'd be totally out of it when he got up. If he stayed awake, he'd get a second wind when the sun rose. From experience, it would be the difference between feeling weary and feeling totally awful. Well, when the army moved out, he could doze on his mule.

"Do you want some coffee? I could make you some."

Wizenbeak nodded. The expedition to the mediplano was getting off to a rocky start, but right now a cup of coffee sounded like the best that could be done in the circumstances.

The Lagualian coffee was strong and sweet and left a thick, bitter sludge in the bottom of the tiny cup. Wizenbeak studied it for a moment and accepted a refill from the long-handled copper pot Jankura had prepared for them. He took a tiny sip and set the cup carefully on his plate. Already he was beginning to feel more human—an encouraging sign.

They sat at a little marble-topped utility table in the back of the kitchen, where peas were shelled and bread was kneaded. There was one lamp throwing shadows among the pots and pans hanging from the walls.

"So," the king-patriarch said at last. "We could maybe create time for ourselves by staying awake longer." He gave a sigh. "God forbid we should ever need time so badly. How are Mischka and Branka doing with sign language?"

Jankura shrugged. "Mischka has a few signs—'yes,' 'no,' 'love you,' and something else, 'later,' which he uses when he doesn't want to do what you ask him. Branka has two—the standard 'no' and something he picked up." She extended her middle finger. "This. Ask him to do something he doesn't want to do and you get a no. Insist and you get the finger."

"I don't know why we put up with the little son of a bitch," the king-patriarch said. "And what in *hell* are we going to do with Marjia?"

"What's the problem?"

Jankura was there, Wizenbeak thought irritably; she *knows* what the problem is. Then he blinked his eyes, and the discomfort reminded him of his sleep deficit. Maybe she just wants to know *which* problem. "Shaia's gone. Even if the kid remembers, it will be like a dream."

"You think she'll be disoriented—Marjia?"

"No, she won't be disoriented." He took another careful sip of coffee. "Well, at least I hope not. But the stuff Marjia needs to be queen, why Shaia did what she did, what she thought, and how she decided, that's lost. Gone for good. The best I could do was the restoration of the memory of what happened to Marjia physically while Shaia was in charge."

"She's a minor, even if she is queen," Jankura said. "Put someone in as a temporary regent while you're gone."

"Hunh. Who is there that I could trust? Do *you* want the job?"

"No, no. God, no," she said with a shake of her head. "What about Lady Djilas? She seems like a nice person."

"She's one of Duke Viluji's relatives. A pretty thing with more intelligence than dowry, married into a cadet branch of the family. Viluji himself wouldn't be any worse."

"Lock her up until you get back, then."

There it is again, the wizard thought. Why did I reject the idea earlier, when I was somewhat more able to function? Oh, yes. Out of deference to Marjia's feelings, we never consummated the marriage. He sighed. Shaia had been willing, but the body of Marjia had resisted to the point where Shaia had had to draw back for fear of losing control right then. What has that to do with anything? Oh, yes. My being king, laying claim to the throne of Guhland by force of arms and a royal marriage. Because I married HER. "That isn't a bad idea, actually," he said, "but we can't do it."

Jankura took a sip of Lagualian coffee. "Why not?"

He gave a shrug. "It would be inhumane."

She looked at him for a moment and shook her head. "Hey. You are the King-Patriarch of Guhland, right, Master Wizenbeak? Of course. Right, how could you say otherwise? You have a duty to keep the peace for the benefit of all the poor slobs who are your beloved subjects. Right?"

He rested his elbows on the kitchen table, leaning his chin in one hand. "Of course, right."

"So how can you say it is inhumane to put one little girl in the tower for safekeeping when you maybe risk a civil war if you don't?"

With Shaia gone, Jankura is about all the confidants we have left, the wizard thought. Will telling her put the secret at risk? Marjia knows, and God knows what she'll do. "The problem is this. I married Marjia to become King of Guhland, right?"

"Of course right. So?"

"So the marriage was never consummated. What Shaia said was that she wanted to have a hold on me, to keep me straight."

"Oh, hell." Jankura finished her coffee and put down the cup. "You have a problem."

"Sure. What am I going to do, hold up the march into the mediplano to consummate my marriage?"

"No, go to her right now." She shook her head as she recognized the needs of the healing process competing with political necessity. "No, damn it! She needs however much sleep she needs to restore her memories. Well, you couldn't tell anybody what you were holding up the march for."

"Wait till noon for Marjia to wake up, and then go in and rape her? And then put her in the tower? That's a hell of a way to start a campaign."

"You shouldn't have restored her memory."

"Wizards make interesting mistakes, Jankura."

The chief steward entered through the pantry. "Your Majesty is up very early," he said.

"No, Hobs," the wizard replied. "We haven't been to bed. Therefore, we are up very late."

"Yes, sir. May I fix your breakfast?"

Wizenbeak looked out the window. The sky was light enough so that he was starting to feel better. Breakfast was something within the realm of possibility. "Very well. Scrambled eggs and . . . what were those pancake things you fixed the other day out of grated curu root and onion?"

"Latkis," Hobs said with dignity. "A peasant dish but easy to digest."

"Just what we need," the wizard said. "And serve us here so I don't have to totter into the damn dining room."

"Very good, sir," Hobs said, and moved off to prepare the food.

"What will you do about the queen?" Jankura asked.

"Nothing," Wizenbeak replied. "For every mistake I might anticipate and guard against, she could find three others without even thinking." He yawned. "This way, at least she isn't actively hostile."

8

The Mediplano Campaign

THREE days north of Seven Locks City, King-Patriarch Wizenbeak sat on his big blue mule and watched as the Tarelian Order carried out his strategy. He was on top of a low hill overlooking one of the vast estates the Church held in this area, and his engineers were staking it out into forty-acre plots.

"The enemy, they pull up those stakes as fast as they find them," Pardus Murado said, expressing disdain and a certain skepticism for the whole procedure.

"And take down the signboards," the wizard agreed. The signboards, neatly lettered with a hot stylus on freshly planed wood, simply said that there would be a lottery at some future date to give away those forty-acre plots, free and clear. "Nevertheless, we have the plat plans on parchment, and the word about land reform will spread."

"Yes, sir," Murado replied. "Only what good it will do, I can't imagine." He felt very strongly that one ought not to mix politics with the conduct of wars and said so at every opportunity. Nevertheless, orders were orders.

Ten days north of Seven Locks City the signboards listed the names of the estates and the number of lots they had been cut into. The army of the Kahunist dukes, swollen with recently hired mercenaries to perhaps one and a half times the size of the Tarelian Order and the Royal Cavalry, followed at a distance, frustrated in their efforts to force an engagement and baffled in their attempts to anticipate the wizard's moves. Duke Bhumraji himself commanded the center, with Duke Lascajao commanding on his right flank and Duke Yssemer on his left. Several times they had tried to maneuver in front of the swiftly moving Tarelians, and there had been a few clashes of light cavalry, but in the main the Kahunists had found themselves having to choose one place to defend, leaving the Tarelian Order free to sweep through the other. The possibility of defending both targets had been discussed. The stumbling block was that the army would split into two groups, one twice as strong as the other, and none of the commanders wished to be in the small group.

Fourteen days north of Seven Locks City the signboards started to list the information that the drawing to distribute the plots of land would be held "soon" at a place to be named later. The signboards listing the estates and the number of their forty-acre plots were now being posted separately, one to each of the staked-out Church landholdings. The regular signboards had only the current summary: As of today's date, fifty-two estates have been divided into 7,487 plots.

Twenty-one days north of Seven Locks City, marching in a meandering fashion that had touched most of the great Church estates in the central mediplano, King-Patriarch Wizenbeak sat on a stool before his tent and looked at the half dozen prisoners kneeling before him.

"We understand that you are all mercenaries," he said softly. Nobody made any reply, but it was true. "In one week's time we will hold a drawing, a lottery. The nature of the lottery is this: It is open only to mercenaries who have sworn never to bear arms against their king. Each winner will be seized of forty acres. No oath is required of you now, but one will be when you appear at the site where the lottery is to be held." He paused, waiting for someone to ask where that would be. No one did, and he smiled. "A site which is shortly to be announced. *Then*, the act of writing your name on the numbered chip which may or may not be drawn from the barrel, *that* constitutes your oath. Which is binding whether you win or not. Think about it."

He turned to his guards. "Give this lot their arms and horses and release them." They would return to their comrades with news of the lottery, and the word would spread.

The guard squad pushed the two-wheeled caisson into the cordoned-off area. A couple of troll-bats flittered around

Bythanastros for a few moments and then went back to instruct their humans.

One of the eunuchs took out a posthole digger and made a neat hole in the hardpan dirt. Others put the top of one pole in the hole and traced a small arc with the top of the other pole at the end of the bracing rope. A second hole was dug on the arc, and both poles were set into the ground. From each pole the bracing rope was pulled taut and secured to a peg driven into the ground, followed by the guy rope.

Then the diamond-shaped tarpaulin was unrolled, and the long ends were secured to the pulleys at the top of the poles. The four sidepieces were quickly tied on to the edges of the tarpaulin, and the tent was lifted up, forming a sad-looking canvas bag. Guy ropes were fastened to the short ends of the diamond and pulled taut. The tent roof snapped into a smooth saddle shape, with the sidepieces hanging limply. The guards quickly dug a drainage ditch around the four sides of the tent and secured the bottom of the tent on three sides. The fourth side was lofted on a pair of shorter poles to form an awning. At night, when the tent needed to be closed, the poles were taken down and laid over the edge of the canvas to hold it in place.

"Well," Yosie said, unfolding her cot and winding it taut, working each end in turn, "we have ourselves a place out of the rain, at any rate."

"Say what?" Melissa asked, walking around inside the tent. "The rains aren't going to come until autumn."

"Real luxury," Yosie said. "This is real luxury. Three humans and two troll-bats in a tent that should hold ten of each. And they bring us our meals. How long is this going to go on?"

Until the trives come to an agreement, Bythanastros said. There was a faint whiff of urine and vinegar cynicism. Hashma Trive wants to resume fighting, but Sisulia Trive has threatened to come to the support of Goldentrive if they do so before the barn-burning incident is resolved.

"That's us," Heather said, slipping the sticks which she had used as a lever to wind the cords into their keepers. "The official barn burners. I offered to go up and plead guilty, and they didn't want to hear it."

"Animals can do a lot of things," Oskvas said, "but violating a truce appears not to be one of them, according to Hashma Trive.''

''Depends on who's talking,'' Heather said, sitting on her cot.

''What would you know?'' Oskvas asked. ''The arguments were too complex for a human to follow.''

''Well, sure,'' she agreed. ''From what I could make out, it smelled as if you were downwind of a burning sausage factory. But it wasn't all that hard to make out what they *meant*.''

''It beat the hell out of me,'' Yosie said. ''What-all were they saying?''

Heatherfields-Hsven folded her legs into the lotus position. ''Start with Hashma Trive. Bythanastros can correct me if I get it wrong, right?''

The troll-bat pulsed the avricod and cinnamon smell of affirmation.

''One faction of Hashma Trive wants to continue the war, to put down Goldentrive. When we burned their barn, they lost enough dragons so that some of their uncommitted supporters switched sides and said, well, maybe a conference is a good idea. So the hard-liners, the warhawks, have to go to a conference where they now profess to believe that Goldentrive's humans are dangerously sentient.''

''Sorry, no,'' Bythanastros said. ''Dangerously sentient is—'' He projected a dense, complex scent with aldehyde highlights. ''What they said was—'' He projected essentially the same suite of odors with a slightly different emphasis. ''—inconveniently intelligent. The difference is important.''

''Not to humans,'' Heather replied. ''Of Hashma Trive's opposition to the war, half believe that humans are dumb animals, and the other half think it doesn't make any difference, that it's a phony argument because of who is making it. The swing votes, the ones who have supported the war up to now but would just as soon back off, they don't know what to think. Mostly they don't buy the argument that humans have enough smarts to worry about because then they'd be committed to keep on with the war.''

Yosie pulled up an empty ration box and sat down. ''How about it, Bythanastros? Is that how the argument went?''

''A crude approximation,'' the troll-bat conceded, ''missing the complexity of nuance, the intensity of feeling, the sheer passion of the argument. It will do for humans."

"Thank you," Heather said. "In Sisulia Trive, our own beloved parents, the majority, those who *still* want to coerce Goldentrive are split into two major factions. The ones who fear us, who want Goldentrive to use conventional animal husbandry because humans, dangerously sentient or inconveniently intelligent, have smarts enough to worry about. The other faction—" She paused and pulled at her nose. "Generally they are those who envy Goldentrive the success it has enjoyed, the wealth it has accumulated. In the past they blocked our efforts to attain full trival status."

"How about it?" Yosie asked.

Bythanastros flicked his ears. "Oversimplified but not actually wrong, so far."

"Glad to hear that my rough-and-ready interpretation meets with your grudging approval," Heatherfields-Hsven replied. "Then there is the minority group that opposed the coercion from the beginning." She sighed. "Our allies but hardly our friends, speaking of course as a husbanded animal."

"What about them?" Melissa asked.

Bythanastros produced the smell of half-dried dragon dung thrown on the fire.

Heather nodded. "They are the enemies of our enemies, loving ideas better than reality. They would make bad masters, I think."

"What about Goldentrive, then?" Yosie asked.

Her mother hesitated. "Goldentrive is listening rather than talking. My sense is that they are stalling, hoping to run the truce past harvesttime. Bythanastros?"

The troll-bat scratched his fur with a vigorous hindleg. "They were the ones that touched this whole thing off, you know, with their insatiable greed. Trying to get you humans to produce more than anybody could reasonably use, seeking advantage in peace, better weapons in war. The deal they made with the devil gave you your games and your god-kings, and in return you made them rich."

"What's wrong with that, Bythanastros?"

"It has to be against nature to seek wealth grossly beyond

what you can use, piling it up as an instrument of war. It isn't the troll-bat way."

"You little buggers seem to have taken to it naturally enough," Yosie said.

"Not all of us. It was the same thing when Goldentrive tried to use . . . did use humans to gain advantage in war. Wars have always been fought with dragons. Always. Since time immemorial. The whole community, not just the trive, would participate, the females and children and Kachkas all gathered together in the flues to provide the lift that flew the dragons, while the young males, the warriors, would ride their dragons into fiercest combat to seek glory or death."

The warrior troll-bat fell silent.

"That was then," Yosie prompted him. "What about now?"

There was a complex odor suggesting resignation and sadness. Once Goldentrive started using more and more humans, with fewer and fewer dragons, they began winning. They called it progressive, and it didn't matter what anyone else called it; that was the way to fight if you didn't want to lose.

"They call us names and imitate us," Yosie said. "Why is that, do you think?"

"We were winning, darling," Melissa replied.

"Shut up, you two," Heather snapped. Hot oil and garlic suggested her annoyance. "Bythanastros, what was it that the others called the new way of fighting?"

"Unnatural," the troll-bat said. "More and more, we were having less and less to do with the wars we fought."

"We? What we, troll-bat?"

"The warriors, Yosie, the young males that rode the dragons. Humans do our job now, and there is no way to achieve glory. Not on the field of battle, not anywhere."

"Without glory," Oskvas said, "no male could hope to become an Honorable Kivu."

Heather looked up. "Kivu? I never heard the word before."

Oskvas twitched an ear. "It is the masculine equivalent of Kachka. An Honorable Kivu is a male who is a participating member of the trive."

"Fascinating," Heather said. "Does this have anything to do with the roots of our war?"

"Who can say?" the troll-bat asked. "For whatever reasons,

instead of spinning off Goldentrive into Golden Trive or whatever name they might have selected for themselves, Sisulia Trive conspired with Hashma Trive to cut Goldentrive down to manageable size."

"In the beginning," Heather said softly, "the argument Hashma Trive put out was that the war was against the excessive ferality that Goldentrive permitted."

"There are some in Sisulia Trive that think the barn burning was human ferality given official sanction," Bythanastros replied, "but they can't come out and actually *say* it, because if they did, they'd be obliged to join Hashma Trive against us."

"What a mess," Yosie said. "When are we going to get out of here?"

Heather laughed. "When the fall rains come, maybe."

On the evening of the twenty-third day north of Seven Locks City a lean old man with a black eye patch openly rode up to Wizenbeak's camp. The sentinels stopped him and, after a little discussion, handed him over to the officers, who brought him into the presence.

"Good evening, your Majesty. My name is Gowan, sometimes called the Fox, and I am here on behalf of my former comrades."

"How do you mean, 'former'?" the wizard asked.

"There was a time when I had a small reputation in this part of the country," Gowan replied, "but I am now too old for a soldier's life." He smiled, showing strong white teeth. "A deputation of some of my old friends asked me to check up on this lottery you plan to hold three days hence."

"We are sincerely dedicated to land reform," the king-patriarch said. "The current count is eighty-seven estates, split into 16,904 plots of forty acres each."

"If all the mercenaries in Bhumraji's army went along, each one would have about two chances in five of winning," the one-eyed man mused. "Good odds for a lottery. Only the thing is that it won't work the way you've got it set up."

"Indeed? I am new to this part of Guhland." Wizenbeak turned to his adjutant. "A chair for our guest, and a bottle of wine." When Gowan was seated and a bottle of Jamreaux

Peennon Wahr was set out with small silver goblets, the wizard himself poured each of them a drink. "Your good health, sir."

"And yours." The former mercenary took a sip and put the goblet down. "Not bad for a Jamreaux red. I had heard that they don't travel well."

"They don't. We picked up several cases from the cellar of one of the local estates."

Gowan nodded. "They live well, the clerisy. Even their lackeys that have to run the latifundas live well. The people." He smiled, not pleasantly. "Well, let me tell you a little local history, then, if you care to invest the time." Wizenbeak sat back in his chair and nodded for him to continue. "At one time the mediplano was a whole lot more densely populated than it is now. Smallholders mostly, and many of them raised their families on less than the forty acres that you're offering."

"I tried to find out about that history," Wizenbeak replied. There hadn't been time. "What happened to them, the smallholders? The Church histories are unclear."

"Then listen up, young trooper," the former mercenary said. Wizenbeak grinned. "No offense intended, your Majesty."

"And none taken. Continue, please."

"The main crop was anacuru gourd. Still is, for that matter. The seeds are pressed for curu oil, the seedcake and the vines are first-rate fodder, and the curu root—well, they use that for pig feed nowadays, but it used to be a staple for poor folks."

"Nothing wrong with curu root," Wizenbeak said. "I rather like latkis."

Gowan nodded. "So do I. That reminds me of a joke, but never mind. Anyway, after three or four years you go out and pull up a root six or seven feet long that weighs maybe eighty pounds. You don't need many of those to get you through the winter." The old man coughed and reached into his pocket, producing not a handkerchief but a device of rope and woven tape. "A curupu'." He held it up. "You dig around the top of the root, maybe six to eight inches down, and slip this over it. Then you give it a few gentle pulls to get it set." He put the tapes over his fist and pulled the rope handles with his other hand. "It gets tighter the harder you pull."

"I see," the wizard said as Gowan opened his fist and slipped out of the curupull. "It's like having handles on top of the root."

"Right. The vines won't do for a big one. You squat down and pull with your legs, and once it gives a few inches, it'll come right out."

"Fascinating. And the smallholders, how do they live?"

"Did. They fed the seedcake and the vines to the livestock and lived on curu root, milk, and garden vegetables. The meat you raise can be eaten or sold, depending, but curu oil is your main cash crop. Even a farmer needs money, right?"

The king-patriarch nodded. "Go on."

"Maybe two centuries ago the Syncretist Church swept in and established a monopoly on pressing curu oil. Also a monopoly on buying and selling the oil. Which was all right as long as they continued to accept curu oil in kind for the tithe."

"They shifted to a cash economy?"

"About a generation later. And not all at once, but a single latifunda at a time as they became the places to support absentee . . ." He hesitated. "Not landlords. Life tenants? No. The clerisy don't own the properties—the Church owns them—but the clerisy collects the rents as long as they hold down some particular job."

"Being patriarch, I understand how the clerisy is paid," Wizenbeak said. "What was the word you used?"

"Latifunda? What you were calling estates on those signboards you were posting."

The wizard opened his diptych and made a note. "Go on, please."

"The way it worked, the Church set the tithe based on a high price of curu oil. And then they lowered the price of oil without touching the tithe the smallholder had to pay. And after they got the people off the land, they switched to raising sheep."

"Indeed?" Wizenbeak continued writing. "I seem to recall reading about riots and rebellion and all sorts of contention."

"Well, nobody liked being forced off the land. The sheep were more profit and less trouble, by and large. That's when the Yssemers and Bhumrajis got established. They were given title to their estates for supporting the Church. With fire and the sword, as they say."

"What about the Lascajaos?"

"New rich," the old man sniffed. "The current duke is hardly more than a mercenary adventurer."

"And who works the farms now, Master Gowan?"

"Day laborers for the most part. They get paid when they work. The shepherds come around with their dogs at shearing time and bid for the job of herding the sheep next season. The millers, the supervisor, and a few foremen are all from one or another of the monastic orders. They don't *need* all that many people, the latifundas."

"So why won't my land reform work?"

"Because you leave the oil mills in Church hands, your Majesty. Or should I address you as your Holiness? All set to grind down the poor smallholders one more time. The mercenaries were very keen on taking the land until they were reminded." Gowan smiled and took a sip of wine. "It was, you see, something they knew but didn't want to remember."

"Interesting. With all the rebellions and religious wars, it was the oil mills that did them in." Wizenbeak sat back in his folding canvas chair. "Historians never write about oil mills for some reason. What ought to be done about it?"

"Hire some proper historians."

"Hunh, hunh. Well, no, what to do about the oil mills."

"What do you want to achieve?"

The king-patriarch sat for a moment pondering his answer. "I want to make a difference in the world," he said at last. "Something that my successors won't be able to scratch out with the stroke of a pen."

"Like putting smallholders back on the land?" Gowan asked softly.

"That, too. We also have a rebel army to defeat."

"Yes, yes, yes." The one-eyed man sat for a moment considering the matter. "The oil mills. They are the key to the whole business. And even if someone beside the Church owned them . . ." He shook his head. "Times change. A bad man, they could corrupt. A good man, they could take the mill away. Or kill."

"Each latifunda was built around its oil mill?"

"Yes. Some of the larger ones sort of ran together, so they have several."

Wizenbeak refilled his goblet and took a sip as the idea floated up of its own accord. He turned it over a few times, inspecting it for obvious flaws. There were none. At last some of the research he had done before coming here was paying off, though not at all as he had expected. "As king I can charter mercenary companies," he said, giving it a shot, "and as patriarch I could charter such a company to perform a religious purpose. Such as pressing curu oil."

"What? I don't follow you."

"A latifunda with, oh, say, one hundred plots and one oil mill would be chartered as a mercenary company. Each smallholder would have one vote to elect the officers. So far, so good?"

"Well, the smallholders would initially be mercenaries, so the idea might be familiar," the old man said. "But no. Communal farming won't work."

The wizard took a sip of the Jamreaux red. "The *farms* are not communal," he pointed out. "Each man owns his forty acres and needs must work it himself. It is the *oil mill* that is communally owned."

"By the freshly chartered mercenary company?"

"Right. The purpose of the company, however, would be religious, not military. To press curu oil. And sell it."

Gowan the Fox sat bolt upright. "Son of a bitch!" he said. "That just might work!"

"Sure," Wizenbeak said. "We give them the forty acres and a company charter for the oil mill on each latifunda."

"But who would own the mill?" the other asked. "I mean, who'd own it really?"

"Sometimes a mercenary company owns a ship," Wizenbeak said. "Title vests in the company so that acts of piracy don't become acts of war. The company elects the officers and the captain, usually for the duration of the voyage. If a company can own a ship, it can own an oil mill, right?"

"The officers are permanent, then?" Gowan was sharp, but he was working his way through a totally new idea. "What's the duration of the voyage for an oil mill?"

"Whatever the owners of the company decide at the outset. A year. Two years. Get someone good running the oil mill, you can reelect him."

"Hah, I see. And who owns the company? The smallholders of the latifunda?"

"Sounds good to me," the king-patriarch said. "What do you think?"

"A very strange concept," Gowan said at last. "But—" He refilled his goblet and took a nominal sip as he turned the idea over in his mind. "If you put it in writing, I will tell my friends that they ought to attend your lottery."

Wizenbeak pulled a fresh diptych from his field desk and wrote out a draft. Gowan examined it carefully. "I haven't got the foggiest notion what these laws you refer to are," he said at last. "It could be a trick to fool the unlettered."

"Hunh, so much for my vaunted scholarship," the wizard replied, smoothing out parts of what he had written with the stylus. "How about if I write it plain and put the legal footnotes in as a comment, for, for—what do they call it?—nonbinding guidance?"

"Try it that way," Gowan the Fox replied. "If we can get the words smoothed out, the idea sits very well with me."

Wizenbeak looked up from the diptych. "Guidance for the lawyers, not for you."

"Lawyers need all the guidance you can give them, your Majesty," Gowan said. "But the idea of owning your own land, *plus* a share of the oil mill, that was the idea I liked." Maybe I could even trust him to have the legal references right? No, said his hard-won wisdom. Trust no one in power.

"How's this, then?" the king-patriarch said, passing over the diptych. Gowan read it over, then read it over again, slowly, carefully, to be sure he had it right.

"Good," he said at last. "Put it on parchment, set your hand and seal to it, and you've got your lottery."

Wizenbeak summoned his secretary and handed him the diptych. "Make two copies on parchment," he said. "I want them as fast as you can get them done. And send in another bottle of wine."

After they had cracked the second bottle, the wizard sat back in his canvas chair and pushed his emerald glasses up on his nose. "Well, then, Gowan, old boy, where do *you* think would be a good place to hold our lottery?"

On the last night of his life Duke Lascajao's sleep was troubled with a strange dream. He was at a circus or a carnival, standing in a crowd, and a wizard wearing a kingly crown came out on the stage. "Hola," he said, "I will perform such feats of magic as will amaze and astonish you!" Whereupon he did a couple of card tricks, and Lascajao booed him for a fraud and a faker. "For this next trick," the wizard said, "I shall need assistance from the audience." He pointed to Lascajao, and suddenly the duke found himself on the stage with five of his soldiers, four mercenaries, and an officer of his guard. "Now, then," the wizard said, setting his crown straight, "before your very eyes we shall make an army disappear upon the field of battle!" He reached into his pocket and handed each of the mercenaries a numbered slip of brightly colored wood, and when he waved his hand, Lascajao stood alone on the stage with his officer, and the audience had turned into the Tarelian Order.

He sat up in his darkened tent. The sentry standing at his door turned toward him. "Are you all right, sir?"

Lascajao shivered and lit a candle. "I dreamed the campaign went badly," he said, slipping into his dressing gown. In his army four out of five were mercenaries. And the silly stakes that they had been pulling up as they went chasing after the Tarelians, they were to divide the latifundas into small holdings to be distributed . . . The light went on in his head. *That* land was what was going to be distributed at this rumored lottery they'd been hearing about! The wizard in his dream had been giving his mercenaries lottery tickets! "I'll sleep no more tonight," he told his guard. "Would you get me a cup of coffee."

The man returned a few minutes later, visibly shaken. "Sir, sir! The mercenaries are gone! What shall we do!?"

"Bring me my cup of coffee, please," the duke said calmly, and then, reacting to the guard's obvious distress, "Bring in the pot and join me."

Very shortly after, on another part of the field, Duke Bhumraji was roused abruptly.

"Master! Master! Our sentries have had their throats cut, and the mercenaries are gone!"

"What?! Ceton, you whey-faced loon! What the devil are you talking about!?"

"The mercenaries are gone," Ceton said. "All of them."

Bhumraji shook his head and sat up. "Our sentries would have reported them leaving," he said grimly.

"The mercenary sentries are gone. Our sentries had their throats cut."

Bhumraji stood up. Sentries dead, mercenaries gone. An attack must be imminent. "That damned wizard was responsible for this!" he snarled.

"What shall we do?" his orderly wailed.

"Ceton! My armor!" the duke roared. He had resigned himself to death when he had resolved on the rebellion, and he wasn't going to quit now. Once he was fully accoutered, he took his two swords from the rack and thrust them into his sash. With his general's helmet and black horsehair plume he was a fearsome figure, and he stepped out of his tent to rally the men of his household. In the distance, coming out of the east, he heard the Tarelians. "Boom, boom. Yah, yah, yah! Boom, boom. Yah, yah, yah!" By the sound they were maybe two miles away and coming closer.

He looked around. His house guard was gathering about him, and Duke Yssemer, leading his great roan war horse. They were not yet defeated, by God!

"Look west," Yssemer said, sourly.

Bhumraji looked. It was still dark to the west of his encampment, but the sun was picking up clouds. Clouds of dust were moving slowly to close their line of retreat. The horses and men were shrouded in darkness, but they were there; they were waiting for him to try to escape across those gently rolling hills.

Ceton brought up his own black stallion. "Where's Duke Lascajao?" Bhumraji barked. "We can mount a spoiling attack at any rate and slip out to the north!"

Duke Lascajao was in his tent with his sons. He was not wearing his armor but, rather, a silken dressing gown embroidered with the token of his house.

"Father, put on your armor!" the eldest protested. "We can still fight and die like men!"

"Vanija, it is your duty to obey, not instruct!"

"Then give us orders we *can* obey!" the younger said urgently.

"You will obey the orders I give!" the duke snapped. "But

perhaps it will be easier for you, Nerono-bonehead, if I explain them. First, God has turned His face from us, and the holy war has ended in catastrophe. Accept it, as I do, and seek the most resolute method of coping."

"Charge into the Tarelian swine and cut our way to freedom!"

"Ah, Vanija. You talk like a child. Freedom is not so cheaply bought. There is little time. WILL YOU DO WHAT I TELL YOU?"

Stunned at the intensity of his outburst, Vanija and Nerono stepped back. Then Nerono bowed.

"Yes, Father. I will obey."

"Good. Vanija?"

"The Church is nourished by the blood of martyrs!"

"Imbecile! Half-wit! This day will provide the Church with a bloody surfeit of martyrs!" His eldest son stood grimly silent. "Guilliam and Edsvart weren't enough?"

"We must avenge them," Nerono said sullenly.

"By dying uselessly? By throwing your lives away to look *stylish*? I forbid it!" He paused. "Come on, Vanija. Play out the hand!"

"Your way?"

"Yes, imbecile! A small chance is better than no chance. Will you do as I tell you?"

A sigh. "Yes, Father."

"Good." He picked up his short sword. "I must die shortly in any event." He wrapped his hands around the grip and placed the point at his sternum. "When I give the word, you, Vanija, will trip me, and you, Nerono, will strike off my head. When this is done, you will instruct our retainers and men of the house guard to lay down their arms. You understand?"

His sons nodded.

"Good. You will then take my head to King-Patriarch Wizenbeak and apologize to him."

"What?"

"Apologize. You know, say you're sorry! Nerono can do it for both of you, just like at home. Don't ask for mercy. Don't ask for anything. Just apologize and see what happens. IF the king-patriarch asks whether you are willing to serve him or take oath to him, YOU ARE TO SAY YES! WILL YOU?"

"Yes, Father."

"Vanija?"

"Mother won't like it."

"Your mother can take herself to the nunnery of her choice. Will you obey?"

A long, sullen pause. "Yes."

The thunder of the Tarelian advance was coming closer. Boom, boom. Yah, yah, yah! Boom, boom. Yah, yah, yah!

"Now! The trip, Vanija!" He fell on his sword, and Nerono cut off his father's head with a single stroke. Then they put the head on a pillow and went outside to tell their men to lay down their arms.

The heads of the enemy commanders were lined up on the table before him, each neatly impaled on a steel spike for inspection: Duke Bhumraji, his brother, two nephews, two cousins, and three sons-in-law, Duke Yssemer, his son, his brother-in-law, an uncle, a cousin, and two sons-in-law. Unrelated officers were not prominently displayed, but their heads were neatly piled outside for tallying. At the end of the table was Duke Lascajao, all by himself.

Wizenbeak passed in review before the heads, as was the duty of the victorious commander.

"What do you think?" Captain Nick Sejenics asked, walking beside the king-patriarch.

He had been wondering how his own head would look on a spike, garnished, perhaps with troll-bats. "I am reminded of my own mortality," was his reply.

"A splendid battle," Pardus Murado said. He didn't understand the theory, but he approved of the effect. A formidable army in rebellion had suddenly disintegrated, and the leaders were dead or taken. "Splendid. Bhumraji and Yssemer fought to the bitter end. They went down leading a charge at the Tarelian gonfalon with hardly a score of retainers. Duke Bhumraji had made it to within ten yards of the banner, unhorsed and alone, when the spears pierced him! It is a good thing war is so terrible, otherwise we would love it too much."

"We saw," Wizenbeak said tersely. "And what of Duke Lascajao's officers?"

"His men laid down their arms." Murado sounded a little

disappointed. "His sons came out with their father's head and said they wished to apologize to you. I accepted the head, their weapons, and told them to await your pleasure."

"What should I do with them, the Lascajaos?"

"Kill them," Count Braley said. "You killed the father; it is necessary to kill the sons."

"That might well be true," Wizenbeak agreed. "Should I hear their apology?"

A longish pause. "I suppose so," Braley said. "If you're going to kill a man, it doesn't hurt to be polite."

"Yes." He gave a sigh. "Ought I accept their apology?"

Braley and Murado looked at each other with mild astonishment. "No, sir," Murado said at last. "I don't believe you should."

"To what end, sir?" Braley asked. The idea of accepting the enemy's apology implied forgiveness, moving into a strategic mode which he understood most imperfectly.

"To show the imbecility of fighting to the death," the wizard replied. "It might instruct our future enemies. Bring the Lascajaos before us."

After a moment the guards brought in three men, stripped of their battle gear, with their hands tied behind them.

"From the left," Count Braley said, "the new duke, Vanija Lascajao; his brother, Nerono; and his brother-in-law, Javadh Kirwanis."

"We are told you wished to apologize," Wizenbeak said. Vanija looks very like Edsvart, he decided, while Nerono looks more like Guilliam. His eyes flicked to the father's head on the table. The family resemblance was unmistakable. "You have our permission to speak."

"Thank you, your Majesty," Nerono said, clearing his throat. "We wish to apologize for raising war against you. We are very, very sorry."

"Indeed? And do you speak for all or only for yourself?"

The three looked at other and said nothing.

"In this case silence is taken to mean assent. Your apology is accepted. Your lives are spared and the lives of your men." He raised his voice slightly. "Guards. Unbind their hands."

A man will forgive the loss of his father before he will forgive the loss of his patrimony, Wizenbeak thought sadly. He watched them massaging their wrists for a moment, thinking about seeing another sunrise. They will never love me, but there are enemies and then there are enemies. "Before you take your leave of us, would any of you choose to pledge your loyalty to the Crown of Guhland?"

"I will," Nerono said firmly.

"And I, also," Javadh said.

There was a long pause, and Vanija mumbled something inaudible.

"What did you say, please?" the king-patriarch asked.

"Me, too," Vanija muttered softly.

"Oh, good. Do you, then, Vanija Lascajao, pledge your loyalty to the Crown of Guhland?"

"Yes, your Majesty."

Wizenbeak sat back in his canvas folding chair and sighed. "Your reluctance to swear is manifest, young man. Why did you do so?"

"Because my father made me promise I would. Just before I pushed him onto his sword."

The king-patriarch looked over at the duke's head on the table, sitting in splendid isolation. "Kahun was most fortunate to have such a supporter," he said at last. "Count Braley, bring in the map of the Lascajao latifunda."

Count Braley brought the map in, and Wizenbeak unrolled it on the clearest table, beside Duke Lascajao's head. The Lascajaos owned a latifunda with thirteen oil mills and extensive grazing land. It was almost certainly too large a holding to be left in hostile hands. On the other hand? He took his silverpoint and outlined a division into three parts, following old boundary lines. Two with four oil mills and a central one, which included Castle Lascajao, with five.

"Nerono, you spoke for the family. Which property do you choose?" The second son studied the map for a moment and selected the larger central portion. Wizenbeak printed his name neatly above the castle.

"Javadh, you spoke next. What choice do you make?"

Javadh unhesitantingly picked the smaller portion to the south. Perhaps it was better watered, or maybe he lived there. The wizard didn't ask. He simply put down Javadh's name.

"Vanija, you are a young idiot, but you kept your promise to your father, who was a man of character and understanding." He wrote Vanija's name in the third portion. "This holding is hardly suitable for a duchy but is more than adequate for a count."

He returned the silverpoint to his pocket and pushed his spectacles back up on his nose. "Still, better three live counts than another dead duke."

"You didn't have to split up the duchy," Vanija said sullenly.

"Quite so," Wizenbeak agreed pleasantly. "The duchies of Bhumraji and Yssemer have gone into the royal pocket, entire, for distribution to my friends and allies." He turned to his guards. "The three counts and their men are free to depart. All are to have a pair of swords apiece, with horses for the officers. Armor and banners we shall keep as souvenirs."

He smiled. "And now, gentlemen, I must get over to see how the lottery is progressing!"

9

Home, Sweet Home

IN the cutting garden Gorabani and Darussis were having breakfast al fresco, hot popovers in a wicker basket and Lagualian coffee set out on a round marble table, when Count Tylsos, their host, entered the garden through the tall glass doors in the dining room. With him was an unkempt soldier in travel-stained clothes.

"Good morning, revered guests," he said. "This is my cousin, Jerid, an officer in the household of Duke Yssemer. He has news of the rebellion in the mediplano, and I thought it best that you be informed at once."

Gorabani took a sip of the potent Lagualian coffee. Ah, indeed? If it were good news, our effusive host would have brought the word himself. "Good thinking on your part, Count Tylsos. We appreciate your continuing efforts on our behalf. What word have you, Captain Jerid?"

"Lieutenant Jerid, your Holiness," the young man said, somehow reluctant to begin. "You are aware of how the campaign was being fought up till now?"

The former patriarch nodded and took a bite of popover, savoring the fresh, warm bread. "Yes. Our side has three commands of about equal size under Bhumraji, Lascajao, and your own master, Duke Yssemer. The usurper, with the Tarelians and some cavalry, has been avoiding the forces of light, dancing all over the mediplano."

"That's right, sir. The usurper, with seven men to our ten, was trying to defeat us in detail, one ducal army at a time. Duke Bhumraji's strategy was to force him to stand and fight our whole force."

Gorabani took a sip of coffee from the tiny cup. "Yes, yes. If the usurper couldn't defeat you in a reasonable time, he would lose as rebellion and discontent inexorably spread at home, a perfectly sound strategy for Duke Bhumraji to have followed. What happened?"

"There was a battle near the hamlet of Brugah."

Impatient, Darussis wiped his lips with a snowy white napkin. "Go on, Lieutenant. A decisive battle?"

"Yes, sir," Jerid said, rubbing the growth of beard on his cheek. "The three ducal armies engaged the usurper at dawn."

"Your demeanor does not suggest a happy outcome," the pudgy clerisiarch declared. "What happened?"

"Our mercenaries deserted. All of them. En masse, during the night. And the usurper attacked at dawn. Duke Bhumraji and all his household fought to the death, as did Duke Yssemer." He wiped his nose on the back of his hand, leaving a muddy smear in the dust. "I was a courier or I would have died, also, but it was too late. I came back too late."

"No one questions your bravery, Jerid," Gorabani said gently. "You obeyed orders like a good soldier, and it was the will of God that you survived. What happened to Lascajao?"

"The duke fell on his sword, and his sons presented his head as an apology. At least that's what I heard. In any event, his men laid down their arms, and the usurper spared their lives."

"Brugah Field, eh?" Darussis said. "Sounds like a total disaster. Now what?"

Gorabani stood up. "First things first. See that the lieutenant is fed and has a chance to get some sleep. Then we can consider what further steps ought to be taken."

After one of the servants led Jerid off to the kitchen, Count Tylsos picked a red rose from one of the trellises and inhaled its fragrance. "I am afraid, your Holiness, that one of the first steps you will have to take is to find new living quarters."

"You fear to take risks in the face of adversity? We understand."

Tylsos smiled, showing a missing dogtooth. "Of course you do, your Holiness, but I shall explain, anyway. Jerid, here, is the grandson of my maternal aunt, who married an Orthodox merchant conditional upon his permitting their children to be brought up Syncretist. Have I made myself clear thus far?"

Gorabani nodded. "Such marriages were lawful at that time, though they would now be attainted with heterodoxy."

"Heterodoxy sometimes runs in families, unfortunately," Count Tylsos said, turning the rose in his fingers, "and Jerid has a brother, Rovijas, an unalike as day and night. They fought all the time, and if Jerid was one thing, nothing would do but Rovijas should be the exact opposite. Jerid became a passionate Syncretist . . ."

"And Rovijas became Orthodox?"

"Not exactly, Archdeacon. Rovijas became a very lax Syncretist, rejecting his brother's passion while keeping the forms of his religion in a deliberately sloppy fashion." The count smiled unpleasantly, showing the gap in his teeth. "An unacceptably sloppy fashion. Anyway, Rovijas married a pretty young girl, Orthodox unfortunately, whose parents owned this very house. When the mother was accused of witchcraft . . ." Tylsos paused and pulled at his nose.

"Go on," Darussis prompted, suspecting that it might have been Count Tylsos himself who had levied the accusation.

"The Holy Inquisition burned her and her husband. Being well connected, I was able to pick up the property from the Inquisition at a very reasonable price."

The archdeacon raised an eyebrow. "There were no other heirs?"

"They had two sons who fled to escape arrest. One was hanged for the murder of a bailiff; the other died of wounds at Sifoty Field when King-Patriarch Kahun, of blessed memory, fell."

"I see," Gorabani said coldly. "So you are turning us out to make room for your kin?"

"Oh, no, your Holiness. I would happily let Rovijas and his Orthodox bitch sleep under bridges. And when the courts asked me to return this property to the heir in exchange for a somewhat more valuable piece of Church property, a vineyard that abuts a vineyard I already own, I refused."

Gorabani and Darussis exchanged glances. "Then what seems to be the problem?" the pudgy archdeacon asked.

"There is a deadline in the law that King-Patriarch Wizenbeak enacted," Count Tylsos said grimly. "If court-ordered exchange has not been made by Saint Homma's Day, then the tax rates on all the property owned by owners in noncompliance goes up ten percent."

"Ten percent is nothing!" Darussis said. "You'd throw us out for a few pieces of silver?"

The count flushed angrily. "Use your head, you fat fool! I don't want to find myself on any list of landowners that are enemies of the king-patriarch!"

Gorabani looked around the flowering garden. A pity to leave this place, he thought. Such a mixture of comfort and security will be hard to find again. "Saint Homma's Day is still a few months off, Count Tylsos. Perhaps we could defer our departure until then."

A shake of the head. "I would prefer that you left at once. When the news of Brugah Field is announced, there will be a great rush of noncompliant owners coming in to make the proffered exchanges, and as there is safety in numbers, I intend to be one of them."

"You're trimming, Count Tylsos."

"Call it what you will, your Holiness," the count said, casting away the rose. "I will not betray you nor lend succor to our enemies. But neither will I give up my land!"

After he had closed the glass dining room doors behind him, Darussis looked at Gorabani and shrugged. "Not the most genial of hosts, Count Tylsos. Do you think he denounced his Orthodox in-laws to get the house?"

The tall clerisiarch composed his black-gloved hands in an attitude of prayer as he considered the question. "The house was incidental," he said at last. "The denunciation was surely a blow struck at the detestable Rovijas."

"Your Holiness," Darussis said, "is being excruciatingly kind."

After a moment Gorabani nodded. "Perhaps. If the in-laws had been poor, our noble host wouldn't have bothered. Now what?"

The archdeacon stepped on the rose the count had dropped and ground it under his heel. "Keep moving," Darussis replied. "Keep moving and hope that something will turn up. Otherwise we may have to use plan B."

* * *

Duke Bedirny stood leaning on his wooden practice sword and holding his side where his swordmaster had countered his attack. "Enough for a while," he said when breath had at last returned. "What am I doing wrong?"

"There is the briefest hesitation during your attack, sir," his instructor replied. "This is the basic combination." Swordmaster Gevas went through the moves very slowly and smoothly. "Pivot, step, turn, cut, recover." He paused. "Grossly exaggerated, what you did was this: pivot, step, turn—" He made the turn, coming to a full stop, only then to start raising his wooden sword for the stroke. "—cut, recover. The moves all flow into one another. Don't wait for the completion of the turn before beginning the cut."

"I know," Bedirny said. "And I shouldn't think of the moves as being separate but only as the way to cut my enemy."

That's my boy. He can recite the lesson, now he has only to master its application. The swordmaster thrust his practice sword in his sash with a decisive gesture. "You shouldn't think at all," he said as they walked slowly toward the center of the room. "You should look for the opening and let your body move reflexively to take advantage of it. What takes the time you can't spare is when you have to discover the proper way to coordinate each awkward and unrehearsed part of your body."

The young duke bit his lip for a moment, awkward and unrehearsed. "What do you know about women?" he blurted.

Gevas laughed. "Less than I know about the way of the sword, and that is God's truth."

"Look, I've become a favorite of Queen Marjia."

He feeds me month-old gossip as a revelation? Perhaps our boy is leading up to something. "Is this about women or about politics, another subject of which I am hardly a perfect master?"

When Bedirny hesitated, the swordmaster gently prompted him. "The two are mixed in this case?"

"Yes. Before the king marched into the mediplano with the Tarelian Order, I had, uh, I had socialized with her Majesty as a sort of game. Up to that time she was very, well, aloof. 'Proper,' maybe, is the word."

Socialized, he says, Gevas thought, raising his bushy black eyebrows. Our young duke inadvertently involves himself in a borderline royal scandal and thinks nothing of it. However, since he has asked my advice: "She was flirting with you, perhaps?"

The muscular young duke looked down at his feet. "Uh, yes, uh, no. Well, maybe that was what she was doing. In a kind of awkward, clumsy way. She is, after all, only thirteen or fourteen . . ."

And you are only three or four years older. Gevas sighed and let his discipline take hold. At that point recriminations were wasted motion. Focus on where to cut. She *is* very young, and there had been malicious gossip to the effect that she was totally repulsed by the ugly old wizard she married, that she had had to marry. "So after her lord and master marched off to war, what happened?"

"She, uh, she sort of stopped . . ." The sentence sort of trailed off into embarrassed silence.

Don't lead the boy; let him tell it as much as he can. "Stopped what?"

"Stopped holding me off. Several times . . . uh, several times, I think she was willing to go further than I uh, than I uh . . ."

"Try talking about the situation in the third person," the swordmaster suggested. "As in, 'Several times the queen appeared more willing to what? than the duke.' Try it."

"The queen appeared willing to go further than the duke wanted to."

"My congratulations on belatedly showing a little sense," Gevas said, observing the doors to the exercise room without looking. "In the past flirting with high treason unnerved many a bold courtier. Now that King-Patriarch Wizenbeak is coming back, what will happen?"

A long pause. "Marjia said we'd have to be discreet."

"Did she, now? What do you suppose her Majesty wants?"

"I don't know."

We may be in this too deep already. The swordmaster drew the wooden sword from his sash and stepped back. "High guard," he said, "and circle to the left as I pivot, facing you. Concentrate on your footwork." Bedirny began to move. "Good, good. Now remember, don't let your opponent's chatter distract you. Perhaps her Majesty wants to marry somebody young and pretty, like yourself?"

The duke didn't miss a step. "Don't be impudent! But yes, I think she does."

"Someone who is also a duke, like yourself, so she could continue being queen?"

Bedirny circled to the left and said nothing.

"I hear gossip," his teacher said, probing. "They say you are already past the point of no return with her."

"I've not yet bedded her, Master Gevas!"

"The lead foot is floating a little. That's better. If the queen said you did, could you deny it?"

Duke Bedirny flushed like a schoolboy but did not break step. "It would be her word against mine, wouldn't it?"

"I phrased that badly, your Grace. Let us attempt to anticipate the ene—" Gevas attacked with his wooden sword, and Bedirny parried. "—my sword cut. Good, good. Now circle right." Bedirny resumed his guard and changed direction.

"Suppose, once again, that your Grace is in her quarters, she having enticed you there on some pretext or other. And she comes right out and asks you to come to bed. What do you do?"

"Well, for one thing," Bedirny said, moving with satisfactory smoothness, "I wouldn't go."

"You refuse? A wise decision, however belatedly taken," Gevas said softly. "But it is not what she wants to hear. So her Majesty says that if you *don't* come to bed with her, she will tell King-Patriarch Wizenbeak that you forced yourself upon her. Now what?"

The duke's jaw dropped, and he almost stumbled.

"Keep circling, sir. You're open on the low line and off balance." He is off balance for a fact. Just as well I don't hit him unnecessarily; he might fall down, which would be disgraceful. "It'd still be your word against hers, sir, but who's going to believe *you*?"

Bedirny took a deep breath as he struggled to regain his composure. "Ah, ah, why, ah, I don't think she'd do a thing like that."

"I hope you're right. The king-patriarch turned a blind eye to much in the past. Unwisely in my opinion. He should have locked the little slut up and thrown the key away. But if her Majesty decides to make a public issue of the matter, which is already close to a scandal, he must address it. What if she does?"

"She's too young to think of such awful things," the duke protested.

"You have me to advise you on the way of the sword," Gevas said, patiently. "Who is advising her Majesty?"

In his mind Bedirny ran through Marjia's courtiers and ladies-in-waiting. He hadn't much liked them, but he'd never imagined they were dangerous before. Now he was appalled, and it showed on his face.

The bushy eyebrows went up. "If she makes the move on you, which we devoutly hope will never happen, your Grace has two choices. Either you bed her or you can leave the country. And if you bed her, you may be sure that you have committed yourself to becoming king." A sigh. "Your wishes in the matter are of little consequence."

"And if I leave the country, I suppose my estates get confiscated?"

"Entirely possible, sir. It would depend on the whim of a thirteen-year-old girl whose favors you spurned."

"And if I reach for the Crown, I get my head handed to me," Bedirny said sourly.

"Not necessarily," Gevas said, attacking on the high line. Bedirny parried and counterattacked with a clatter of blows. "However, if you *do* reach for the Crown . . ." Bedirny attacked with unexpected smoothness and scored on the swordmaster's hip.

They stepped back and faced each other at middle guard. "If I do reach for the Crown?"

The swordmaster let his breath out slowly. "You'd better want it pretty damn bad."

The sky was full of dragons, wheeling and turning, the long, slender dragons favored by Heiketrive, with bodies of burnished copper and scarlet wings, and the dragons from Tairatrive, colored the same, but with thicker bodies, heavier heads. The Honorable Kachkas of Imperial Trive, from which the Heike and Tairatrives were descended, were carried by several enormous dragons, glorious in golden and purple, which were airborne only by the most prodigal waste of energy. The delegations from a dozen lesser trives, in a confusing melee of colors and breeds of dragon, held their altitude and slowly circled on the perimeter, awaiting their summons to enter the great pendant that had been mounted in the central flue at Bythanastros Field.

The arguments were neither orderly nor dispassionate, and since they were nasal rather than oral, it would have been difficult to impart their precise flavor. Nevertheless they proceeded with a certain logic and with considerable force. The first day was spent arranging the seating within the great pendant, while the second day was devoted to setting the agenda for subsequent discussion. The problem of setting the agenda was extended into the third day and then the fourth, until the Honorable Kachkas of the Imperial Trive lost patience and established a working agenda by the sheer vulgar force of their collective personality.

On the fifth day the question addressed was historical and broken down into small, easily chewed bites. First, where was the location of Alanji Field, also known as Posalanji Field, which was the site of the great trival meeting that had incorporated humans into the trival economy? There was no argument. The site was known, marked, and celebrated in history and legend. The collective memory of the trives extended far deeper into the past than such a recent event.

The second bite was to ask what the name of the field had been before the great trival meeting. Here the several collective memories of the trives provided diverse answers. Hashma Trive, the most radical, maintained that it had always been Alanji, or Posalanji, Field. In contrast, Sisulia Trive held that it been known as Gesisul Ridge after the ancient warrior who had founded their trive. Other memories were less vivid. A consensus was reached, placing Gesisul Ridge at the northern edge of the field in question, which had up to then been nameless.

The third bite was to ask why this nameless field had come to be designated with the name Alanji or its variant, Posalanji? Who or what was being so honored? The day ended with the question unanswered, but much subsidiary information had been dredged up suggesting that the conference had been called to settle a war which subsequently had been effaced from conscious memory.

Heatherfields-Hsven sat out under the starry sky with Bythanastros and Oskvas huddled beneath her jacket for warmth.

"What are we doing out here in the cold?" Oskvas asked.

"Melissa and Yosie are consoling themselves in their captivity," Heather replied, adjusting her woolen blanket about her. "Can't say as I blame them, either. It looks like that great trival conference of yours is going to go on forever."

"The Honorable Kachkas are making progress," Bythanastros replied. "Today, finally, they started establishing the agreed-on basis from which the argument will be resolved."

"Where are they, eight centuries in the past?"

Bythanastros twitched an ear. "There or thereabouts. A start has to be made somewhere, after all. When they adjourned, they were trying to establish who or what Alanji Field was named for."

"It was named for Lady Alanji of the Flowers," Heather said. "Sometimes she called herself Posalanji."

Both troll-bats stirred. "What?" Oskvas asked.

"Who was this Alanji of the Flowers?" Bythanastros asked.

"She was the founder," Heatherfields-Hsven said. "She delivered us from oppression, from slavery."

"She was human?"

Heather nodded. "She was human. In those days the world, the human part, anyway, was ruled by human males. 'Women were property, things to be used and discarded at the pleasure of the men.' " She paused. "There's a whole lot more, in rhyme to bind it in memory, citing chapter and verse."

Oskvas scratched with a vigorous hindleg. "What's rhyme?"

"It's like when you couple the fragrances of onion and garlic for emphasis," she said. "Anyway, after Alanji was totally fed up with men, she went into the wilderness and learned to converse with troll-bats. When at last she understood them, she realized how, with their help, a more perfect social order might be realized."

"And how was that?"

"What we have now, Bythanastros. The boy children are emasculated when they reach puberty, except for the nine who are chosen to compete in next year's games. They spend the year in training, and three days in the games determines the winner. Who becomes the new god-king."

"What happens to the losers?"

"They are emasculated, just like their fellows, at the hand of the old god-king. Then the old god-king is sacrificed to ensure the fertility of the tribe, and the new god-king is crowned."

"Interesting," Bythanastros said. "But why did they need troll-bats to change their social order?"

"Did you ever work the god-king?" Oskvas asked. "They impregnate up to ten or twelve women a day, every day, and they can't do it without help."

"What sort of help?"

"The flow of blood out of the penis is controlled by a little involuntary sphincter muscle that chokes off the vein. After two or three times the god-king loses concentration, and you have to help the poor son of a bitch out. The other thing is the regulation of the seminal fluid that carries the sperm." Oskvas projected a warm sweaty musk. The god-king lies on his back, while the troll-bat sits on the belly and keeps him up. Then the woman straddles him, and the troll-bat sees that she gets her ration of passion. Afterward she goes off with her own troll-bat, who ensures that the sperm will reach the egg.

Heather stirred uneasily. "With a breeding population the size we have, one man couldn't maintain it without help. Lady Alanji looked to troll-bats for salvation from men, but maybe that was a mistake."

10

His Triumphant Homecoming

UPON his return, Wizenbeak found that the Privy Council Chamber had changed a little; the chairs and table were an elaborately carved and polychromed set taken from the castle of the late Duke Bhumraji. Four silver candlesticks, set with semiprecious stones and bearing the arms of the late Duke Yssemer, illuminated the parchment map of Guhland spread out on the table even as they held its corners in place. From the lofty ceiling hung the standards of Bhumraji, Yssemer, and Lascajao, taken at Brugah Field. Other trophies and souvenirs were on display elsewhere in the Citadel.

King-Patriarch Wizenbeak entered the room and motioned Jankura and Gowan the Fox, now Count Gowan, to be seated as he eased himself into his ornately decorated chair at the head of the table. So, he thought, bunching and shifting around in the royal robes to make himself comfortable. Here we sit surrounded by the spoils of war. The question is, How ought they to be divided? He looked around at his councillors and pulled at his mustache. The trick was to keep your balance by moving forward, except, of course, that forward wasn't necessarily straight ahead.

He shrugged and took the plunge. "Now that the Syncretist resistance to returning Orthodox land and accepting Church property in compensation has collapsed, is there any reason why we shouldn't proceed at once to make the contemplated distributions?"

Jankura pushed a diptych across the map of Guhland. "Which

contemplated distribution?" she said. "Gowan and I have looked into this, and it depends on the chances you want to take."

"Oh?" He opened the diptych she had given him. "What's this, then?"

"This division takes you at your word when you said you wanted to make the maximum immediate impact possible. Of the available land, five parts will be raffled off to mercenaries willing to pledge their loyalty. Three parts will be given to the loyalist dukes. And the remaining two parts will be retained by your Majestic Holiness."

"What do I need it for?"

She shrugged and ran a hand over her pate, which was starting to grow out. "Most of it is to maintain the Tarelian Order, which you will absolutely need as a force in being for as long as you want to hold the throne."

The king-patriarch shifted under the weight of the gold chains of office. "Yes, yes. Where am I being challenged that I need the Tarelians?"

"In the short term," Gowan agreed, taking out a diptych of his own, "there is no challenge in sight. Disarm yourself and rebellion will spring up like mushrooms after the rain."

He slid the diptych over the table. "A somewhat slower distribution will have a better chance of success. This plan, which is still pretty risky, recommends three parts to the smallholders, three parts to the loyalist dukes, and four parts retained by the Crown. I personally recommend the third plan to demonstrate that you are in this for the long term."

"In the long term we are all dead," Wizenbeak protested. "If I was in this for the long term, I would keep all the land myself and dole it out an acre at a time as a reward for devoted service."

"You aren't giving thought to your dynasty, your Majesty," Jankura said, stroking the soft fur of a troll-bat who had emerged from her robe.

The king-patriarch sighed and sat back in his chair. "We have given thought to our dynasty," he said. "The fact is, I'm too old to found one."

Gowan laughed. "A man is never too old."

The wizard held out his finger, and Mischka leaped onto it. "Not to make babies, of course. With little Mischka here to help me, I can make babies for the rest of my life.'' He rubbed the troll-bat's ears and produced a dried avricod, which the little animal nibbled daintily. ''Any time I find a volunteer for the hard labor.''

''That's what it takes, isn't it?'' the one-eyed man asked.

''Alas, no. To found a dynasty requires having an heir that can take the reins of power. You want the long term, Fox? How old would this child I have not yet made have to be to hold the throne against these rapacious dukes who surround us?''

Gowan the Fox rubbed his clean-shaven jaw, feeling the growth of stubble. ''Seventeen or eighteen, if you trained him well. Twenty would be better.''

''And thirty would be better still. However, ten or eleven is what you'll likely get if we make the attempt.'' The king-patriarch shook his head. ''I don't even want to see the third option. You'd be setting Guhland up to have an eighty-year-old king and a ten-year-old crown prince.''

''As you wish,'' the one-eyed man said. ''However, you ought to consider the option even if you choose not to follow it.'' He held up a third diptych. ''One part to the freeholders, two parts to the dukes, the rest to the Crown.''

Wizenbeak sighed and took the third diptych. ''What will this accomplish?''

''What can I tell a wizard about deception?'' Gowan asked. ''Except for the distribution changing mercenaries into free-holders, a distant echo of Brugah Field, it displays dynastic intent. Even if you don't intend to found a dynasty, you need to think deeper in time than the next holy day.''

Wizenbeak sat back, looking at the candle flame through his emerald glasses, and rehearsed the mantra for clarity of understanding. The essence of deception, he thought, is to persuade the audience to watch the right hand while the left hand does the business. So if I'm not trying to found a dynasty when that is what the audience expects, there could be some interesting possibilities. ''You're right, of course. I wanted to clear out, and it can't be done.''

Jankura almost smiled. ''I know the feeling,'' she said.

Darussis sat in one of the back booths of a grubby canal-front tavern, drinking country-brewed black coffee and watching the door. Things have not gone well, he thought morosely, contemplating the room. He saw whitewashed brick walls, varnished at shoulder level by constant contact with humanity, and a tile floor that would have been white if they had washed it. There were dark wooden benches, carved with professions of love and the names of people fighting anonymity. The white plastered ceiling was supported by massive beams of black oak, low enough to crack the head of a tall man. A couple of dispirited whores were waiting for customers. The old lock tender sat by the door to keep out of the rain. Things haven't gone well, Darussis thought. Hell, they haven't been going well now for some time. At this very moment, for instance, old Wizenbeak is well on the way to dismantling the Syncretist Church.

He removed the saucer from the top of his cup and took a sip of the strong, bitter coffee. Not the Church itself, perhaps, but Syncretisty Hall had been converted into a museum with a restaurant, and the College of Clerisiarchs was suddenly devoid of income and therefore of influence. They were a ragtag lot of beggars, lay preachers in velvet gowns, selling what little they had managed to steal to keep body and soul together.

There had been a rumor, untrue, or maybe only a little premature, that the king-patriarch was going to call a convocation of deacons, each one representing some particular congregation of peasants and tradesmen that in the aggregate made up the body of the Church. And what was he going to tell them? Nothing. He was going to ASK the deacons, in all humility, whether they thought that the position of patriarch ought to be abolished. Gorabani had been very upset by that rumor.

Darussis took another sip of coffee. It could happen, he supposed, reducing the Church to nothing but churches, supported by the tithes of the faithful. Where, then, the rewards for learning, for study? Ignorant merchants would hand them out to those they deemed worthy. He snorted derisively. Those promised rewards had not been disbursed honestly in the memory of living man. The clerisy, alas, was also a self-perpetuating clique of fanatics. Imbeciles, too. How many he could name—and how many had received advancement over him! Still, there were scholars among them, like Dr. Raskidenji, who was supposed to have been here half an hour ago.

Listen to you, Darussis, he thought bitterly. You make old

Wizenbeak sound like a bloody reformer. He took another sip of coffee. Even under the saucer it was beginning to cool, forcing upon him the harsh choice of drink or discard. Harsh choices were no stranger to him. Having decided to destroy Wizenbeak at any cost, why was he now hesitating at dumping this cup of mediocre coffee? Possibly because the price for a second cup had become serious money.

A tall, lean man came in the door, wearing the traditional but currently unfashionable cape of black wool. The whores looked up for a moment and then returned to their conversation. He removed his wide-brimmed hat, looked around the room as rain dripped off his cape, and finally spotted Darussis sitting in the rear. Raskidenji wasn't unhandsome, but his face was stamped with a stern spirituality that did little to encourage intimacy.

"So, old boy," he said, hanging hat and cape on the hook beside the booth, "I hear that you wanted to see me. What have you got?"

"A spell," the shorter man replied. "A variation of the major weather spell. One that we'd like you to vet, you being the expert and all."

"Huh. Maybe, maybe not. You have a working copy with you, I'll take a look at it and give you an estimate for a proper review."

Darussis reached inside his robe and pulled out a shabby leather scroll case as the waiter came over. Raskidenji looked up and ordered coffee.

After he had been served, he twisted open the case and read through the spell, first swiftly, to see what it was about, and then more carefully, to see how it had been composed and how grammar and syntax interacted. "This is well done," Raskidenji said at last. "Elegantly done, in fact. Who was helping you?"

"A mutual friend," the smaller man said cautiously.

"Right. It shows too much originality to be yours alone." Raskidenji read through the scroll one more time. "It could work, Darussis, but you must know that it's crazy."

"How much to vet it?"

The lean man shook his head. "I could use the money, but the fact is, I wouldn't touch it. What our mutual friend has done is clever as hell, all right." He warmed his hands on the coffee cup and hunched forward. "But one of the virtues of the weather spell was the inhibitions that were worked into it. There were all sorts of double meanings, raising the Lord of the Troll-Bats and calming him at the same time. Here . . ." He took a careful swallow of hot coffee.

"Here what?" the archdeacon asked.

Raskidenji rolled the parchment back up and slipped it into the case. "Here you are summoning the Lord of the Troll-Bats—Vohar, Demon Lord of Thunder—to do your bidding, and when you are finished, you tell him, 'Thank you so much, have a nice day.' If he isn't in a good mood, you're in it up to your neck! You understand?"

"You want to strengthen the mantras of dismissal?"

"No." The other shook his head. "The mantras of dismissal are as good as you'll get them. The problem is architectural in that your intent is liberating rather than constraining. For what you want to do, this is about as good as you're going to get. But—" He pointed a bony finger for emphasis. "—in my judgment far too dangerous to use."

Grimacing, Darussis finished his lukewarm drink. "Do you think it will work?"

A long pause. "Probably, yes."

"And you can't make it safer." It was a statement rather than a question.

Dr. Raskidenji shook his head. "No one could."

"I suppose you're right," the little archdeacon said. Well, he thought, sometimes you have to go with what you've got. "Thanks for your trouble."

The Privy Council Chamber had been enhanced with the personal armor of Duke Bhumraji and Duke Yssemer flanking the door, while that of Duke Lascajao stood in one corner. King-Patriarch Wizenbeak, wearing one of the more elaborate military uniforms in his extensive wardrobe, sat at the head of the table, flanked by Pardus Murado of the Tarelian Order and Lasco Genzari, general of the Royal Army, on the right, with Count Braley, his strategist, and Count Gowan on his left. At the other end of the table sat Duke Viluji, come to receive his reward.

"Your Grace and his family have done great service to our cause," Wizenbeak said, "and it is appropriate that you and yours should be rewarded. In our wisdom we have determined that your third son, Aran Viluji, will receive the fourth part of the Bhumraji holdings in the mediplano.'' Count Gowan unrolled a parchment plat plan and laid a keeper on it to hold it flat. The king-patriarch stood up and traced out the red-marked boundaries with his forefinger. ''As you can see, a substantial holding.''

Viluji nodded, his eyes hooded. Aran was by far the brightest of his boys, and his help would be missed. ''Our family is honored, your Majesty.''

''It is amply deserved, your Grace. The second fourth, here marked with green boundaries, as you can see—'' Wizenbeak traced them out on the map. ''—it goes to your nephew, Archdeacon Ulfjahr Viluji.'' He smiled and reseated himself. ''He was one of the very few clerisiarchs who was willing to give me the time of day when it was my duty to serve in Syncretisty Hall, and in some measure this repays a debt of gratitude.''

''Such debts are most often honored in the breach, your Majesty,'' Viluji said watchfully. Hit high, hit low, he thought. The boy is a good-natured lightweight, nothing more. What was it he had told his sister-in-law? If Ulfjahr had been properly born, he might have been a first-rate bartender.

''Yes, yes,'' the king-patriarch agreed cheerfully. ''It was also through his good graces that we came together, your Grace, so that in some measure we both owe him for the success we presently enjoy. We were given to understand that Ulfjahr's younger brother, Gerd, is the husband of Lady Djilas.''

''She has born him two sons, your Majesty,'' the little duke said, his face impassive as he did not lie but also did not correct the king's misapprehension.

''Excellent. Queen Marjia has become quite fond of Lady Djilas, so this third fourth—'' He leaned over the map and traced out the borders marked in blue. ''—here, we assign to Lady Djilas. Her husband will, of course, assume full right to the property under Guhlish law unless and until he divorces her.''

Oh, hell, Duke Viluji thought resignedly. He gave me a chance to correct his error, and I passed it by. I wonder how much the crafty old bastard knows? Gerd is married, all right, but not to Lady Djilas, who isn't married at all. ''To whom is your Majesty assigning the fourth quarter, the one marked in purple?''

"To me, your Grace," Count Gowan said politely. "For services rendered at Brugah Field."

"I understand," Viluji replied, sitting back in his chair. The land was going to Lady Djilas because the queen wanted it that way. Had he tried to explain the minor deception involved in getting her the position of Marjia's lady-in-waiting, matters would not have changed one iota. He sighed. Gerd had always made his harebrained brother look good.

"And for you, your Grace," Wizenbeak said, pulling at his mustache to hide his smile, "this matched pair of swords forged by the incomparable Tomiji, perhaps his best surviving work." Count Braley set the glazed black stand on the table, displaying a pair of truly beautiful swords.

"Ah, why, I don't know what to say," Viluji faltered. "Thank you. Thank you very much."

The wizard beamed. "They are worthy of your Grace," he said softly, "swords of the most noble lineage. They are truly priceless artifacts and fit expression of our high esteem."

That's it? Viluji thought. Two lousy swords. And a wizard's high esteem? Good God!

"The box, please," Wizenbeak said, and Count Braley produced a small chest of brassbound linden wood. He opened it and began removing legal parchment, piling it in a stack beside the chest.

"You owed the boys in Syncretisty quite a bit, didn't you?" the king-patriarch asked. "We are pleased to mark it paid."

"There were also pledges I gave to the Church in times past," Viluji said hopefully.

"And as patriarch it is my pleasure to return them," the wizard replied. "At least those that can be identified." He reached into the chest and took out a massive gold seal ring with the Viluji arms carved in carnelian. "This is all we have at the moment." He took the ring between thumb and forefinger and spun it like a top. Spinning, it danced across the table until it stopped, wobbled, and fell over with a clatter in front of the duke.

Viluji picked it up and slipped it on his forefinger. "Thank you, your Majesty."

Wizenbeak pushed his emerald spectacles back on his nose. "Perhaps we could add a line to one of the more popular selections in the Book of Common Prayer,'' he mused. ''Something like 'Forgive us our debts as we forgive our debtors.' What do you think?''

''That seems a little radical, your Majestic Holiness,'' Braley said.

''Perhaps you should consult with the clerisy,'' Pardus Murado suggested.

Genzari closed his eyes and shook his head. Count Gowan covered his mouth to hide a smile but held his peace.

''I appreciate the sentiment,'' Viluji faltered, ''and as it applies in my own case, I am grateful. But I have to tell you that it seems inappropriate as an official policy.''

The king-patriarch sat back in his chair, struggling a little to make himself comfortable in robes stiff with bullion. ''Perhaps you all are right,'' he said at last. ''Theology has never been one of my strong points. Duke Viluji, it has been a real pleasure doing business with you this afternoon. Who's next?''

11

Gambling for High Stakes

DEEP beneath the Cymdulock Cathedral former Patriarch Gorabani made his way through niter-streaked passages, his globe lantern casting a feeble light around him. After many twists and turns, with not a little backtracking to avoid the guards posted at key intersections, he at last arrived at his destination and rapped for admittance at the massive oaken door.

Max, the apprentice, opened the peephole, then let him in. "Master Darussis said you'd be coming, Master Gorby."

"Gorbidal," the clerisiarch corrected, using his alias. He removed his hat and gloves, putting the gloves in his hat and the rings . . . he wasn't wearing any rings. He looked in his hat for a moment, as if seeking the missing jewelry, and put it on the upper shelf.

"Yes, sir. Master Darussis will be here very shortly. He said to make yourself at home."

Gorabani slipped out of the scholar's robe he was wearing. Black velvet it was, for formal occasions, hood lined with the red silk of theology and the front richly purfled with gold and maroon as befitted a tenured lecturer. He'd "borrowed" the garment from his host before last, but it was clearly unsuited for the work at hand. He hung it on a peg and selected the least decrepit black robe from among the several that were hanging in the closet. He slipped it on and went over to study the chalkboard.

Darussis, he decided, had done a better than passable job in revising the mantraset they had worked out. Most of his objections had been taken care of, insofar as possible. Here and there a word choice might be questioned—he remembered questioning some of them—but there were no errors. At least no gross errors. At least no *obvious* gross errors. He was engaged in one more compulsive, meticulous review of the spell they were about to use when Darussis arrived, carrying a small cage covered with a dark cloth.

"Good to see you," the smaller clerisiarch said, who was no longer as portly as he had been in happier times. "Are you sure you don't want to hold off until you see what comes of the reported intrigue between her Majesty and the young and handsome Duke Bedirny?"

"Feh." He shook his head. "Palace intrigues are a waste of time, even when you are the one conducting them. Besides, suppose it were true? Bedirny is a weak reed to rest one's hopes on, not at all the sort of champion the faithful need."

"Your Holiness appears less than enamored with the young man," Darussis said. "However, the procedure we are following is also not without risk, as you are well aware. A small delay would cost us nothing."

The tall man sighed. Time, he felt sure, was against them. "Except, perhaps, our resolve. The other item that we needed—do you have it?"

Darussis shifted to Ursprach. "My assistant here is eager but disposable. It can be arranged for him to doze off whenever I say the word."

Gorabani rubbed his naked hands together, an echo of past exuberance providing a little warmth against the cold. "Let's get on with it, then."

"The drum, Max. The one in the cabinet that we cleaned up. Bring it over, please." The little archdeacon took the drum from his assistant and set it on the bench before him. Two feet in diameter it was, and covered on one side only. The drumhead was made of yellow-stained human skin, and the drum itself was a smooth wooden hoop about eight inches wide.

From a shelf above the bench Darussis selected a jar and a bottle of milky liquid, nearly full. The bottle he set aside; the jar he opened and, using his fingers, smeared the drumhead with the dark salve, applying a smooth, even coat. When he had finished, he wiped the salve remaining on palms and fingers on the back of his hands and wrists. He then turned to see the blackboard where he had written the spell, and, using his forefinger, began to inscribe the opening mantra in the dark salve. When he finished, the former patriarch read it over to make sure he had it right.

"So far, so good," Gorabani grunted, and removed the cloth from the wire cage. A troll-bat, sluggish and with lackluster eyes, stared back at him. Good. The little monster was awake but too far gone on kimjii root to make any trouble. The archdeacon opened the cage and removed the troll-bat, spreading the webbed fingers of one hand. The apprentice, who had been well instructed in the procedure, opened the bottle of milky fluid and splashed a generous dollop on the troll-bat's webbing.

"That's way too much," Gorabani said, spilling some of the liquid on the floor. The rest he massaged into the troll-bat's webbing, going from finger to finger quickly but gently. Then he spread the other hand. The little animal began to cry. The fresh solution must hurt like the devil, he thought absently, his own fingers starting to tingle. Max decanted a smaller amount on the other wing, and Gorabani rubbed it in.

That's step one, he thought. For step two, he took the troll-bat and spread-eagled it facedown on the besalved drum, being careful not to smear the spell written on the drumhead. He took a deep breath as he held it in place and counted to ten according to the old timing rhythm. Fine, the little monster can cry all he wants; he is well and truly placed. The whimpers became louder and more resonant as the drum amplified them. Gorabani picked up drum and troll-bat, hanging them on the wall. So far, so good.

"All right, Darussis," he said, speaking in Ursprach. "Time to place the sacrifice."

The archdeacon nodded. "So, Max," he said. "This is going to be pretty dangerous. Come on over here, and we'll hide you in the commode so you can listen without being seen." He drew the musty cloth curtain, and Max obediently climbed onto the wooden box that concealed the buckets of night soil, which he dutifully emptied as needed, seating himself on the closed lid.

"Is this all right, master?"

Darussis nodded. "Absarka, Max." Max's eyes closed. "Do you hear me?"

"I hear you, master."

"Good. Now, this is what I want you to do: Go to sleep for an hour or so, but stay behind the curtain and don't snore." He finished with the regular closing he had been using on the boy. "When you wake up, you will remember everything you heard." Max pulled his knees up and rested his back against the stone wall, fast asleep. Darussis pulled the curtain closed and went back to the business at hand.

Together, he and Gorabani recited the mantra written on the drum. And then, leaving the taller man to work the troll-bat, he went into the spell proper.

My fingers are numb already, Gorabani thought, feeling distinctly apprehensive. I'd better sit down before I fall over. He had just eased himself down onto a sack of dried kimjii flowers they had been using, when Darussis invoked the name of Vohar, Demon Lord of Thunder.

The temperature in the room plunged, producing a fine mist, just as it was supposed to do. Gorabani's teeth chattered, and he clutched his numbing hands together to keep them from shaking. The drum began to grumble, a deep bass complaint without specific words but nevertheless fearsome.

Darussis, with the serenity born of imperfect understanding, produced a silver *tau* nabla and held it before the drum. "Vohar, Lord of the Troll-Bats," he intoned. "Come thou before us!" The grumble changed pitch.

So far, so good, Gorabani thought, shivering uncontrollably, his jaw clenched to silence his chattering teeth. But why do I get the feeling that Vohar is seriously agitated about something?

"VOHAR!" Darussis shouted. "I BID YOU SPEAK!"

"You again?" an unexpectedly mild voice said. "Fewmets! What is it you want, human?"

"I want you to destroy Guhland's king-patriarch, the wizard William Wizenbeak!"

"Oh, really?" There was a rumble of distant laughter. "And how is the weather to single out one puny, tiny human?"

"ANY WAY YOU WANT!" Darussis yelled.

"I could change the climate for the whole kingdom," the drum mused. "Surely that would destroy your victim. Surely it would." The drum began a wobbly humming.

"Don't do it!" Gorabani croaked. Darussis turned to him and shushed him fiercely.

"You don't want your climate changed?" the drum rumbled, expressing grim amusement.

"No! But Wizenbeak must be destroyed!" Darussis said, concerned but not yet alarmed by the turn matters had taken.

"But not with the weather," the drum said, giggling. "We have other means to attempt this feat you ask of us. Vohar, Lord of the Troll-Bats, will undertake this task you set him." Gorabani, in considerable distress, noticed that the demon had omitted asking for his customary sacrifice to seal the bargain and croaked a warning.

Darussis looked at him and shrugged. Matters were off the track, and he didn't know what to do. Even so, he found his best remaining chance. Missing the cue he was expecting to receive, he skipped directly to the final mantraset enclosed in the spell, the binding and dismissal.

"Excellent," he said when he had finished. "Splendid. Thank you. You are dismissed. You may go now." Nothing. Darussis then repeated the lines from the mantraset expelling the elemental. Again the magic didn't bite.

The drum laughed, and the room began to get colder. In one corner a tiny ball of light gathered and grew larger; a ball of light that looked curiously unlike the phosphorescent owl described in ancient manuscripts was dancing and floating. Gorabani closed his eyes. The dancing figure of light, or maybe it was fire, came over and touched Darussis on the forehead.

Darussis screamed and fell to the floor, his clothes burning all over his body. The flaming manifestation of Vohar's will, now bigger than ever and displaying an intense, flickering blue at its heart, rolled over to Gorabani, and the drum laughed like thunder! There was a violent explosion, and the drum shattered into a dozen fragments.

Max the apprentice awoke. The room was filled with foul-smelling smoke and lit by a single globe lantern that had fallen onto the floor. He picked up the lantern and peered around in the gloom. Master Gorby was lying in shards like a broken pot that had spilled its contents. Master Darussis was dead, charred and black, his clothes still smoldering around the edges. Of the troll-bat, nothing was to be seen.

Max shivered and let out a frosty breath. How had it gotten so cold? Perhaps being a wizard was not such a good idea, after all. Master Darussis and Master Gorby had been powerful wizards, masters of the art, and look where it had gotten them. What was he going to do, go back to his father and work in the fish market? Incredibly, the idea seemed attractive, the smell of fish wholesome, and his father a decent and concerned man. Touching nothing, Max slipped out of the room, locked the door, and left Cymdulock Cathedral.

12

Letting the Chips Fall Where They May

WIZENBEAK pushed his way through the knot of courtiers that surrounded him until he reached the judicial chamber behind the King's Bench. Originally it had been one of a pair of half-round towers that guarded a sally port. In later years it had been a guardroom, and later still the private chapel of the tragic Queen Kejate. The pair of stained-glass windows, set into stone walls two feet thick, were from that time. The ceiling was rough-hewn beams supporting hand-split planking, entirely of chestnut to keep away the spiders. Otherwise, the curving walls were hung with tapestries to ward off the drafts.

The furnishings were rather austere, reflecting the fact that the room was used by whatever judge was serving in the courtroom on that day. There was a wardrobe, a tall pier glass, a table with several unmatched chairs, and a shabby leather bench.

"Deacons," Wizenbeak said. "We thought they'd never stop talking. Almighty God, how they went on."

"Your Majestic Holiness is patriarch, after all," Count Braley pointed out. "You could have shut them up whenever you wanted."

"Yes, yes, but they were doing what we wanted for once." He pushed the emerald spectacles back on his nose. "But maybe we should have done that rude and unseemly thing." As several well-intentioned courtiers oozed their way into the chamber around him, Wizenbeak took a deep breath. "Braley," he said, "we're running late. Bring me something to eat—coffee, a sandwich, maybe a piece of fruit. Janko, help me with the damn robes. The rest of you, clear out."

Nobody moved except Count Braley.

So much for the theory that courtiers hang on your every word. "It is not that we do not appreciate your presence, gentlemen," he said firmly. "However, the time has come when we prefer your room to your company. You." He tapped an exquisitely dressed young man on the shoulder.

The fellow had a winning smile, spaniel-like eyes expressing pleasure at being noticed, body language suggesting things difficult to put into words. "Oh, *yes*, your Royal Holiness?"

"Please leave, sir." And when that brought no more than a pained look of incomprehension. "OUT!"

After the gaggle of courtiers had made their exits, bowing and scraping and twittering like magpies, Jankura closed the door.

"What time are we supposed to open the Jamreaux thing?" he asked, as she helped him off with the ornate patriarchal robe of white and gold, tastefully embellished with scarlet thread worked into symbolic designs. It has a name, he thought, but I can never remember it. Damn. It's a prop, and I can still name all the props I used back in the old days. What's the matter with me?

"Half an hour ago," she said, "but it's all right. Everybody is sitting in court, waiting very patiently because they know you're in here." She hung up the gold and white robe and helped him into the relatively simpler robe of black velvet on black silk worked with gold thread which the king wore as judge.

"How do we look?" he asked.

"Frazzled," she said. "A little grooming is clearly indicated." Jankura sat him down and combed out the snarls in hair and beard and smoothed it down until he once again looked fully regal. There was a knock on the door, and she admitted Count Braley with a wicker basket covered by a linen napkin, which he whisked off to reveal a cork-stoppered flask of coffee, a chicken sandwich on dark bread, a pickle, and a bunch of green grapes.

"A hell of a thing," Braley said, only half joking. "Having your strategist bring you lunch."

Wizenbeak wolfed half the sandwich and washed it down with coffee, sweet, with milk, the way he liked it. "No, no, it had to be you, Braley. We couldn't trust those other imbeciles to be timely. They'd make a production and bring it in when we wouldn't have time to eat.''

''It's all right,'' the count said, mollified. ''An army marches on its stomach.''

The king-patriarch demolished the other half sandwich in three bites, then commenced eating the grapes one at a time and spitting the seeds into the napkin. ''Janko, did you review the evidence on this thing we're about to hear?'

''Of course. You asked me to, right?''

''Right.'' He popped a grape and slowly chewed it. Having one's orders obeyed, one's wishes deferred to, is profoundly unnatural, he decided. The worst part is, you could get used to it very easily. ''Is there anything we ought to know?''

''No surprises,'' she said. ''It looks like everything is pretty much straightforward. The ears match.''

Wizenbeak folded the napkin around the grape stems and seeds and finished his coffee. ''Straightforward, eh?'' he said; blotting his lips. ''That's nice. What was that about ears?''

''They match,'' Jankura said. ''You'll see.''

''Probably so.'' He sighed. ''We want you both to attend the session. Mainly so we can consult with you before handing down a decision. You understand?''

''Didn't you want Gowan, as well?'' Braley asked.

A slow shake of the head. ''On this one, we know what he thinks without asking.''

''What about the troll-bats?'' Jankura asked. ''I was looking forward to getting back to them.''

''You said you had someone taking care of them, someone good. We need you here.''

She pursed her lips and nodded. ''Right now I have a fellow named Doctor Raskidenji. A recently unemployed professor of hagiology or some such. He *is* good, but for the past week I've seen about as much of Mischka and Branka as you have. Now what do you want from me?''

Wizenbeak picked up the pickle. ''We'd like to spend lots of time with the little monsters,'' he said, pointing it at her. ''Failing that, we'd like *you* to spend lots of time with them.'' He took a bite of the pickle. She's taking up some of the slack that the queen used to handle before reverting to her useless brattish self. Would we like her to take up some more? Yes. Probably as much as she could handle. "However, there is a lot to be done, and time is the one thing we can't give you." He took another bite. "We need you here."

Jankura nodded. "I understand," she said. "I can remember the same problem from when I was regent. There just isn't a whole hell of lot of use for troll-bats when you're mucking around with affairs of state."

"Too true," the king-patriarch said, finishing the pickle. "Any questions before we convene the court?"

"Why did you save the pickle for last?"

He stood and swept his robes about him in an increasingly practiced manner. "It sets my mouth for passing judgment."

If he had not had a harelip, or perhaps if he hadn't stammered when he got excited, Brother Skerboj might have become a lay preacher. He was, all agreed, a good hard worker and orthodox in his beliefs if not very bright. This final assessment was unjust, because Skerboj was a considerably better thinker than he was a talker. In time he had become associated with the housekeeping of Cymdulock Cathedral, and when the king-patriarch had dismantled the economic infrastructure of the clerisy, he was an EF-3, ecclesiastical functionary, third class, and far removed from the great sea change that had swept away so many of his superiors in the administrative superstructure. He was in charge of the keys inside the cathedral, signing them in and out as requested.

He looked with professional satisfaction at the board which he maintained. Each peg had a number burned into the wood with a heated stylus, and from each peg hung a key with the corresponding number, or else a wooden chip with the name of the person who had taken the key, and the date it had been taken. He knew that board and the keys and the rooms that the keys unlocked. Of the people who took them, he knew the regulars and which ones he could make allowances for.

The key for Room 537 was still out. He looked at the tag, which was signed out for the night before, and scowled. Darussis had given him trouble before. If one of his keys was missing, there was going to be trouble. Picking up the ring of master keys, he sorted through them until he found the one that would open 537. He took it and went off to see what was the matter.

All too often these high and mighty clerisiarchs had taken to sleeping in rooms intended for other purposes. If that overbearing Darussis was sleeping late, he'd roust the son of a bitch out.

Skerboj made his way through the long dank passages under the cathedral until he came to the guard station. No problem. The guards knew him, and he signed in to pass beyond the sign that said: UNAUTHORIZED ENTRY FORBIDDEN. He knew where Room 537 was, but he still missed it on his first approach. Turning back, he found the room, and, holding the globe lamp in his teeth, he used one hand to jiggle the door a little until he could turn the key in the reluctant lock with the other.

The stench was appalling. Holding his globe lamp high, he advanced cautiously into the room. Something was wrong here, and it made the hairs on the back of his neck stand up. Then he saw the bodies, one burned to the point where the charred spine and some of the ribs stood clear of the carcass, the other shattered, lying in a pool of dried blood. He gasped and slowly lowered his shivering lamp to the face of the corpse that still had a face.

"Wuh-wuh-wuh-well," he said to himself, "I do buh-buh-buh-believe that might buh-buh-be Patriarch Gorabani." For whom there is a reward out, dead or alive. The other body was probably Archdeacon Darussis, who had signed for the key, but he had no interest in taking a closer look. Now what?

After checking out at the guard post, he went up to the tiny room that held the Officer of the Day, the ensign in charge of what was surely a boring detail.

Composing himself, Skerboj went in and bowed. "Uh, your Honor, sir?" he said. The ensign looked up, recognizing one of the staff without knowing the name.

"What is it?" he asked.

"Puh-puh-puh-Patriarch Guh-guh-guh-guh-Gorabani, sir. I know where he is."

The ensign stood up from his desk, delighted at a break in the boring routine. "Sergeant!" he barked. "Come in here!"

The sergeant made a carefully timed appearance. Not prompt exactly, but not so tardy as to merit a rebuke. "Yes, sir?"

"This fellow says he knows where ex-Patriarch Gorabani is. Right, harelip?"

Skerboj nodded.

"You hold the place down, Sergeant, while I get a couple of men and collect the son of a bitch," the ensign said.

"There's a rewuh-wuh-wuh-ward," Skerboj said. "I'm entitled to the rewuh-reward."

The ensign sighed. "Right." He adjusted the block and pushed down on the froe to slice off a fresh three-by-five wood chip, on which he wrote the date. "What's your name?"

"Skerboj. I'm an EF-3."

"On this date EF-3 Skerboj reports finding Patriarch Gorabani." He looked up. "Satisfactory?"

Skerboj nodded, and the ensign signed it and had the sergeant sign it as well. "Here's your testimonial for the claim, Skerboj. All that we need now is Gorabani."

"Fuh-fuh-fuh-follow me, then. I'll take you to him, but he's duh-duh-dead."

The ensign nodded. "Right. Sergeant, get some of the police from across the square so we don't have to handle the corpse."

"Corpses, sir. There was two of them."

"You heard the man, Sergeant. Get moving."

Wizenbeak sat on the King's Bench looking down at Chancellor Tolikna, a balding man of about forty with a stocky, muscular build. Braley had said he was a first-rate swordsman. Now, neatly dressed in gray silk, he was presenting the case for the Jamreaux heir, his once and perhaps future lord.

"Now, wait," the king-patriarch said. "We want to be sure we understand what you have been telling us. The Kahunista soldiers came in and wiped out the Jamreaux family, root and branch, except that they missed one."

Tolikna nodded gravely. "That is correct, your Majesty. They had a list, which included my master, Polje Jamreaux, who was five days old at that time."

"Yes, yes. We understand. Now, how is it that he was not killed, so that he stands here before us?"

"One of the Lady Jamreaux's attendants, her wardrobe attendant, Gruisha, had given birth within hours of her mistress. The morning before the Kahunistas arrived, and at the direct request of one of the officers, the late Captain Nuris, she exchanged her own baby with the Jamreaux heir before leaving the manor house. She gave direct testimony to that effect."

Wizenbeak rested his head in his hands. Gruisha had indeed so testified, and as nearly as he could tell, she believed she was telling the truth. Her grief in recounting the death of her child, which she had evidently not anticipated, was probably genuine. Curiously, the fact that she had not anticipated that her own child might be killed in the circumstances tended to lend credibility to the story. She was a kindly, simple person who had been used in the furtherance of the dynastic ambitions of the Jamreaux retainers.

"So a substitution was made." Probably it had been; almost certainly it had been. "Even so, how do we know that the young child whom you have presented to the court is Duke Polje Jamreaux and not a pretender of some sort?"

The chancellor made a slight bow. "We have, first, the testimony of Gruisha. Second, the testimony of the mother, Lady Kaula, whom the Kahunistas spared, since she was a member of the powerful Viluji family."

How many relatives does Viluji have? the wizard wondered. Well, maybe that isn't a problem. Lady Kaula had had six children, all now dead except Polje. She'd be unlikely to remarry, and probably have little to do with the duke in any event. "Yes, yes. And you have the birth certificate, with the tiny footprint, and the scrolled silk pedigree, and the locket with the infant's hair, which, we have no doubt, matches the young man whom you represent. All of which are artifacts of the most persuasive sort but capable of being forged."

Chancellor Tolikna looked amused without actually smiling. "The artifacts and the testimony, your Majesty, bear on the legitimacy of the heir. The final line of evidence which we wish to present is intended to show an actual connection of the blood. Please show the court Exhibits Four, Five, and Six."

The exhibits in question were paintings of two dukes of Jamreaux, Polje's uncle and his grandfather, and the wedding portrait of his parents. Both dukes were in armor, the grandfather on horseback.

"Your Majesty will note the color of the hair, a characteristic flaming red. The court is invited to compare the hair color in the paintings with that of the child."

"There is a similarity," Wizenbeak conceded.

"The second point of similarity concerns a murret-colored

birthmark on the left shoulder, in shape somewhat resembling a nabla." The chancellor turned to the retainers sitting on the front bench with Polje and nodded. The child stood up, and one of the women pulled his shirt down to display the birthmark to the court. Wizenbeak nodded.

"Exhibit Seven is the Jamreaux family record of births and deaths, a rather unwieldy collection of parchment and annotated scrolls. From this has been selected five cases of similar birthmarks, described with sufficient detail to match that of the heir." Chancellor Tolikna walked over to the table and picked up a single piece of parchment. "These cases have been set forth in Exhibit Eight, here, and each case has been verified by officers of the court as being in agreement with Exhibit Seven. Exhibit Eight is submitted in evidence, in lieu of Exhibit Seven, which is available for scrutiny."

"This is suggestive, Chancellor," Wizenbeak said, "but hardly constitutes anything resembling rigorous proof."

"I understand, your Majesty. Exhibit Nine is a plaster cast of Polje Jamreaux's right ear, made in the presence of court officials and attested to by them."

An ear? the king-patriarch thought uneasily. They have the child right here. What do they need the plaster cast of his ear for?

"Exhibit Ten," Tolikna said, removing a black cloth from a rather large glass jar, "is the head of Arvan Jamreaux, the child's father, preserved in brandy. Lady Jamreaux has testified that this is, indeed, the head of her husband. We have other witnesses, if they are needed, to establish the identity of the head."

"In the past we had somewhat to do with Arvan," Wizenbeak said, studying the head in the jar that was set before him. "He seems a little the worse for wear, but that's him, all right." He cleared his throat and looked around the courtroom. "That is to say, the court is satisfied, in the absence of compelling evidence to the contrary, that Exhibit Ten is indeed the head of Arvan Jamreaux, youngest brother of the last duke."

Chancellor Tolikna merely nodded, as if no other outcome had been possible. "Thank you, your Majesty," he said gravely. "The third and final point of similarity to establish the paternity of young Polje, here, is the comparison of Exhibit Nine and Exhibit Ten. Specifically, the right ear of the child, as represented by this plaster cast, with the right ear of the father, easily visible through the glass jar.''

He handed up the plaster cast, and the king-patriarch looked back and forth from cast to embalmed head. There was a mantra to aid pattern recognition, enabling one to perceive hidden similarities, but it wasn't needed. Except for size, the two ears appeared to be identical. Now what? Consult with Braley and Jankura, of course.

''Court will adjourn for a quarter of an hour,'' Wizenbeak said, ''After which we except to hand down the verdict.''

Underneath Cymdulock Cathedral, Inspector Kokolskaia looked around Room 537, his manner expressing a certain benign skepticism. An officer was outlining the bodies with a piece of fat yellow chalk, and others were searching drawers and closets for the key which Skerboj insisted was missing.

Lieutenant Jetay walked into the room and snapped his diptych shut. ''Well, sir,'' he said briskly. ''Several witnesses have identified the one body as that of Patriarch Gorabani. The burned body is probably that of Archdeacon Darussis. We have men going over to his room overlooking the canal to see if they can find any evidence.''

Kokolskaia nodded. ''The key, perhaps?''

''Yes, sir. Or Darussis himself. That burned body, it could be anyone. About Gorabani, it would seem appropriate to inform the king-patriarch at once.''

''Is that all the information we need?'' the inspector asked mildly. ''When the king-patriarch asks how they came to die, what shall we tell him?''

''Why, that they died attempting to work a dangerous sorcery. The blackboard, the working notes we found, all bear that out.''

Kokolskaia nodded impassively. ''So I am told.'' That theory was plausible but by no means definitive. The door had been locked, after all, and the key was missing. ''Have your men found the key yet?''

''No, sir. But it may turn up.''

''The men are thorough,'' the inspector said. The key wasn't there, and at that point the search was pretty much intended to answer the question of where one had looked, namely, everywhere. ''The key is not in the room, so obviously it must have left the room. And therefore some person or persons unknown took it with them when they left."

The lieutenant considered this for a moment and made a note in his diptych. "Yes, sir," he said. "Should we try to find these persons or person unknown?"

"That would be a good idea," Kokolskaia murmured. "Then, when the king-patriarch asks about them, we can say we're looking for them."

The lieutenant made another note in his diptych and snapped it shut. "Very good, sir! I'll get on it at once."

He's so eager, Inspector Kokolskaia thought. He wants to be off and running and never stops to sniff what direction he wants to run in. Well, let's see if we can't guide him a little. "Good thinking, Jetay. Do you recall the state of the commode?"

"It was behind the curtain, sir. Both lids closed."

"So it was, and so they were. What about the bucket?"

Lieutenant Jetay looked baffled. "It was there. What about it?"

"The log the guards kept shows that Darussis had come in every evening for the last eleven days. Yet except for a little urine, the bucket was clean. What does that tell you?" There was a long pause that gave every sign of going on indefinitely. "What it tells you, Jetay, is that someone cleaned the bucket."

The younger man opened his diptych and made a note. "Yes, sir."

"Probably the someone who cleaned the bucket was not one of the two dead clerisiarchs."

"Yes, sir. How can you say that, sir?"

The help you get these days, Kokolskaia thought sadly. Well, take him through it. Someday maybe it will register, and he'll start to think on his own hook. "Because the key was neither on its nail by the door nor in the room, someone took it out. Therefore, there was someone else in the room. Since the commode was clean, someone must have cleaned it. One may surmise that the person who cleaned the commode and the person who left with the key were the same."

Jetay nodded and made a note in his diptych.

"You have that? Good." Kokolskaia's face relaxed a little into what might have been the start of a smile. "What that means to you and to the officers who are going out into the city looking for this person is that the two clerisiarchs probably had a flunky. Young, male, very likely willing to apprentice himself to a couple of wizards for little or no pay."

"Yes, sir. That's very impressive, sir."

It was obvious. It should have been obvious to anyone, but to Jetay it was a revelation. Well, he'll learn. I hope. "Thank you, Lieutenant. Now, go out and start looking for this fellow, starting perhaps from around the room of Archdeacon Darussis."

"Yes, sir. What about telling King-Patriarch Wizenbeak, sir?"

Kokolskaia pulled at his nose. The news was hot; better not delay too long in passing it on. Skerboj wanted to cut off the head and deliver it personally to ensure that he got the reward. I told him it wasn't necessary, but God knows who he's been talking to. "Probably best to take a sedan chair over to the Citadel and tell him myself."

One of the officers came up. "Sir, we have the stretchers here. Shall we move the bodies to the morgue?"

The inspector shook his head. "No. Just cover them with sheets for now. I have to go over to the Citadel to tell the king-patriarch, and he may want to see them just the way we found them."

In his chambers behind the King's Bench, Wizenbeak turned to Jankura and Braley. "We are convinced. Polje Jamreaux is the heir to the Jamreaux holding. What's the argument against ruling in his favor?"

Jankura ran one hand over her tonsure, which now looked more like a crew cut. "Dynastic, basically. A strong king needs land to support his armies, and the Jamreaux holdings are strategically located."

Wizenbeak nodded vigorously and pushed his spectacles back on his nose. "We understand. Count Braley?"

The handsome strategist looked thoughtful. "Observe," he said, making an irregular circle in the dust on the table. "Here's Jamreaux. To the north—" He traced a wobbly figure. "—Church lands, already in your pocket. To the east—" Another wobbly figure, sharing the common boundaries. "—the same thing." He traced another boundary. "To the west it's also Church land, but supporting the Tarelian Order. To the south it's Duke Bedirny, except for a couple of counts who are married into the Bedirny family."

"Do you argue that we have to hang on to the Jamreaux lands?"

"Well, your Majesty, strategically it gives you a very solid position." Count Braley tugged at his sash, tightening the companion sword he was wearing. "Of course, that cuts both ways. If you were forty, I'd say hang on to it and break the dukes one after another to consolidate your rule."

"Hunh," the wizard said sadly. "We parted company with forty long since. Besides, we have no wish to break anybody."

"You may have to fight a small war now to avoid a much fiercer war in the future," Braley said. "Viluji is ambitious, and he isn't the only one."

Wizenbeak pulled out a chair and sat down at the table. "Let the future fight its own damn wars," he said. "Will we be any the worse off making little Polje the fifth duke of Jamreaux?"

"He *is* a redhead," Jankura said. "He'll be making trouble for somebody, eventually; you can depend on it."

"That's eventually. What about now?"

Count Braley tugged at his sash. "You'd be dealing with Chancellor Tolikna, who is—" He hesitated. "I hate to call the man a master strategist, but the fact is I don't know of anyone better. In the short term he'd be consolidating the Jamreaux position. Absent any threat, I'd look for him to have his horns in."

That might be the way to go, Wizenbeak thought, restore Polje Jamreaux with the Crown named as his heir until he reaches what, seventeen? No, no. Keep it simple so even a three-year-old like Polje can understand it. Give it back and appoint Tolikna guardian until when? "We could live with that," the king-patriarch said at last. "Suppose we make Polje the fifth duke of Jamreaux and appoint Tolikna his guardian until when? When the boy is eighteen?"

"You aren't going to hold it, then?" Braley asked. Wizenbeak shook his head. "Eighteen seems a little low."

"Try twenty or even twenty-one," Jankura said.

Braley nodded in agreement. "Twenty-one is good. Are we going to make the Crown the heir until then?"

There was a knock on the door. Wizenbeak turned to Jankura. "See what they want."

She went to the door and opened it a crack to receive a little wooden chip from the other side. "Inspector Kokolskaia is here with someone named Skerboj, who wants the reward for finding the late Patriarch Gorabani."

"So Gorabani turned up dead?" the king-patriarch said. "Where did they find him? Wait. No point in talking through the door. Ask the gentlemen in."

Jankura admitted Inspector Kokolskaia and Skerboj. "The king-patriarch wishes to know where Gorabani was found," she said brusquely.

Skerboj started to stammer and looked appealingly at the inspector, tugging at his sleeve. Kokolskaia patted his hand. "EF-3 Skerboj, here, found the body in Room 537 of Cymdulock Cathedral, your Majesty. In the course of carrying out his duties."

Wizenbeak nodded. Was that three levels down? He didn't remember. "Skerboj is eligible for the reward, then. How did he die, the patriarch?"

"With considerable violence," Kokolskaia replied. "The theory at present is that the two of them were casting a spell which backfired on them. There was a blackboard covered with Ursprach and other paraphernalia."

"Two? Who was the second person?"

Kokolskaia opened his diptych. "Probably Archdeacon Darussis," he said. "The second body was burned beyond recognition."

Wizenbeak sighed. "There's no help for it. We'll have to go down under Cymdulock Cathedral and see for ourselves. Wait until we dispose of the case before us, and we'll be over directly." There were spells? He turned to his assistant. "Janko, who do we have that can read Ursprach in cold print?"

Jankura considered the various wizards and charlatans on the royal payroll and settled on the new troll-bat handler. "Doctor Raskidenji," she said at last. "I'll bring him over." She opened her diptych and made a note. "What did you want to do about your meeting with Duke Falenda?"

A week later Jankura sat in the Privy Council Chamber with Gowan the Fox. Below the captured battle flags hanging from the lofty ceiling a crystal chandelier had been installed, and on the floor an ornate and richly colored carpet, pulled from some warehouse or other. "Well, sure, Braley has a point," she said, leaning on the carved and polychromed table. "But the king has a point, too. If he isn't going to found a dynasty, what's the best he can do for the country?"

Count Gowan fingered the black eye patch he wore. "He has a duty to found a dynasty in order to prevent civil war."

"Right. Braley and I have hashed this over a few times with him. His point is that attempting to found a dynasty and founding one are not at all the same thing." She hesitated a moment. No sense telling Gowan that Wizenbeak had *never* bedded Queen Marjia. It would only get him upset. "Forget the dynasty. What else could he do for the country?"

Why did I ever agree to advise this lunatic? Gowan wondered. He would have given me the land anyway, but no, I thought I could do some good in the world, lending the king-patriarch my wise and sagacious counsel. "All right, Janko," he said at last. "Guhland's civil war is the problem. Right now it has its fires banked, but when he dies, it figures to flare up again." What could anyone do? Buy a little time, maybe. Better to die later than sooner if you have a choice. Better to go down fighting in any event.

Count Braley entered, putting his long sword on the rack by the door. "Going over the succession, old boy?" he asked, taking a seat at the table. Gowan nodded glumly. "Wrong question. The problem is to avoid renewing the civil war."

"Any ideas?" the Fox asked.

"Basically, the king is buying time to let things cool down. Did he talk to you about abolishing the clerisy?"

"Now and again," Jankura replied. "That was what he was setting up with that conference of deacons he called in."

Braley leaned forward with his elbows on the table. "Not a bad idea, that. Weaken the opposition, right?"

"That's the theory, anyway," Gowan agreed. "But when he dies, it will all be undone."

"Not necessarily." Count Braley hesitated a moment. "The king has a policy. At least I think he does."

"Buy time and hope for the best?"

"No, Janko. Look what he's doing. He *is* pushing land reform. Abolishing the clerisy—for all practical purposes that's done. Decentralize the Church—that's done, too, once he resigns as patriarch. It's like razing the wall around Rosano. Once the wall was gone, the hard-liners in Rosano were never able to dig in their heels to make a stand."

Jankura looked at Gowan and then back. "I missed something," she said. "What does the wall around Rosano have to do with anything?"

"It got torn down in the war, and we never let them rebuild it, all right? When the three dukes raised the flag of rebellion in the mediplano, Rosano would undoubtedly have joined them if the wall had been there." Braley leaned back and folded his arms. "It'll be the same with the institutions. Once they're gone, those pious bastards, those sons of bitches that made a living being holier than thou, stinking clerisy with their flaming hypocrisy—well." He paused for breath. "They won't have the leverage anymore!"

He always was too pretty to take seriously, Jankura thought. This time, however, he has a problem with logic. "True," she said mildly, "but most of the land going up for land reform only *used* to be Church land. It is now the *Crown's* land, and by giving it up, the king is weakening us as well as them. Am I right?"

"Of course," Count Braley agreed. "Now, this is speculation on my part, you understand. Given that the king-patriarch is not looking to establish a dynasty, who figures to take over when he dies?"

"What sort of estimate do you want to hear?" Gowan asked skeptically. "If it's policy you're making, you ought to be looking at the worst case."

"Right," Braley said. "That's exactly right. What I think is that the king is trying to minimize the possibility of civil war, even if the Kahunistas take over the throne."

Gowan the Fox shook his head. "I disagree. Well, not with you, Braley, with the king, if that's what he thinks. Less is not stronger. Giving land to those who are not your supporters will weaken you now and in the foreseeable future."

The door was opened to admit Wizenbeak and Duke Falenda. The three at the table rose and stood as both men placed their long swords on the rack by the door, resuming their seats when the king-patriarch took his place at the head of the table.

"After a protracted debate," Wizenbeak said, adjusting his stiff and voluminous robes, "Duke Falenda has persuaded us that the Crown ought not to be giving away land which it could easily sell. Specifically, we refer to the Old Harmony Church Latifunda, which borders the Jamreaux estates on the north, and the Syncretisty University Latifunda, which borders the Jamreaux estates on the east."

Falenda looked rather depressed for one who had just won such a signal victory.

Wizenbeak removed a couple of color-coded diptychs from an inner pocket and pushed the red one across the table to Jankura. "This is a copy of the decree permitting the tenants now working the land to sign a seven-year lease with an option to buy. Get it copied on parchment for mounting on display at the latifundas in question." Mounting for display meant putting the official decree inside a flat, clear block of glass.

"The terms are generous," Duke Falenda said with a sigh. "Excessively so, in my opinion. However, if your Majesty's argument is correct, the Crown will reap a considerable flow of tax revenues."

Wizenbeak tugged at his mustache. "The royal argument," he said softly. "Was the duke able to refute it?"

Falenda shook his head. "No, sir."

"What *was* your Majesty's argument?" Count Braley asked.

"Why, basically that the supervision and oversight required to run such establishments is expensive and not terribly efficient," the king-patriarch replied. "In terms of revenue, we should do a lot better collecting taxes from the owners."

"It might well be true," Gowan said. "The owners, working for themselves, will work harder than you could make any serf or day laborer work."

"Except with the most rigorous supervision," Falenda said, echoing a recent argument.

"Which is not often forthcoming," Wizenbeak said, "and is besides easily corrupted. Now, this—" He pushed the purple diptych across the table to Jankura. "—this is the authorization for the free landholders on each latifunda to organize themselves into a mercenary company, the purpose of which is mutual support and self-help.''

''In the best of all possible worlds this might be a good thing,'' Falenda said. ''However, it appears that this is directly aimed at the rural moneylender, replacing that kindly and beneficent soul with a group, a wolf pack, rather, of mean-spirited, horny-handed avaricious sons of toil who will ruthlessly exploit their weaker brethren.''

Gowan swung around to look at the duke with his good eye. ''Did you ever have to deal with a rural moneylender, your Grace? Kindly and beneficent they are not.''

There was a knock on the door. ''See who it is,'' Wizenbeak said, and Jankura went to see.

''It's Inspector Kokolskaia,'' she said. ''You wanted to see him right away if he ever found anything new, and he has the missing witness in tow.''

The royal party went down into the subterranean depths of Cymdulock Cathedral: King-Patriarch Wizenbeak; his troll-bats, Mischka and Branka; their handlers, ''Janko'' Jankura and Dr. Raskidenji; his strategist, Count Braley; his adviser on general policy, Count Gowan; and from the Cymdulock police, Inspector Kokolskaia with Maxijao Grodus, better known as Max or Grotty Max. With them went a crowd of courtiers and hangers-on as well a strong company of soldiers serving as the king's bodyguard. Cymdulock Cathedral was still a place of dread reputation.

Count Braley and Count Gowan waited with the bodyguard and courtiers outside Room 537, where Patriarch Gorabani and Archdeacon Darussis had died. Inside, the party contemplated the chalk marks that outlined the bodies of the two clerisiarchs, the dried blood that awaited cleaning, the blackboard that displayed the presumably fatal spell, and the generally oppressive ambience. Perhaps it was the ambience: Branka left Wizenbeak's shoulder and joined Mischka in the pouch Jankura carried.

When all was in readiness, Wizenbeak put Max under a light hypnotic trance and took him through everything he remembered, one step at a time. ''Wait a minute, Max,'' he said when the young man switched to another language. ''We didn't quite catch that last phrase. Would you repeat it, please?''

Max paused and took a breath and repeated the phrase in an eerie rendering of Gorabani's voice.

''Ursprach,'' Raskidenji said softly. ''Gorabani is saying something about resolve. Then, 'The other item that we need, do you have it?' ''

The king-patriarch nodded. ''Go on, Max.'' Max repeated a second sentence, this time mimicking Darussis.

''They switched to Ursprach to hide what they were talking about,'' Raskidenji said. ''Darussis just said, 'My assistant here is eager but disposable. It can be arranged for him to nod off whenever I say the word.' ''

The human sacrifice, Wizenbeak thought uneasily. Well, the spell was intended to call on Vohar. ''Go on, Max,'' he said, and followed him through the procedure step by step until Gorabani switched to Ursprach again.

'' 'All right, Darussis,' '' Raskidenji said, translating, '' 'time to place the sacrifice.' ''

Wizenbeak led Max around and beyond the word Darussis had used to put him to sleep and followed the procedure as best he could from what Max had heard behind the commode curtain. Then, in the voice of Darussis, came the cry, ''Vohar, I bid you speak!'' and the mumbled response in Ursprach.

''What did he say?'' Raskidenji asked, and Wizenbeak had Max repeat it. '' 'You again? Fewmets.' I don't know 'fewmets.' ''

''It's an archaic word for troll-bat feces,'' Wizenbeak said. ''Go on.''

''Used as an ejaculation, then,'' the doctor said, and finished the sentence.'' 'What is it you want, human?' ''

''Go ahead, Max,'' Wizenbeak urged, and Max, speaking in Darussis' voice, repeated the next sentence.

Raskidenji looked up, almost apologetic. ''Darussis said, 'I want you to destroy the wizard, Guhland's king-patriarch, William Wizenbeak.' ''

Jankura shivered. ''Is it my imagination or is it getting colder in here?''

''We hope it's your imagination, Janko,'' Wizenbeak said

with a flash of irritability sparked by sheer panic. He rehearsed the mantra for calmness and the related mantra for serenity. Conjuring Vohar wasn't going to be done without a whole lot more effort than had been expended here, and she ought to know it. "Go on, Max," he said at last, taking the boy through the next steps.

"Darussis is speaking," Raskidenji said at the next critical point. "He doesn't want the climate changed, but 'Wizenbeak must be destroyed!' He insists on it."

"Go on, Max," Wizenbeak said. The mantras for calmness and serenity had taken hold, leaving him feeling somewhat uncomfortable nevertheless. Max said something in Ursprach and giggled. It made the hair stand up on the back of the neck.

Raskidenji took a deep breath. "Now Vohar replies. 'But not with the weather,' he agrees. 'We have other methods to try this deed you ask of us. Vohar, Lord of the Troll-Bats, will attempt this task you set him.' "

Wizenbeak shivered in spite of himself, pulling at his nose in a nervous gesture. "Go on, Max," he said, and Max went through Darussis' attempts to dismiss the elemental they had conjured up, trying the magic that didn't bite again and again.

"Then somebody screamed," Max said, "and there was a rumble of thunder followed by an explosion, and after that nothing happened until I woke up."

"That will have to do," Wizenbeak said, more shaken than he cared to admit. "Let's get out of here."

Jankura found herself opening the door and turned back to the room with an effort of will. "What do you suppose Vohar is going to do?"

"I don't know," Wizenbeak replied, dropping the royal "we" which he had trained himself to use, "and I don't want to know." As they stepped out into the corridor, Braley and Gowan were waiting with a travel-stained messenger, while the courtiers were standing at a discreet distance so as not to be associated with any bad news.

"This is Sergeant Lukijian, from Damuso, your Majestic Holiness," Count Braley said with a formality that he would not have wasted on any sort of good tidings. "He's had a long hard ride."

"Let him approach," Wizenbeak said. Damuso, where is that? Probably in the north somewhere, certainly in the north, maybe a day's march west of Springhill.

The messenger, obviously fatigued, saluted. "I bring evil news, your Majesty," he said. "The north country has been invaded by dragons."

13

A Weapon for Dragon

"GINGALS!" Pardus Murado shouted. From across the parade field, a sergeant echoed the command. "Gingals, post!" and three teams toiled to get their gingals in position. Murado waited until the three teams were set and waved the red flag to signal the release of the target.

The target, a tightly packed bundle of straw wrapped in burlap, was set loose from the tower and went gliding down the rope straight at the three teams. All three released their quarrels and all three missed, knocking tiny chips out of the stone wall down range. The target thudded into the post behind them and was dutifully winched back to the tower.

"Again," Murado said. And the crews repeated the drill and repeated it again. Eventually they scored one hit out of sixteen shots taken.

"That will do, Pardus," Wizenbeak said, climbing down from the wooden reviewing stand. "Let's take a look at these damned things."

The king-patriarch and the captain-general of the Tarelian Order walked over the neatly cropped grass to the three gingals and the Tarelians who had manned them. The gingal was a large crossbow, intended for siege work, wound by an inertial wheel. The gunner engaged the crossbow and gave the wheel a powerful heave, and when it was moving fast enough, the crossbow was engaged by pulling a lever. The wheel then spent its kinetic energy cocking the crossbow, moving against increasing resistance as it did so. In the process a rachet clicked off to make sure that the crossbow stayed cocked, and when the final step of the rachet clicked off, the crossbow disengaged itself, making it impossible to overwind. Mechanically somewhat more complex than the windlass-and-rachet system which it had replaced, inertial cocking had the advantage of permitting a faster rate of fire.

The gingal was mounted on the tail of a two-wheeled pushcart, its iron-rimmed wheels, about four feet in diameter, designed for easy moving over irregular terrain while keeping the inertial wheel clear of obstacles. On the front of the cart was mounted a large wooden shield to protect the gingal's crew from arrows fired from the besieged wall. There was a slit in the shield, and the tail could be pivoted through an angle of about thirty degrees to shoot through the slit. Wizenbeak walked around the cart and studied the way it was put together. Finally he turned to the sergeant in charge of the three crews.

"The shield," he said. "Isn't it usually a lot thicker?"

"Yes, sir," the sergeant said. "In a siege you'd have a double shield, the outer one wickerwork and both of them covered with green hides so they couldn't be set afire."

"We're going to be hunting dragons," Wizenbeak said. "Do you think we need the shield?"

"Why, ah, I don't know, sir."

"Nor do we," the king-patriarch said. "Pardus, the shield on front of the cart. Do you think we need it?"

Murado rubbed the bristles on his chin. "Against dragons?" he said dubiously.

"Of course against dragons," Wizenbeak said, hitching his sash to tighten the two swords. "We need to march against them as soon as possible."

The captain-general of the Tarelian Order studied the gingal and tried to imagine what his patriarch had in mind. The effort was useless, and at last he shook his head. "I don't rightly know, sir."

"Good. Then we'll do without it. That's, what, a hundred pounds less to haul around?"

"It's made to go on and off, sir," the sergeant said. "Here, a couple of you chaps dismount the shield." The men fell to work with a will, and Wizenbeak saw that it would be very easy to remount or replace with something a little thicker.

"With the hides and all it would be more like two hundred

pounds, sir," the sergeant said. "Maybe two-fifty in an exposed position."

Wizenbeak pulled at his mustache and contemplated the granite curtain wall they'd been peppering with their quarrels. At last he quoted basic Tarelian tactical doctrine back to them. "Against any enemy, including dragons, you need mobility, the better to attack them when they present themselves. And don't worry about an exposed position. In the field with dragons you'll always be in an exposed position."

When the soldiers had finished removing the shield, the king-patriarch stepped behind the gingal and put it to his shoulder to practice aiming. It went up and down easily enough, but to turn it from left to right he had to pick up the tail of the cart and set it down.

"Dragons," he said, quoting from one of the ancient texts he had read. "The sons of bitches fly all over the place to get at you. Now, what's the best way to get the gingal to turn so you can follow them?"

"A swivel," the sergeant suggested, "sir."

"Naah," the older of the two men said, who had dismounted the shield. "That gives you the swivel up and down, and the swivel turning besides, and a man will ne'er be holding the damn thing steady when he tries to squeeze the damn trigger."

Pardus Murado started to reprove him for speaking out of turn, but Wizenbeak checked him with a gesture. "How would you do it, young trooper?" he asked.

The man grinned. "I don't rightly qualify as a young trooper, your Holiness, being as how I've been busted from sergeant eight or nine times, but for turning left to right what you want is a spring-clamp hand brake."

You take your expertise where you find it, Wizenbeak thought. "That might be what we want," he agreed. "What is it?"

"Your Holiness wants to turn on the axle? The first thing you needs to do is pull on the hand brake to release it. Now it will turn, and you turns it to where you wants it and lets go. The spring puts the hand brake back on, and it's steady for you as you takes your aim, jiggling only up and down."

Wizenbeak produced a diptych from his robes and handed it over to the soldier. "Can you draw me what you just said?"

The man opened the stylus and made a sketch, then rubbed

the wax smooth and revised it. "Something like this, your Holiness."

The king-patriarch, the captain-general of the Tarelian Order, and the sergeant all studied the sketch for a few moments. Nobody said anything, but perhaps they weren't mechanically inclined, Wizenbeak thought. From working with various props and stage devices he had a bit of a feel for machinery, and this looked as if it might work if they could find someone to execute the design.

"This looks reasonably promising," he said finally. "Let's try it. Pardus, see that this man gets his stripes back and put him in charge of making one. And we want it done yesterday. You understand?"

"Yes, sir," Murado said. He took out his diptych and made a note. "Sergeant Jhesmu, you *will* stay sober until you have a working model, and that's an order."

The newly promoted Sergeant Jhesmu grinned and saluted. "Yes, sir," he said. " 'Tis dragons we're about to slay, and I would not miss it for the world."

Far to the north, Bythanna Group work crews toiled to erect a portable flue twenty miles to the south of the previous site. Heatherfields-Hsven, riding the spool of glazing, put her fingers in her mouth and whistled directions to the crane operators after the manner of dragonriders. The piercing whistle carried the speech which modulated it over a considerable distance with great clarity. The crane operators and their crews, who pulled in unison to move the spool along slowly and smoothly, unreeled the glazing over the framework of the flue without skips or flaws, their proficiency greatly improved with recent practice.

Just before sundown they completed the glazing operation, and a cheer went up from the crew. They tied fast the loose rigging, downed tools, and went off for supper. Holding on to the rope for support, Heather walked along the narrow wooden beam to the brake house, where there was a ladder she could climb down. On the brake house platform Melissa was waiting for her.

"Well, now," she said with a hint of a swagger, "that's not a bad day's work for a couple of ferals."

Melissa grinned. "Not bad at all. What's on the slate for supper?"

"Mush and gruel," Heather replied as she started down the ladder. The slate had been posted in the mess hall that morning, but not everyone had paid attention. "And they're out of gruel. What the slate said was red beans and rice with vegetable soup."

"Again?" Melissa followed the older woman down the ladder. "What's the problem?"

"You have to haul the stuff a long ways, darling. And you know how it is—first the dragons get fed, only then the other livestock."

They stopped by their tent to pick up bowls and spoons and got into the mess line. Sure enough, the kitchen had run out of soup. Going through near the end of the line, Melissa and Heather got a little red gravy poured over their rice. They were standing together eating when Yosie came up and joined them.

Melissa put her spoon back in the bowl. "Well, look who's here. When did you get into camp?"

"This morning," Yosie said. "I was on the wagon train bringing in the framing for the dragon barns, and the great love of Daffy's life wanted to trade places with me so they could be together again."

"And you, being a simple-minded romantic, couldn't say no?"

Yosie shrugged. "No big deal, but it was Daffy asked me to do it, of course."

"We don't seem to have the glamor and flash we had when we were flying dragons, do we, darling? Are youth and beauty slipping through our fingers?"

"Oh, shut up, Melissa," Heather said. "You were born old, and you worked your way up to ugly. Now get off her back."

Melissa laughed and took another bite of rice. "A few more years and I'll work my way up to *you*. I'm just delighted to see Yosie again. You know that, don't you?"

The older woman shrugged and carefully scraped out her bowl. Yosie kissed Melissa on the cheek as she turned aside a physical overture. "Right, darling, we both know it. Hey, Heather . . . whatever the hell happened to our trial for that barn-burning episode?"

"You were there. What do you think happened?"

"I haven't a clue. One day all the troll-bats in the world are raising an unholy stink about everything you can think of, and the next it's as if the trial never happened. Goldentrive packs us up and marches three groups under the mountain, and we're off and running."

Heather nodded. "That's what happened, all right."

"Sure, but the trial was going hot and heavy, and then it just wasn't even there. What happened?"

"Good question, Daughter. I asked Bythanastros, and he said the trives shared a dream." She uncorked her canteen and took a swallow of water. "Doesn't happen very often, I guess, and he wouldn't say what it was, but you saw what they did."

"Well, they moved that boulder in front of the tunnel," Yosie said. "That was pretty impressive. How did they know the tunnel was there?"

"I asked. What Bythanastros told me was that they remembered. So I asked the little bastard how it was they could remember about some godforsaken tunnel when they couldn't remember about Lady Alanji." Heather shook her head. "He told me that pride triumphs over memory."

"What does that mean?"

"That's what he said, Melissa. What it means, what I think it means, anyway, is that the troll-bats don't remember Lady Alanji because she dealt with them as equals. Memory says: this is so, and pride says: this could never have happened. And after a while, memory goes away."

"If you say so, darling."

Heather nodded. "That's what I was told. All right? The trial was a really big thing, getting bigger and stickier all the time, asking hard questions, asking about what the trives had agreed to at Alanji Field. My guess is that they didn't want answers, not the trives and not the troll-bats, either, so they all had this dream and decided to invade some long-forgotten foreign land instead."

"Curious. How could they all have the same dream all at once?" Melissa asked, collecting the three empty bowls and spoons.

"Troll-bats are strange," Yosie said. "But we knew that already, didn't we?"

* * *

Late in the evening the king-patriarch was seated at the desk in his chambers, stacks of diptychs at his elbow and a bronze candelabra providing light. He was laying cards out before him one after the other when the guard admitted Jankura.

"You wished to see me?" she asked as the door closed behind her.

He nodded and played another card in the flickering candlelight. "Yes. Maybe 'needed to see you' would be nearer the mark. Here, have a seat."

His longtime confidante pulled up a chair at the corner of the table and sat down beside him. She moved a stack of polychromatic diptychs, unanswered correspondence that was likely to stay unanswered, so she could see his face. "You always said that you can't read the cards for your own problem."

"It's true," Wizenbeak said softly, gathering the cards together. "You see what you hope for or what you're afraid of. On the other hand . . ." He put the cards in their case, the case in his pocket. "On the other hand, she had six fingers."

Something's bothering him, Jankura thought, maybe worse than usual. "On the other hand, what?"

He pushed his emerald glasses back up on his nose. "Sometimes the cards tell you what you believe."

"You *know* what you believe, don't you?" Maybe if we approach this sideways, he can tell us. "I mean, doesn't everyone?"

"We know what we're *supposed* to believe, anyway."

"Well, sure." She hesitated a moment. "What do the cards tell you?"

He shook his head. "Not much, Janko. They tell me that very likely I won't come back."

"Is that what you think or what you're afraid of?"

"Yes." The king-patriarch changed the subject. "The Tarelians have had such a rush of volunteers that they've reorganized themselves into three regiments: Blues and Reds and Greens."

"That's nice. What about cavalry?" The rumor that cavalry wasn't going to be used had been reverberating around the Citadel all afternoon.

"Hunh." He shrugged. "We had a big meeting this morning. Some fool, it might have been Duke Bedirny, asked the same question. We told him and told him, but he didn't want to hear it."

Jankura waited for a moment and then prompted her master. "What didn't he want to hear?"

"That dragons spook your horses. The old texts are pretty explicit on the point." Wizenbeak shook his head. "That's why we're using oxen to draw the baggage train."

"You aren't using cavalry at all?"

"A few scouts, maybe. We, as befits our Majestic Holiness, will be riding a mule."

She smiled at the irony. "Excused by your advanced age?"

"Whatever. Mules are more comfortable than sedan chairs, less strenuous than walking."

Ah, he needs to unload, that's all, Jankura thought. "What did you want to see me about?"

He sat back in his chair and looked at her over his emerald spectacles. "We probably need a minimum of fifty gingals per regiment. You've done a hell of a job on this, Janko, but we'll be lucky if we can start off with thirty, total. Will we get any more?"

That had been a top-priority assignment, rounding up gingals and modifying them. "You ought to pick up another dozen on the march north," she said. They had been promised fifteen, but finding them had been like pulling teeth. Viluji had ten, of which he had offered two, going on up to three and then four with great reluctance. And the modifications . . . you couldn't trust the donors to do anything right. So the artificer, some sergeant, had his people making conversion kits. "The Tarelians figure to do the modifications en route."

He nodded. "Good enough. What about building new ones?"

"We have a batch on order, but it takes time. If you march a week from tomorrow instead of tomorrow . . ."

Wizenbeak sighed and settled back in his chair. "It would help if we knew that they worked, too. But one can't have everything. Jankura?"

"Yes?"

"The Yssemer holdings in the mediplano." The candles flickered in the draft that blew down from the lofty ceiling, spilling wax down their sides and setting the shadows to dancing. ''Would you like to be seized of them? I'd like it to go to someone I can trust.''

She blinked. That would make you a duke, she thought, maybe not quite as fancy as being queen, but something a bit out of the ordinary. Of course I wound up being throughly hated by all sorts of people who never even knew me, and if I became duke, they'd probably remember. I'd really have a head start in life, wouldn't I? ''Well, no, thank you,'' she said at last, not knowing why she was refusing. ''The mediplano is not my place.''

''Take your duchies where you find them, Janko,'' the king-patriarch said, and then a thought struck him. ''Where is your place?''

''In the north.'' Now, why did I say that? Jankura wondered. I hate the north.

''Think about it,'' Wizenbeak said, gently pressing the offer. ''For a new duke we need somebody loyal, somebody we can trust.''

She put her hand on his arm. ''What about Lasco?''

''Genzari? He's a good man.'' Then the king-patriarch shook his head. ''Only we can't spare him from heading up the Royal Army. Are you sure you won't take it?''

Jankura sat perfectly still for a moment, listening to her heart. There were mantras to help one do this very thing, the sorting out of what one truly wanted from the distractions of present opportunity or present danger, but it was something she did naturally. I don't want a duchy, she decided, not in the mediplano, not anywhere. And then, in reply to another part of her mind: If Wizenbeak isn't king, we wouldn't be able to hold one, so it doesn't matter. ''I'm sure,'' she said.

''In that case you'll be marching north with us.'' Wizenbeak put his hand on top of hers. ''Some clouds *do* have silver linings.''

''My home was in the north,'' she said for want of any better remark. ''To tell you the truth, my time in Cymdulock has been very stimulating, but I can't really say it was entirely enjoyable. What about Raskidenji?''

''A gentleman and a scholar,'' he replied. ''We'll take him, of course, so you have more time to attend to my general well-being. Too bad for Mischka and Branka.''

"He does all right with them," Jankura said. "It may even be good for the little monsters to have a firm hand once in a while."

Wizenbeak rubbed his eyes. "It's settled, then. We'll take the whole menagerie."

"We've both packed our gear," Jankura said gently. "Now, why don't you get some sleep?"

"We aren't sleepy," the king-patriarch said, producing another deck from an inner pocket. "Would you like to play some cards?"

"What does your Grace see?" Count Tylsos asked, deferentially approaching the young duke across the polished parquet floor. The three of them were standing beside one of the tall windows in the lesser drawing room, overlooking the Blue Regiment of the Tarelian Order in the courtyard below as they prepared to march north.

"Not much," Duke Bedirny replied, watching the soldiers milling around the unfamiliar gingals. "His Majesty is still breaking his fast with the queen, I guess."

"A touching demonstration of domestic felicity," Tylsos said without the faintest hint of irony in his manner. "And afterward he will get on that blue mule he rides, and she will stand on the balcony and wave good-bye." Your opportunity will be at hand, your Grace, don't waste it for God's sake. "Then what?"

"Then he goes to fight the dragons invading the north. I wish I were going, as well."

The young lout, Tylsos thought. He could reach out his hand and make himself king, and he can't see it. That foolish child-queen plainly dotes on him, and he dithers about in an agony of indecision. "Indeed. Why, then, are you not going?"

"Except out of bitter necessity a noble does not go to war leading freshly hired mercenaries," Swordmaster Gevas answered, "and the men of my master's household are mainly heavy cavalry."

"True, true, your Grace. Yet a war must be fought whether one rides or walks." The count hesitated, considering what had just gone by. "You offered your services? Well, of course, that goes without saying. But why did Wizenbeak decline?"

"The reason he gave was that dragons frighten the horses,

lore he'd gleaned from the perusal of ancient texts.'' Duke Bedirny growled. ''Viluji and Falenda protested, as did I, but old Wizenbeak was adamant, and later dispatches confirmed that this was indeed the case.''

Count Tylsos nodded. It was plausible; it might even be true. ''The king has responded with admirable promptness to this threat. Admirable. Almost, it could persuade one to forgive his treatment of the Syncretist Church.''

''Gently, sir,'' Gevas said. ''Once the Church involved itself with high treason . . .''

''Yes, yes,'' Tylsos agreed impatiently. ''There are some who say that the Church killed one king of Guhland too many.''

''Of which I am one,'' Bedirny said, ''though there are, of course, two sides to any argument.''

Gevas raised his bushy black eyebrows and tried to change the subject. ''Historically, the situation of the Orthodox Church at the birth of Syncretism was very similar to that of the Syncretist Church when the late Prince Kahun made himself first king and then patriarch.''

''There are similarities,'' Count Tylsos agreed, smiling wolfishly to show his missing tooth. The swordmaster was wary, and rightly so. He might well be the reason Bedirny had not yet responded to the queen's overtures. Something that should be looked into, perhaps. ''But there were differences, also, the most notable being that Syncretism had already come into being. Now, it is true that God works in mysterious ways,'' he continued amiably. ''To punish the sins of the Orthodox, He raised up Syncretism. The sins, if any, of the Syncretists did not merit anything so . . . so emphatic.''

''What *did* God do to punish the sins of Syncretisty Hall, then?'' Gevas asked. ''Raise up Wizenbeak? Or would you deny that the king-patriarch is *also* doing God's will?''

One could get in trouble arguing with Gevas, Tylsos decided. Better to agree with him. Except that Bedirny is wavering. ''Of course the king-patriarch is doing God's will,'' the count said smoothly. ''He humbled the clerisy, as God intended, and if in the press of circumstances he dealt a little harshly with the Church, God is perfectly capable of taking any corrective action He deems necessary.''

''Do you think the invasion of dragons was God's judgment

on the king-patriarch?'' Bedirny asked, echoing a scurril popular among the clerisy.

A herald announced the entrance of Queen Marjia, and everybody turned to face the queen, paying his respects as she swept into the lesser drawing room, walking regally across the hardwood floor to the appointed French windows, which opened onto a little balcony overlooking the courtyard.

When the queen appeared in the window, there was a fanfare of trumpets. Wizenbeak mounted his big blue mule, and they exchanged salutes. Then the captain-general of the Tarelian Order gave the command to march, and the massed companies moved out to the skirl of warpipes and the rattle of snare drums. They marched past the queen, dipping their spears in salute, and out of the Citadel. Wizenbeak, accompanied by Count Braley, his strategist, who was also riding a mule, fell in behind the third company. Queen Marjia dutifully remained on the balcony until the last of the Blue Regiment was gone. Then she and her entourage withdrew from the lesser drawing room.

''Oh, no, your Grace,'' Count Tylsos said, continuing their previous conversation.

Bedirny looked confused. He had been totally absorbed in the smooth movement of the regiment. ''No, what?''

''No, the dragons are not God's judgment on the king-patriarch,'' the count replied. ''There has surely been enough rank impiety and crabbed Orthodoxy in the north to warrant an invasion of dragons long since.''

''We should, perhaps, rejoin the queen's court,'' Gevas suggested, watching the stately exodus of courtiers from the room now that the king's departure had taken place.

''An excellent suggestion, your Grace,'' Tylsos said as the three of them drifted away from the window to flow easily with the crowd of courtiers. ''Her Majesty, I am sure, will be pleased to see you. And yet . . .''

Bedirny took the bait. ''And yet?''

''God's will, your Grace. It's hard for mere mortals to divine. Yet suppose the dragons were to eat the king-patriarch and go home? You could never persuade the pious of any other interpretation.''

14

The Campaign Begins

THE Tarelians arrived at Damuso on Saint Jugao's Day, marching up Old Damujao Road under overcast skies and a slow, drizzling rain. Damuso was the administrative seat for Count Darji-Damuso, a motte and bailey fortification perhaps two hundred years old. It consisted of a circular motte ten yards high and about a hundred yards across at the top, with the bailey set into the motte's east edge. From the bailey's gate a drawbridge spanned the ditch, touching a path of beaten earth that ran east a quarter mile to connect with Old Damujao Road running north and south.

The bailey itself was an eight-sided tower, deviating from the circular style of its time because it had been built in great haste with dressed stone taken from an unfinished Orthodox cathedral. It was twenty yards tall by thirty yards at the base, and statues of some of the saints collected with the rest of their building still stood among the battlements, bringing confusion to the enemy.

Touching the bailey on top of the motte were a pair of what had originally been slate-roofed stone barns. Departing from strict rectangularity to make better use of the available space, they came together at a narrow gate facing due west to enclose a triangular yard. Augmenting a reliable but parsimonious well, the water draining off their slate roofs was collected in a cistern. Both barns had been modified to include barracks on the upper floors, and in times of peace the hay which had been displaced by the cavalrymen had been stacked inside the yard and around the perimeter of the motte.

The king-patriarch met with Count Darji-Damuso in his great hall, a cold, cheerless room hung with the banners of his relatives and supporters, greens and blues mostly, figured with black boars. With the king was his court: Pardus Murado, Count Braley, "Janko" Jankura, and included Dr. Raskidenji, simply to keep him out of trouble. Around the master of the hall were several hounds and some of his retainers, all evidently somber and depressed.

"Well," Wizenbeak said, handing his damp cloak to a servant and putting his long sword in the rack. "We've read your dispatches." He walked stiffly over to the fireplace to warm himself. "What else can you tell us?"

"They panic the horses," the count said glumly. His hair was streaked with gray, and he seemed far older than the dashing young commander the wizard remembered from Sifoty Field. "And they have riders on back that shoot arrows. Did I mention the riders?"

"I don't believe so," Braley said, putting his sword in the rack. "You shot back, of course?"

"From the back of a galloping horse, shooting backward and up?" Darji-Damuso shook his head. "Nobody hit anything. The dragons flew as fast as the horses could run, whistling and screaming, and their archers picked us off until they ran out of arrows."

"Wait a minute," Jankura said. "This sounds like a major battle. You never mentioned anything like that in the dispatches. When was this?"

"Four or five days ago. I was tired of sitting and taking it. Cavalry is not meant to endure a siege, you know." He hesitated. "So . . ."

"So?" Jankura prompted.

"The Tarelians were very close by then. If we lost, it wouldn't be a catastrophe."

"What did you do?" Murado asked. "I mean, what was your plan when you went in?"

The count turned and walked over to the improvised sand table, a shallow box set on sawhorses, the raw, unfinished wood in sharp contrast to the dark, elegant formality of the dining room suite. "Here. This is Damuso. We're in the piedmont. Above the piedmont is the altiplano. Right at the western edge of the table is Springhill. The dragons pushed south over a front about fifty miles wide."

"Did they attack Springhill?"

"Not yet, your Majesty, but they overflew it many times, whistling and screaming. They pushed about fifty miles into the piedmont, to the Jidderswash, about ten miles south of here."

"But we still hold Damuso, do we not?" Dr. Raskidenji asked. A classical scholar and a master of magic, he sometimes asked questions that were unduly subtle for everyday living.

The count sighed. "Well, yes. We are here, as you can see, but Damuso was always a cavalry post, not some mighty rock to withstand the pounding of the siege."

The king-patriarch studied the sand table. "A nice turn of phrase, that," he said easily. "Nevertheless, Damuso, for all its weaknesses, seems to be our natural base for now." The king had given his explanation, and now he gave his order. "Would it be possible for us to stay here?"

Count Darji-Damuso shifted his weight on the flagstone floor. "It would be an honor, your Majesty. For how long?"

"For the duration of the campaign," Braley replied, "or until we need to move elsewhere."

"Your Majesty is welcome to such poor hospitality as we can offer," Darji-Damuso said apologetically. "But the farmers have been driven from the land. Even the haystacks we kept on top of the motte were set ablaze. As time goes by, we expect the dragons to range farther south, which will make it harder and harder to keep this place supplied."

"Tell us a little about the dragons, then," Jankura said after a moment. "Your dispatches were rather terse."

"I'm sorry. The dragons, if they're coming after you, swooping down to do you mischief—you understand?" Count Darji-Damuso fidgeted, pulling at one ear. "They fly in groups of four. You see one dragon, the son of a bitch will be high in the sky, spying out the lay of the land." He bit his lip, trying to recall his facts for orderly presentation. "Until we went after them, we never saw more than two groups at once."

"They don't show up much before nine in the morning," one of his retainers volunteered. "And by late afternoon the wretched beasts are all headed for home."

"Don't they fly at night?" Wizenbeak asked.

"No," Darji-Damuso said. "They don't even fly after dark. Well, maybe they can, but I've never seen them do it."

"That's interesting," the wizard said. "What about your most recent engagement, then?"

Darji-Damuso gave a sigh. "We assembled a force of about six hundred light cavalry and maybe a thousand foot, local militia with a couple of mercenary companies. Here, at Damuso."

There was a pause. Wizenbeak drew his strategist to one side and whispered in his ear. "Cavalry? His own dispatches said that dragons spooked the horses. Cavalry is useless here."

"That's something a cavalryman would rather die than admit," Braley replied softly. "Wizards make different mistakes, all right?"

They studied the sand box. The area afflicted with dragons had been sprinkled with dark sand. Damuso was a little white-painted wooden model deep inside enemy territory. Or maybe it wasn't enemy territory, just an area that couldn't be defended. Spotted around the dark sand were little red flags, each annotating an attack with the date and number of dragons.

"Did you have any specific objective in mind?" Murado asked.

"No," the count replied. "We were just going in, looking to put ourselves in harm's way." He sighed. "We did it, all right. We marched north about ten miles, with dragons flying over us all the while. First a group of four, flying pretty high, then, suddenly, another group of four, whistling and screaming. I counted maybe a dozen or more before the battle was actually joined."

He pointed to a double red flag. "Perjio's Farm. A thatched-roof house and barn with fieldstone walls about a hundred yards off the road. Fieldstone fences, too, marking the boundaries. The first time the dragons burned him out, he put on his sword and started to rethatch the roof on his barn. The second time they killed him and his son. We ran into archers behind the walls. Maybe a couple of companies. I ordered the cavalry to take them in the flank, and when they started to go over the fences, dragons on the ground reared up, ten or fifteen feet high, and bit off the heads of every horse they could catch. The charge just dissolved in panic. Then the flying dragons swooped down, screaming and shooting arrows, and it was every man for himself, back to Damuso."

"How many men did you lose?" Braley asked.

"Out of six hundred cavalry, we had two hundred and six standing to the colors when we got home. When the women went back for the dead, they found one hundred and thirty." He gave a shrug. "The mercenaries and the militia never stood muster."

"Didn't you say one mercenary company held ranks?"

Darji-Damuso nodded. "Well, yes, but they headed south, and we never saw them again."

"When the women went to pick up the dead," Wizenbeak said, "was there a truce with the dragons?"

"No. The women just hitched up some hay wagons and went. A few dragons were watching, but they left them alone. Mostly it was the arrows that killed them. My cousin Lenji, the horse fell on him." A hound came up and pressed his muzzle against the count's leg. Darji-Damuso patted his head absently. "A few they brought back had been bitten in half. What the women told me was that they'd find the lower half of the body and, some distance away, the upper half, terribly mangled."

"You saw this yourself?"

"A couple. My standard-bearer was one." He patted the dog's head. "I asked them if they'd found the flag he carried. They said no."

So the enemy collects souvenirs, Wizenbeak thought. "What about the infantry?"

"The militia ran, your Majesty. They wet their pants, dropped their arms, and ran howling. Altogether they might have lost another hundred."

"What about the mercenaries?" Braley asked.

"One company ran with the militia; the other held formation and marched back. The only bright spot of the day."

"What have you been doing since then?" Jankura asked.

He shrugged. "Licking our wounds. Moping. Waiting for the Tarelians. What could we do?"

"What about the archers? I mean, what can you tell us about them?"

"They were small and shrill, your Majesty. I think they talk to the dragons by whistling."

"No prisoners, I suppose?" Murado asked. "Or enemy gear?"

"No, sir. We have some of their arrows, is all."

Wizenbeak nodded and pushed his emerald spectacles back on his nose. "Fascinating. Pardus, after the oxen are fed and the men are taken care of, join us at supper. Until then," he sighed. It had been a long day and looked like it might run on quite a bit longer. "We think a nap might be a good idea."

There was a log burning in the fireplace at the end of the great hall of Damuso bailey, and candles lit the central table. The banners hanging from the ceiling were lost in darkness, while below the illumination was too feeble to set the shadows dancing, so they huddled together, smelling of cold stone and wet wool.

After a cheerless supper Wizenbeak sat down with his staff to consider the next day's action. The steward discreetly refilled his glass with Jamreaux red, and the king-patriarch took a morose swallow. "If anyone has any ideas as to how we ought to proceed, we are, by God, open to suggestion." Pardus Murado looked at Count Braley, Count Darji-Damuso looked at Jankura, and nobody said anything.

"Well, you know, this afternoon I went over the count's record of dragon attacks," Dr. Raskidenji said, breaking the silence. "I had the opportunity to discuss that record with the men who kept it for him. The attacks display a certain amount of order, a pattern almost."

"A pattern?" The king-patriarch's ears pricked up. "What sort of pattern?"

Raskidenji smiled. A master quick on the uptake was more likely to appreciate the brilliance of his servant. "Patterns, your Majesty. What I found, well . . . The dragons are less active on cloudy days. Aside from that, they maintain a pretty regular schedule." He pulled a face, raising his black eyebrows as he savored the moment. "There are intervals, however, when they don't fly at all."

"That's interesting," Count Braley said, unimpressed. "Did you find anything else?"

"I haven't finished," Raskidenji said with a touch of asperity. "The intervals, there were four in all, were each three days long, and after each such interval dragons struck farther south by maybe ten or eleven miles.''

''Go on,'' Wizenbeak prompted.

''After Count Darji-Damuso's unhappy encounter five days ago, there were three incidents in the next two days, which were cloudy, while on the third day numerous dragons were observed in flight though no attacks were reported. The fourth day there was nothing, and when we arrived today there was also nothing.''

''It was raining when we arrived,'' Jankura pointed out. ''Maybe they just weren't flying, the dragons.''

''Maybe,'' Raskidenji conceded. ''However, I believe that we are in one of their three-day interludes, which will continue through tomorrow, after which they will again strike farther south.''

''Then if we went looking for them tomorrow, we might not find them?'' Pardus Murado asked.

''Not in the air,'' Wizenbeak said, twisting his whiskers around one gnarled finger. ''You think we might catch them on the ground?''

The scholar hesitated for a moment. Although he had anticipated that question and the next, the rapid transition from theory to practice was unsettling. ''The possibility exists,'' he conceded.

''Where?'' The obvious question. ''We mean, where would you suggest?''

''Let me show you on the sand table, your Majesty,'' Raskidenji replied. ''We changed the even periods of activity from red flags to white flags.''

The king-patriarch picked up a tall brass candlestick and walked over to the sand table as the others followed. The pattern that displayed itself on the sand table was five arcs, with very little overlapping. The northernmost arc, the oldest, was red, spilling over from the altiplano into the piedmont.

Raskidenji leaned over to indicate one of the earliest flags. ''The messenger was sent off to Cymdulock at this time,'' he said, tossing his dark hair back. ''The next ten days the dragons struck at the sites marked by the red flags in this arc. In the next band, the white flag marking the southernmost point of attack is about ten miles farther south than the previous southernmost point."

The arcs weren't clean, the wizard decided. The line of demarcation between red and white was blurred. Not always the dragons' fault, perhaps. Perjio's Farm was a pair of white flags in a white band, with a red flag added to it where Darji-Damuso's ill-conceived sortie had been routed. But they weren't a set of concentric circles by any means, which might make the proof . . . Wake up, you old fool, he thought grimly. The damned dragons are invading your country, not doing geometry!

"It looks like a series of overlapping, ah, not disks, exactly, maybe fans, doesn't it?" Wizenbeak said at last. "How big would you say they were?"

"What exactly are you asking about, sir?"

"The arcs. They look circular. How big is the circle?"

"The circle? Oh. About fifty or fifty-one miles across," Raskidenji said, removing a diptych from his robe. "Not wishing to disturb the sand table, I copied the map and worked it out on wax. Note that each circle is fixed by at least three points."

The king-patriarch took the diptych and examined it. It was a very neat, very orderly transcription of a sand table which he knew to be a crude approximation. There was a spell to estimate uncertainty, but how did it begin? "Excellent," Wizenbeak said. "Would you mark your center points on the sand table, please."

Raskidenji looked around, and upon finding some blue flags in a box, he placed them carefully on the sand table, forming a perfectly straight line with flags exactly equidistant. "As you can see, your Majesty, they are headed due south, about ten miles at a hop."

A mantra floated to the surface of Wizenbeak's mind. Fight Chaos Eschew Hops Bitterly, each initial letter representing a word in the full spell. He pushed his spectacles up on his nose and began to rehearse the mantra in his mind.

The scholar drew a line in the sand, extending it south. He measured the distance on the scale chalked on the table and planted a blue flag in the sand, about fifteen miles northeast of Damuso. "If, and it is a big if, the dragons repeat the pattern they have been following, they will have their center over here."

"Hunh. Where's here?"

Count Darji-Damuso studied the sand table in the flickering

candlelight for a moment. "Close by Arvijao, your Majesty," he said at last. Wizenbeak nodded for him to continue. "A dozen houses, a chapel, a gristmill, a malt barn with its own alehouse, a livery stable, a smithy. A nice little hamlet until it was burned out."

"What do you think, Braley?" the king-patriarch asked.

"We should go over and take a look, your Majesty," was the reply. If Count Braley was reluctant to charge a nest of dragons, one couldn't tell it. He seemed perfectly calm and matter-of-fact. "I can't imagine what would be at the center, but there's only one way to find out."

"Pardus?"

"A half day's march, your Majesty. We'll break fast at five and be marching with the first light. Do we want the cavalry scouting for us?"

"Probably," Wizenbeak said absently. He pulled at his nose. "Make that a yes. Not far, though, a quarter mile. Half a mile at the outside. Send them off into the distance, they could get chewed up and we'd never see them again." The first word of the spell appeared in his mind, followed in rapid succession by the rest. He focused on the most recent blue flag as he went through the full spell. His glasses blurred, and he was rewarded with the vision of a golden oval surrounding the flag. About one mile north and south by three miles east and west, he decided as his glasses cleared.

"What if they move somewhere else?" Raskidenji asked, a little concerned to find his theoretical discoveries routing the march of whole armies. "What if we don't find the dragons?"

The king-patriarch sighed and shook his head. Well, what if we do? he thought. Isn't anybody worried about *that*? "We'll keep looking until we find them," he said softly. "No problem. Like as not they'll come to us."

15

The First Foeman in the Field

BY the time the sun was lightening the eastern sky, the three regiments of the Tarelian Order were standing at breakfast. Wizenbeak handed his bowl and spoon to an orderly and turned to Pardus Murado. "Morning is wiser than evening," he said. "We've decided you were right suggesting that we leave the baggage train here in Damuso."

His captain-general grinned. "Thank you, sir. We'll move a lot faster without it."

"Yes, yes. What about defending this place?"

Murado pursed his lips and turned to look at the octagonal tower behind him. "One company from each regiment should do it, I think. Three companies and three gingals."

"See to it, then," Wizenbeak said.

Their base camp secured, the Tarelians moved northwest across rank hayfields and ungrazed pastures, past ruined farm buildings. Rolling hills displayed the lush greenery of late summer, hip-high grass sprinkled with wildflowers. King-Patriarch Wizenbeak rode in the van on his big blue mule, Murado on his right, Braley on his left, Jankura and Raskidenji behind. As Raskidenji had predicted, no dragons were seen.

They arrived at Arvijao before noon to find a desolate cluster of burned-out buildings, where a masterless dog slunk away from the homestead that was no longer home.

Murado looked around. "This is the place," he said. "But no dragons. Now what?"

"We send out scouts, of course," the wizard said, preparing to dismount from his mule. "Half a mile all around, just to make sure we don't miss anything big and awful.'' Then what? They had figured to come up empty in Arvijao, but ten miles north of here was Raskidenji's golden oval, theoretically a recently abandoned dragon camp. An orderly helped him to the ground. ''Meanwhile, we can have lunch.''

Murado nodded. ''Yes, sir. Half eat and half stand to arms?''

That was standard practice in enemy territory, a bit of military arcana Wizenbeak was surprised to recall with easy familiarity. ''Of course.''

''Yes, sir. What do we do then?''

Wizenbeak grinned and shaded his eyes against the bright sunlight as he looked up. ''Well, Pardus, we'll just head due north for ten miles and see if we find anything there.'' Murado nodded, satisfied that the king-patriarch had matters well in hand, and went off to carry out his orders.

After an hour's lunch break the Tarelian Order marched north, preceded by a light screen of cavalry.

In midafternoon one of the cavalry officers on the western flank rode up to Pardus Murado and saluted. ''We've found something over the next ridge, sir,'' he said.

''Any dragons?'' Murado asked.

''No, sir. It looks like an abandoned bivouac area.''

''Abandoned, eh?'' Wizenbeak said. ''Let's have a look.''

The Tarelians took up positions along the top of the ridge. Below, they saw that the rather steep northern slope was scarred with a freshly filled ditch. The southern slope across the valley showed unmistakable signs of activity. A roughly oval area embracing most of the southern slope facing them had been burned off, not an easy project considering the relatively wet weather the altiplano had been enjoying. On the blackened ground three circles were outlined by stakes, driven at regular intervals, and at the center of the middle circle was a rather large pit of some sort. On the unburned grass were the traces the scouts had reported. There was an abandoned wagon, broken wheels, a discarded harness of some sort, and evidence of much coming and going.

''Hunh,'' Wizenbeak muttered. The trench, freshly filled in, suggested a mass grave. Not something he would be happy to find out about but something he couldn't ignore. He shook his head. There was no help for any of this. "Pardus, send some men over to see what's buried in that ditch."

"Yes, sir," Murado said. "Anything else?"

"An escort. Janko, Raskidenji, and I are going down there to take a look. One company should be entirely sufficient."

Wizenbeak let the mule find the easiest way down the irregular slope until he came to the excavation in the middle circle. Situated halfway up the side of the ridge, the pit was about ten feet square and four feet deep, with the imprint of great timbers in the bottom, the excavated soil loosely cast around the edge. Branka and Mischka emerged from their pouch as the wizard eased himself over the edge. There was a strong smell of troll-bat, and in the bottom of the pit the smell was stronger. The timbers at the four corners of the pit had been at least a foot square, and he reached down and removed a tiny pellet from the hard, compact ground.

"What did you find?" Raskidenji asked, kneeling in the dirt at the edge of the pit.

"Fewmets," Wizenbeak replied. "The trace of the beast we hunt." He held up the pellet between thumb and forefinger. "Troll-bat dung."

Raskidenji looked about him in the brown soil and began picking up pellets. "Here," he said, scooping up an easily collected handful. "The stuff is all over."

"Give me a hand," the wizard said, climbing out. "You're right. It isn't in the pit but all around it."

Jankura walked back from one of the side circles. "It looks like they planted a huge post of some sort in the center," she remarked. "And there were troll-bats all over the place."

"You found fewmets?"

"Yes, sir," she said, holding out a handful. "I don't know about the dragons, but these troll-bats seem well fed and healthy. And uncommonly large."

Wizenbeak walked around, studying the loosely packed dirt and the charred grass beyond it. A slow circle, then another. "They weren't here that long," he said at last. "My God. There must have been *hundreds* of troll-bats here." He felt the hairs rising on the back of his neck. You couldn't control a trive that size, not for long, anyway.

He walked over to the line of posts, massive stakes of hardwood deeply driven into the ground. The ones near the central pit leaned away from it. The three of them walked from post to post. Always the same thing.

"How big do you think that burned-off area is?" the wizard asked.

"What, maybe twenty acres?" Jankura replied. "Too big for a tent, but I can't imagine what else would be set up like that."

Wizenbeak nodded reluctantly. "Nor I," he conceded, and then, "Fewmets!" He had stepped into a semiliquid mound of dragon dung.

Branka crawled back into his pouch, and Mischka began to whine. Advance warning of a dragon approaching, the wizard wondered, or merely distress at the smell? He stamped and scuffed his foot a few times on the ground and remounted his mule, which an orderly was holding. As they neared the top of the ridge, they heard an excited shout and the snap of gingals. Wizenbeak urged his mount up to the crest in time to see a pair of dragons disappearing into the east.

"East, eh?" he mused. "Well, that's the way the wagon tracks were pointing." Whatever the hell it was, was going to roll back and forth across piedmont and altiplano until it was stopped. A plague of dragons scourging the countryside.

One of the sergeants from the digging detail came up with a couple of officers. "Sir," the senior officer said, "we dug up that trench like you told us."

Wizenbeak sighed and turned to face them. Who had done the actual digging? It didn't matter, but better to get as close to the source as possible. "What did you find, Sergeant?"

"Bodies, sir. Maybe two or three hundred. Most of them wearing a black boar of some sort."

That would be Darji-Damuso's missing cavalry, Wizenbeak thought. "Go on."

"They was bound hand and foot, sir, and their throats was cut."

So the enemy is taking no prisoners. "Very well," the king-patriarch said, wondering what the procedure for field burial was. "Get a count of the dead and have the chaplain bury them with full military honors."

In the end the king-patriarch simply blessed the ground and listened to the chaplain read the burial service as the Tarelians shoveled the dirt back in to the mournful skirl of the pipes. The grave was marked with a wooden plank, dated and inscribed "Here lie 277 prisoners taken at Perjio's Farm. There is no surrender against dragons."

Once the dead had been interred with full military honors, the question was where to go, what to do next. The Tarelians formed up on either side of the ridgeline, spears glinting in the late afternoon sunlight, and waited for their marching orders. King-Patriarch Wizenbeak sat on his big blue mule and conferred with his officers.

"We have an opportunity to catch the sons of bitches," Count Braley said, sitting on his bay mare. "They figure to be about ten miles to the east. We eat supper. Then a night march, and we surprise them in the dark."

"I don't know," Pardus Murado said, shifting his weight in the saddle of his black gelding. "A night march ending in a night attack is bad enough, but to find dragons at the end? I don't like it one bit."

"Dragons attacking are formidable," Braley conceded. "Let's find out how dragons *attacked* are!"

Wizenbeak shook his head. This aspect of Braley's personality—an unwarranted rashness in the face of danger—was new to him. He didn't much like it, but he didn't know what to do about it, either. "I disagree, Hotspur."

"The decision is yours to make, sir," Braley said easily, oblivious to any rebuke. "Still . . . why not go for it?"

How can a man so smart, so experienced, be so totally insensitive to risk? the wizard wondered. Rash seems a gross understatement. Maybe this is the only way he can face fear. Or perhaps he knows something I don't . . .

His line of thought was interrupted by Count Braley. "Why not go for the night attack, sir?"

The king-patriarch sighed. "Two reasons," he said at last. "First, we need to know the strength of the enemy better before we engage them."

"That's conservative," Braley said, nodding in minimal agreement, "but you're probably right."

"Thanks, Hotspur. That could mean any number of things, all the way from talking to prisoners to taking a look at their order of battle in broad daylight.'' Wizenbeak paused for a moment. ''From a night attack we don't figure to learn much.''

''If it was decisive, we wouldn't need to.''

Wizenbeak shifted his weight in the saddle. Perhaps Braley would rather die than retreat. Not exactly. Braley would rather die than retreat when he was afraid. And, of course, fear was something he would not admit to. He rubbed his nose and pulled at his mustache. If that wasn't it, it would do until a better theory came along. ''Second, we found evidence of troll-bats, hundreds of troll-bats.''

''What sort of evidence?''

''Fewmets,'' Dr. Raskidenji said, holding out a sample.

''Those little bitty pellets? How could you tell?''

''Did you ever work with troll-bats, Count Braley?'' Jankura asked. The simulated beard had faded from her face long since. That morning she had picked wildflowers and woven them into a garland which she was wearing like necklace to make her troll-bats happy. ''You can tell, all right.''

''Maybe,'' the count conceded. ''I'll even grant that you could tell the pellet was from a troll-bat, but *hundreds* of troll-bats?''

''I've been involved with troll-bat husbandry all my life, Braley,'' Wizenbeak said, slipping out of the patriarchal ''we.'' ''And in my youth I cleaned out the hutches. Take my word for it, I know what I'm talking about.''

Count Braley looked to the east and shook his head. ''So there are a few hundred troll-bats along with a couple of dozen dragons. Why not cut them up a little, anyway?''

''A night attack with troll-bats was how I beat the Tarelians in the altiplano campaign,'' Wizenbeak said. ''And I only had a few of the little monsters.'' He reached into his black robe and took out a tightly stoppered vial. ''Look. This extract of kimjii root is the entire supply for the whole damned army at this point. A half ounce for three regiments.''

Braley sighed. The point was inarguable, but he was still uncomfortable with this indecisive dancing around.

''Hey, that's right, your Majesty,'' Pardus Murado said. ''In Kalycas Province, Kirndal's army was reeking with the stuff. I remember. They'd loaded up with it just on the off chance that you'd be using that same trick again.''

"It's true," Braley said, conceding the point. "If we're going up against troll-bats, I personally would be a whole lot happier with a sachet of kimjii root around my neck."

"So we head back for Damuso and bring in some kimjii root," Wizenbeak said.

Jankura sighed but said nothing. With the Tarelian Order reeking of kimjii, Mischka and Branka weren't going to be all that sharp if she ever had to use them.

"There aren't any roads around here," Murado said, consulting his map. "On the other hand, there aren't any mountains or swamps, either." He scrolled the map up and returned it to its case. "We'll just head south-southeast across country. Five miles before dinner and an easy march the next day." He looked at the king-patriarch. "Unless you'd rather we made a night march. About twenty-three, twenty-four miles. We'd reach Damuso about daybreak."

Wizenbeak considered the matter. A night march would avoid attack by dragons. On the other hand, it would be a considerable hardship on him, if not on the Tarelians. "No," he said. "We march by day. We went out looking for dragons, we can damn well let them catch up with us."

Murado rode out and ordered the march.

At midmorning the next day Wizenbeak was killing time by passing Mischka and Branka back and forth between Raskidenji and Jankura. For no apparent reason both troll-bats began to fret, and he looked around to see Jankura putting them back in their pouch. He couldn't see any dragons, but the troll-bats were unhappy over *something*. "Mister Murado!" he barked. "Tell the troops to look alert! We may see dragons!"

The word had just started to move down the line when a pair of dragons swept over the hill they were passing and swept down on them faster than a horse could run. They were closely followed by a second pair, and Wizenbeak got a good look at close range. Green they were, with pale underbellies and three pairs of tiny wings on each side. Each carried an archer and another soldier, the driver, maybe, right behind the big ugly head. The archer was shooting into the mass of soldiers, but as the pair of dragons turned, the wizard saw that there was a troll-bat riding the shoulder of the soldier driving the lead dragon.

"Bowmen!" he heard a sergeant shouting. "Bowmen! String your bows!"

His mule was fidgeting but generally seemed under control. The second pair of dragons swept in from the rear, leisurely picking off soldiers with their deadly arrows as the first pair returned for a second pass. A scattering of ineffective arrows went up. All missed. The dragons turned, and the first pair swept back, whistling and screaming as they headed straight at the little knot of mounted officers. Braley, his sword drawn, avoided one arrow by leaning in the saddle and parried the second with a flashing stroke that had to be reconstructed from memory to be appreciated.

That noise was the riders, Wizenbeak thought. The dragons are just too big to sound that high a note. God damn, the son of a bitch is coming right at me! He unhooked his leg from the side saddle and slid off the mule a split second before an arrow whistled through his personal space. As he landed on the ground, he suddenly remembered the gingals. "Why the hell aren't we using the gingals?" he shouted.

There was no answer. There was so much noise, it was doubtful that he had even been heard.

The bowmen among the Tarelians were battle-hardened veterans and they didn't require orders to improve their aim. Wizenbeak watched as the arrows glanced off the dragon's pale green underbelly. Bad angle, he thought. A gingal snapped ineffectively, and a sergeant bellowed at the man to take ever-loving aim and then shoot the ever-loving quarrel the way he'd been taught.

The arrows, though, had had an effect. If the dragons were armored in proof, the riders weren't. And the four dragons spiraled from treetop height to an altitude of about one hundred yards, maybe another hundred yards to the side. There, hanging lazily above the Tarelian Order, safely out of range of Tarelian arrows, they would sit and empty their quivers on the defenseless enemy. Behind him, Wizenbeak could hear the ratcheting clatter of gingals being cranked up.

"Gingals, are you ready?" the sergeant's voice came.

"Gingals ready," the scattered response came.

"Aim your quarrel!" There was a pause. "Shoot!"

There was a staccato sound of gingals being fired in unison.

Of the two dragons on the left, the leader lost its archer. The one following was hit behind the third pair of tiny wings, making a long red welt on the tail. Of the pair on the right, the one forward was hit three or four times. Ugly red blotches appeared on its green side, and it writhed and bellowed, losing altitude in a series of squirming lurches. The one following appeared unhurt, but it swiftly joined the other two dragons as they turned and fled. The Tarelians cheered.

The wounded dragon came down none too gently on the side of the hill, and the Tarelians ran over to surround it with a ring of spears, taking care not to press it too closely. The closest gingals were already pushing their way through the crowd, and the spearmen were like dogs holding a wild boar until the hunters came to finish it off. For all their bravado in talking about hunting dragons, the reality was daunting.

"Take the soldiers alive!" Wizenbeak shouted, running over. He pushed his way through the surrounding soldiers with a rashness that he explained later by saying that he hadn't seen the dragon. "I want those two taken prisoner!"

"Surrender," he told the two dragon riders. "You will be well treated." Nobody paid any attention.

As the wizard was trying to speak, the dragon raised its head man high and bellowed, a horrible deep scream, spraying dark venous blood at its enemies. Julia, the archer, facing numerous drawn bows, made no move to pull another arrow from her quiver. Yosie, the driver, slid her spear from its boot and held it in the guard position. From his vantage point on the driver's shoulder Bythanastros raised the hair on the back of his neck and hissed defiance, his black eyes glaring at Wizenbeak.

Feral human and feral troll-bat stared at each other, and the wizard felt the hairs rising on the back of his own neck. Now what do we do? he wondered. The dragon coughed and made a convulsive attempt to raise itself into the attack position. The deadly head, jaws gaping, rose ten feet high, shuddered, and subsided. Again it coughed, and this time it vomited a great gout of blood mixed with greenish slime. Wizenbeak, gazing into that dying reptilian eye from what he hoped was a safe distance, saw the life leave it. There was a pause measured in heartbeats, and then the head lowered itself gently to the ground.

Yosie unhooked her safety belt and dropped from the saddle

facing the wizard, her spear diagonally across her body. Julia returned her bow to the saddle holster, sliding down beside Yosie and Bythanastros.

The troll-bat glared at her. Craven! You face the enemy with empty hands! The smell of hot oil and smoke was almost palpable, given psychic power by the lingering presence of the slowly dying dragon. Julia shrugged. For fighting on foot, the scimitar was far too long, so she drew her parrying dagger and took it in her right hand.

The two of them stood there defiant. Three counting the troll-bat, the wizard thought. You definitely ought to count the troll-bat. He felt for the vial of kimjii extract and found it.

Behind him, Jankura felt for Mischka and Branka, touching an inert lump in the corner of their pouch. They seemed to be holding each other for comfort, utterly terrorized by the proximity of the dragon. What *is* this with troll-bats and dragons? she wondered.

"Gingals!" someone yelled. "Way for the gingals!"

The king-patriarch turned around to find himself facing a cocked and loaded gingal pointed squarely at his chest. "Sergeant! Point that thing somewhere else!"

The man did a double take. "Yes, sir!" he said, and swung the weapon to its maximum elevation.

Wizenbeak turned to his soldiers. A few of them were looking at him, waiting for him to do something. "We want those two taken alive!"

There was a growl, an involuntary animal noise. Perhaps it was inspired by blood lust, the memory of murdered prisoners. Then discipline reasserted itself, and the Tarelian Order was back.

So far, so good, the king-patriarch thought. Now comes the tricky part. He turned back to the dragon riders. "Surrender," he said. "I, Wizenbeak, King of Guhland and Patriarch of the Syncretist Church, promise you will not be harmed." He loosened the cork stopper in the vial and held it ready. A feral troll-bat promised to be the worst sort of bad trouble.

The archer gestured with the punching dagger and shouted something, defiance, from the tone. The words were strange, but not totally so. Wizenbeak rehearsed the mantra for understanding and cupped his hand behind his ear. Obligingly, she shouted the defiance again. I do believe that's Ursprach, he thought in amazement. It was a bit strangely accented, perhaps, and somewhat ungrammatical, but Ursprach just the same. Telling me to put some noun where the sun doesn't shine and conjugate it.

What do I say? he thought. What's the word for 'surrender'? Wrong question. He looked around and saw Jankura. "Janko! They speak Ursprach! Tell Raskidenji to get over here RIGHT NOW!"

After a few moments Dr. Raskidenji made his way through the crowd of soldiers.

"They speak Ursprach," Wizenbeak said. "We need to talk to them, you understand? Tell them to surrender, *persuade* them to surrender."

The scholar nodded. "Surrender," he said in Ursprach. "You will be well treated."

No surrender, never, never, never! Bythanastros' thought raged. We live with honor! Upon falling down among enemies without honor, to die fighting is glorious! Julia obediently shook the dagger. Yosie looked at Bythanastros on her shoulder, offering the faintly cool minty odor of respectful skepticism. "Let's talk," she said. "What have we got to lose?"

"Traitor!" the troll-bat howled, articulating his contempt.

"Hey, old man," Yosie shouted. "Why should we put down our weapons?" Raskidenji translated.

"Hunh." Wizenbeak rubbed his nose, thinking of yesterday's mass grave. "So you can go on living. Tell them that. Human life is worth preserving."

"That one is the enemy leader," Bythanastros shrilled. "If we can kill him, even him alone, we have won this most hapless encounter!" He shifted back to hot oil and smoke. Even though we die, we have lived for the eternal glory of Goldentrive! From Yosie came the smell of mint, skepticism, but stronger, now tinged with the pungent garlic of doubt.

"Human life is worth preserving?" Julia said. "Who are you people?"

"I am Doctor Raskidenji, and this is my leader, Doctor

William Wizenbeak, Master of the Tarelian Order, King of Guhland, Patriarch of the Syncretist Church. He wishes to converse with you, to understand why you have invaded his land. If you will put down your weapons, you will be well treated."

"Yosie, I think humans are in charge here," Julia said incredulously.

"Not much of an improvement, I should imagine," the driver replied. "Government is government. You think we should sheathe our weapons?"

"I don't know."

Yosie looked at Bythanastros and then back at Julia. "If they wanted us dead, we'd be dead already," she said, grounding her spear.

For the glory of Goldentrive! Bythanastros urged with all the passion in his tiny being. Attack! Engage! Charge for old Wizensnout! Kill! Kill! Kill! Kill! Julia, considering perhaps what Goldentrive had done for her, lowered her dagger from guard to rest.

Bythanastros, despairing of inducing his chattels to attack, launched himself at the king-patriarch, who had been distracted trying to follow Raskidenji's translation of the discussion.

The suddenness of the attack forced Wizenbeak to rely on the most instinctive of defenses. As Bythanastros hit the wizard's chest, there was a blue spark as his own energy was turned against him, and the troll-bat, astonished, stunned, utterly discomfited, fell fluttering toward the ground. Wizenbeak caught him left-handed and opened the vial of kimjii root extract with his right.

"Probably the safest thing would be to wring your scrawny neck, you bloody-minded little monster," he said shakily. Unable to catch the exact meaning of the troll-bat's exhortation, Wizenbeak had nevertheless caught enough of its drift to suspect that the troll-bat might be in charge and not the humans.

Wetting his forefinger with the essence, he restoppered the vial and rubbing thumb and forefinger together, wiped them dry on the troll-bat's ears. As the drug took effect, Bythanastros folded himself up and went limp. Wizenbeak wiped the neck of the vial in the handkerchief, and his fingers as well. He wrapped the troll-bat in the handkerchief and put him into the crown of his hat for safekeeping. He'd have to remember to wash his hands before handling Mischka and Branka, though. The stuff was potent.

"So far, so good," he said, looking up at Yosie and Julia. "Raskidenji, tell them the troll-bat has not been harmed. Tell them, hell, tell them that we drugged him, that he'll be sleeping for several hours."

Dr. Raskidenji translated the message, adding the demand that they surrender.

"We would like to surrender," Yosie said, leaning against the side of the dragon, "but you are ferals, and ferals are without honor or law. Maybe we would be better off dead."

The scholar translated. "I am not sure of the word 'ferals,' " he said. " 'Wild ones' is at best an approximation."

Branka climbed out of Jankura's robe, followed by Mischka. The dragon was dead, there was a whiff of kimjii in the air, and interesting things were happening.

"It sounds as if it might be related to 'feral,' " Wizenbeak said. "Something domesticated that reverted to the wild state. But *we* aren't wild . . ." The thought rose unbidden. Maybe from a troll-bat's point of view we *are*.

The ever-curious Branka leaped nimbly from Jankura to Raskidenji. "Hold on to them," Wizenbeak ordered. "We must be reeking of kimjii."

For the first time Julia saw Jankura, wearing a garland of wildflowers, holding a troll-bat in her left hand underneath her heart. She turned to Yosie. "Look at her," Julia whispered. *"Look at her!"*

Yosie looked and blinked. Then she raised her spear in salute. "We will surrender to the Lady of the Flowers," she declared.

Before Raskidenji could translate, Jankura turned to the king-patriarch. "They want to surrender to me," she said. "Is that satisfactory?"

"They will surrender to the Lady of the Flowers," Raskidenji said. "What does your Majesty wish to do?"

Wizenbeak looked at the dragonriders and back to Jankura. Except for the coloring, they looked like three sisters. And having made that connection, he suddenly realized that the dragonriders carried themselves like Jankura, even sounded like her. "They must give up arms and armor," he said, "but they may surrender to Jankura."

Prisoners taken, the Tarelians hacked off the head of the dragon for a trophy, buried their dead, and marched back to Damuso.

16

The Faces of the Enemy

"How long are we planning to stay put in this place, sir?" Pardus Murado asked. It was midafternoon, and the three regiments were fallen out along both sides of Old Damujao Road, near the intersection with the beaten path leading to Damuso.

Wizenbeak scratched his beard, unwilling to disturb the trollbat in his hat, where the itch was. "Until we get kimjii root for the troops," he said at last. "That will be what? Three or four days, maybe?"

"Or a week. Whatever." Murado nodded. "So it figures to be a permanent emplacement?"

"What's the difference?" the king-patriarch asked, letting his mount crop the meadow grass.

Count Braley, at his left, was looking down the road at Damuso. The drawbridge had been lowered across the ditch in front of the bailey, and several horsemen were sallying forth.

"Well, sir, a permanent camp is one you take a little trouble with."

"Oh? What sort of trouble, Pardus?"

The Tarelian waved his hand in the general direction. "We put up a wall, sir, over there, where we were before, deepening the ditches beside the roads and so forth. After, we dig a well, put in latrines that don't drain into the well, and set up bivouac."

"All this for only a week?"

"Yes, sir. It'll give the men something to do."

There were five riders, three in front with two behind, kicking up a little cloud of dust. The one at front and center was riding

Darji-Damuso's horse, Braley decided. The big black gelding with the white face was unmistakable.

"Same place as last time," Murado repeated, pointing out the barely perceptible outlines of the campsite. "That little rise east of Damujao Road and south of the beaten path running to Damuso. Only instead of unfolded shields tied on spears, we'll dig a ditch and throw up an earthen rampart."

The king-patriarch nodded. "That'll be good, Pardus. Anything else?"

"Yes, sir. Will you be staying in the castle or in your pavilion?"

Decisions, decisions. Wizenbeak pulled at his mustache and shifted his weight in the saddle. He had felt obligated to accept Count Darji-Damuso's hospitality before, but the count's bed wasn't very comfortable. On the other hand, he wanted to put the troll-bat down somewhere until he could give it his full attention.

"We'll sleep in the pavilion, most likely," he began, when Count Braley interrupted him.

"Excuse me, sir. Why don't we see what Count Darji-Damuso wants first?"

Wizenbeak saw the approaching riders and glanced at his strategist. The advice was sound, but he was feeling the long, hard day they had put in and didn't much feel like taking advice. "We'll sleep in the pavilion, Pardus," he said. "Set up camp."

Pardus saluted and went off to mark the outlines of the camp for his three regiments as Count Darji-Damuso rode up.

"Your Majesty," he said, saluting. "While you were gone, dispatches arrived from Cymdulock."

The king-patriarch took the lot and read through them swiftly. They were all routine: necessary logistics, promises of reinforcement, gingals produced, the usual junk and stuff. There was, however, a top priority message bearing the seal of General Lasco Genzari. Broken open, it said simply: "Swordmaster Gevas assassinated. Urge your immediate return." It was unsigned.

"Swordmaster Gevas? Who's he?"

Your Majesty should pay closer attention to the intrigues in your court, Count Braley thought. Then he smiled. Life was getting interesting in the old, familiar way. "He was the strategist for young Duke Bedirny, sir."

"Hunh. *That* intrigue." Wizenbeak felt the beginning of pressure at the back of his eyes and rehearsed the mantra to ward off a headache. It bit, but with a worrying lack of firmness.

"Yes, sir. By all accounts Gevas was a voice for moderation."

Right. Queen Marjia probably wouldn't kill an innocent third party to bed Duke Bedirny. Probably. Which meant that militant Syncretists pushing Bedirny to seize the throne had done it. Unless, of course . . . In his hat he felt the troll-bat he had captured beginning to stir. Fewmets! Going back was out of the question. What to do? He handed the other letters to his strategist. "Take care of these, Braley."

"Would your Majesty honor my poor household at dinner tonight?" Count Darji-Damuso asked. "The cook has prepared some excellent venison pies and an outstanding avricod tartlet."

Wizenbeak looked over at Pardus Murado. The Tarelians had already rolled up long strips of sod and were starting to dig the ditch that would surround their encampment. Oh, hell, why not? "It would be our pleasure," he said smoothly.

In the Royal Pavilion after the evening meal, they sat under globe lanterns clustered around the tent poles, Wizenbeak in the canvas chair, his back to the field desk, Jankura at the end of the cot, and Dr. Raskidenji on the footlocker.

"So what I found was that I could understand Julia and Yosie, but they couldn't understand me unless Doc, here, translated." Jankura pulled her legs up on the cot in the lotus position. "Also, if he moved out of earshot, I couldn't understand them. So I figured, hey, *they* are speaking Ursprach, which Doc understands but I don't, and the thing connecting us is that we each have a troll-bat. So I gave Doc Mischka to hold, and the two of them were back to speaking garbage."

"After that I gave her Mischka and Branka back," Raskidenji said. "The same thing. If we each held one and I could hear what Julia or Yosie was saying, *then* Jankura could understand. But when she *talked*, it came out Guhlish with a northern accent, and I had to translate."

"Yosie saw what we were doing," Jankura continued, "and

she got pretty excited. She said that we had formed a trive with our troll bats."

"Come on, Jankura." Wizenbeak sat back in his chair and folded his hands across his chest. "A trive is a bunch of troll-bats, like a gaggle of geese or a herd of cows. You can be a cowherd all your life, but you never become a damned cow."

"The word Yosie used was 'trive,' your Majesty," Raskidenji said, resting his elbows on his knees. "Of course, the Ursprach she speaks isn't standard, so she might have been talking about something else. Now, if Jankura and I are members of a 'trive,' why, so are are you, most likely."

"Most *unlikely*, rather."

"Easy enough to test, your Majesty." He opened the cage hanging from the tent pole and took out Mischka and Branka. After a little petting and soft talk the two troll-bats were awake, and he handed Branka to the king-patriarch.

Wizenbeak took the little animal and held it against his chest. "Now what?"

"How well does your Majesty understand Ursprach?"

"A few words reading is all. Our formal education was a little spotty."

"I understand. Are you having any trouble understanding me?"

The king-patriarch shook his head. "No. Why do you ask?"

"Because I'm speaking Ursprach." Raskidenji sent Mischka fluttering over to Jankura. "How well does your Majesty understand Ursprach?"

"You just said that, didn't you?" Wizenbeak said, stroking Branka's fur with a gentle finger. "The thing is that now the only word we caught was 'Ursprach.' " He handed Branka back to Jankura. "Fascinating. Put the little monsters back to bed, please."

After Jankura had resettled the troll-bats, Raskidenji continued. "So I thought, well, maybe *their* Ursprach is a little different than *ours*, and I asked them to tell me about trives."

Wizenbeak sighed. Raskidenji was right, of course. Given feral troll-bats, their "trive" was not necessarily the trive he had known and loved. "So? What did you find out?"

"Troll-bats, the ones Yosie and Julia are familiar with at least, order themselves in groups. Up to a point the group takes direction from outside."

"Well, sure," the wizard said. "Tell us something new."

"After the group achieves a certain size, the core of the group does the thinking, makes the decisions, setting the tone, I guess you'd call it, for the rest of them." He hesitated for a moment. "It is this core of the group that they call the trive."

The king-patriarch nodded. Much of troll-bat husbandry was devoted to keeping such a group from forming.

"Not all groups have a core," Jankura continued. "Yosie said that she and Julia were with Bythanna Group, which is too small and too disorganized to have even a rudimentary trive. So they get their orders from Goldentrive, the next step up, which is, what, subordinate? to Sisulia Trive."

"Yosie was confused about the relationship," Raskidenji replied. "At one point she said it was like a mother with a fully grown daughter."

"Some people are no help," she said. "Anyway, the trives own the land, and the trives own the dragons, and it looks as if some trives own the humans, as well. The humans, though, are a relatively recent addition, and what Yosie said was that the trives made their agreement a long time ago with Lady Alanji of the Flowers." A pause for emphasis. "Sometimes called Posalanji."

Wizenbeak felt the hair standing up on the back of his neck. "Relatively recent? Saint Posalanji, also known as Alanji of the Flowers, died what, eight or nine hundred years ago."

"Depends on whose calender you use," the ever-scholarly Raskidenji said. "Anyway, for Yosie it is a matter of faith that *Lady* Alanji was a human who made herself part of the uppermost trive somehow. At which time she cut some sort of a deal for the humans." He peered at Wizenbeak from under bushy brows and grinned. "Now, this may shock and dismay your Majesty, but apparently the troll-bats have forgotten all about Lady Alanji. Some trives own their humans flat out, and the others are thinking about it."

"The two dragonsriders went into more detail than I'd care to rehearse, but that's the gist of it," Jankura agreed. "Anyway, at the games they have this statue of Lady Alanji in the place of honor. She's holding a troll-bat, and they drape a garland of fresh flowers around her neck. And when they saw me for the first time, they thought I was a dead ringer for the statue, so they surrendered to me."

"What sort of games?"

Jankura looked at Raskidenji and shrugged. "She didn't really say, except that it sounded important."

Wizenbeak nodded. "Probably we should look into it."

"Right. Anyway, after that we tried to get an idea of what sort of an army they had."

"What did you find out?"

"They have sixty dragons," Raskidenji said. "Fifty-nine now, I suppose, but they can't fly more than about forty at a time, depending on the weather."

"What else?" the king-patriarch asked, feeling older than he had for quite a spell.

"Well, there's good news and bad news," Jankura said softly. "The good news is that we're fighting eunuchs and women. The bad news is that they're battle-hardened veterans."

The intellectual realization that Bythanastros could talk took a rather long time to sink in, and it was some little while after Jankura had suggested that he ought to be interrogated that Wizenbeak finally braced himself to take the plunge. Shortly after dawn one morning Jankura brought the caged Bythanastros into the Royal Pavilion, as Wizenbeak sat in his canvas chair with Branka and his second cup of coffee. Raskidenji unfolded another canvas chair for himself, with Mischka sitting on his shoulder, and took his place beside his master. Jankura slid the footlocker around and, setting the cage on top of it, perched herself on the cot.

"Here he is," she said.

Uneasily, Wizenbeak took a sip of coffee. He had a feeling things were going to go off the track, and they were pretty strange to start off with. "Your name is Bythanastros?" Raskidenji translated.

The troll-bat's ears stood up. "That is correct."

"What is your rank?"

A long pause. "Senior warrior."

We aren't going to get anything out of this little monster, Wizenbeak thought uneasily.

That depends, came the unspoken reply. What is it that you want?

"Hey," Raskidenji said, looking startled. "What were you saying just now?"

The king-patriarch took a sip of coffee. "Sorry," he said. "All those years of working with troll-bats must have taken their toll. Ask him what his duties were."

"I commanded two dragons and their four riders," Bythanastros replied.

"Right. Ask him . . . ask him how old he is."

A pause. "This is my thirty-fifth summer."

"My little Gruchka was the oldest troll-bat I knew," Wizenbeak said, "and he was only twenty-one when he died." He pushed his emerald spectacles up on his nose. "How old do you guys get?"

"Males often reach for forty or fifty summers. Females . . . well, females live longer."

"How much longer?" Jankura asked.

"Maybe four or five years on the average." Unless . . .

Unless what? Wizenbeak prompted.

Unless the female becomes an Honorable Kachka, a member of the trive. Eighty or ninety is not uncommon.

"Ah, your Majesty," Raskidenji began, but Jankura cut him off.

"Easy, Doc," she said. "I picked that up, and I'm not holding a troll-bat. Bythanastros?"

Inside his cage the troll-bat turned to face her but said nothing.

"What do they call a *male* who becomes a member of the trive?"

Bythanastros twitched an ear. "The title is 'Honorable Kivu,' but since males do not . . ." He stopped. "There have been no Honorable Kivu for a long time."

"Males do not what?" Wizenbeak asked.

"Heroism in battle," the troll-bat said. "In the old days, before humans, the male troll-bats fought their own wars for the glory of the trive and to make a name for themselves. If they were sufficiently heroic in battle, they became Honorable Kivu and took part in ruling the trive."

The king-patriarch took a sip of coffee. "That's interesting," he said at last. "How is it different with humans?"

"You tell humans to fight, and they fight." An ear twitched. "But when you do, you yourself are in very little danger. You administer war instead of fighting it."

"Could you explain a little more fully, please?" Wizenbeak asked. "Why would the successful administration of war not bring you as much glory as personal combat?"

For an instant there was a distant aroma of sour milk. "Administration is for females," the troll-bat said, "and the trive already has more Honorable Kachkas than it can use. You understand? A male cannot make a name for himself doing the work of females." Not when females will judge the results.

Jankura pulled her legs up onto the cot. What's in a name, Bythanastros?

There was a long pause. "To make a name is how the humans say it," he replied at last. "Maybe it should be 'develop an aroma,' because that is what we recognize . . . how we recognize the change that takes place."

Wizenbeak hummed a snatch of a popular ditty with the lyrics bent out of shape. "You can tell by the smell he's a hero sure as hell, troll-baaaat!"

"That isn't wrong," Bythanastros said, "though much has been left out. Such as the female response to courting."

"We can pass on courtship for now," the wizard said. "Otherwise, what happens?"

"What happens is recognition of the change within your own self," the troll-bat replied. "To face death, to slay another and live on, to become a champion of the trive . . . that changes you within your heart, and when the trive recognizes this, they honor you for what you have become."

"Come on. Nobody says you male troll-bats don't have to fight wars," Jankura said.

"You're very swift, Lady of the Flowers," Bythanastros replied, "but that was tried a long, long time ago. Try to fight a war without humans and you lose."

"What about moral courage? Seeking to do right against the will of the trive?" Jankura retaliated.

An ear twitched. The smell is not the same. The Bythanna

Group admires me, but they will not follow. And as for courting . . . The thought dissolved in a mist of fresh-cut onion.

"Did your Majesty follow that?" Raskidenji asked.

"Hunh." Wizenbeak set down his cold cup of coffee. "Yes, actually. Jankura, what the hell is happening?"

Isn't it obvious? Then she laughed. "Well, maybe it's only obvious to me. You and me and Doc and Mischka and Branka have become a trive, sort of. And Bythanastros, here, is an Honorable Kivu, sort of. And somehow . . ."

"And somehow?" Raskidenji prompted.

Jankura opened the cage door, and Bythanastros jumped onto her hand. "Like it or not, Bythanastros has become an Honorable Kivu in the Wizentrive."

17

The Battle of Damuso: Preparation

WAITING enforced gave them time: time to consider the information provided by the human prisoners and by the troll-bat Bythanastros, time to digest that information and derive a strategy from it, time to hash over the strategy in one interminable meeting after another. Dragons overflew Damuso regularly or were seen flying in the distance to spread devastation throughout the land, but always beyond gingal range. The Tarelians strengthened their defenses and waited for delivery of the kimjii root intended to defend them against troll-bats. The king-patriarch and his officers considered the strategy that should be adopted and its weaknesses.

Then one morning the kimjii root was delivered. The sky in the east was sufficiently light to distinguish a white thread from a black one, when three pack mules were led into the Tarelian camp outside Damuso. The sentry admitted Dr. Raskidenji, who shook the king-patriarch as gently as possible. "Your Majesty wished to be awakened when the kimjii root arrived."

"Uh, right. Right." Wizenbeak sat up and donned his robe and slippers. Where are my spectacles? he wondered, and found them on top of his desk where they always were. And his hat. Raskidenji handed it to him; it wouldn't do to make a disheveled public appearance. When he went out to inspect the kimjii root, Pardus Murado and Count Braley were already waiting for him.

"Good morning, your Majesty."

"Hunh. We'll see how good it is." He looked at the little caravan that stood before him. Each mule was carrying six burlap bags, which might weigh what, forty pounds apiece? That was a good sign. The mules were loaded way below capacity, which meant, theoretically at least, that the merchants had culled the stuff when they picked it up.

He selected one bag from each mule and sniffed them. The fragrance was barely perceptible, which meant that the root within was sound. When the merchants opened each bag, he plunged his arm in up to the elbow and pulled out a sample. None of the roots was bigger than his thumb, which was to be expected, but none of them looked stringy, which was good. There was no sign of sprouting, so they were in fact sound. He bit the end off one root and chewed it. It was properly crisp, not mushy or woody. It should grate up nicely. He spit out the slightly sour pulp and considered the aftertaste. Aromatic without any earthiness? This is top-quality stuff. He sorted through the roots in his hand and selected the one that looked the most unpromising. The same thing.

"This will do," he said, dropping the kimjii root back in one of the open bags. "How much?"

The merchant named a price that was scandalously high.

I suppose I should knock it down a little, the king-patriarch thought, but the son of a bitch traveled at night to avoid the dragons.

"There was speculation in the market?" Count Braley asked, who was charged with keeping an eye on domestic affairs.

"Yes, sir," the merchant said. "Duke Viluji cornered the market in the city. This stuff I got by going directly to the growers, but they wanted the market price."

Wizenbeak nodded. "Pay the man what he asked, Pardus."

"Your Majesty doesn't think it's too high?"

It's good stuff. We've got to have it. And it was timely delivered. The wizard shrugged. "Not really."

"There's a war on, you know, Pardus," Braley observed mildly.

The captain-general of the Tarelian Order nodded to his paymaster, who recorded the transaction in his ledger, a newfangled device consisting of ruled parchment leaves bound in a leather folder, before counting out the kimjii merchant's gold from a purse marked with the insignia of the order.

"So." Wizenbeak shivered in the cold light of morning; the dew on the grass had wet his slippers. "Cut this up so that every man gets one ounce, no, make that a half ounce apiece. Have them grate it into the sachet they were issued . . ." He sighed, bringing to mind the realities of military life and the unavailability of graters. "Or put it in the sachet and pound the root to a pulp. Whatever. Then make sure that the sons of bitches hang it around their thick necks. Once that's taken care of, we'll be ready to move out."

"How will we get it to them, sir?" someone asked.

There was a slow exhalation of breath as the wizard rehearsed the mantra for serenity. "The mess line would seem to be the logical place," he said at last. "Don't serve anyone who isn't wearing his kimjii root, you understand?"

He looked around. After breakfast are we going to have another long-winded strategy session in the great hall? God forbid! Things had been settled as well as they were ever going to be; now it was time to move. "Mister Murado, roust your officers up and have 'em here in the Royal Pavilion in ten minutes!"

The king-patriarch finished dressing while orderlies raised the sides of the tent to admit the morning light and went to fetch a pot of coffee from the mess tent. The officers began straggling into the tent before the coffee arrived.

After ten minutes Wizenbeak picked up his diptych and strode over to the sand table. "Here's Damuso, and fifteen miles due north of us is the enemy camp, here. To those of you who rode out at night, our thanks for fixing the enemy position."

He snapped his diptych open and checked the numbers. "So. The information we have is that we will be facing fifty-nine dragons, not all of whom will be flying at any given moment." He paused. Bythanastros had said that there might also be some siege dragons, huge creatures capable of gnawing through solid rock. "Plus maybe a few that can't fly because they're too fat."

"Will a gingal take them, your Majesty?" someone asked.

If not, we may be in real trouble, the wizard thought. "Of course," he replied smoothly. "Of course."

The orderly arrived with coffee and cups on a tray and began serving in strict order of rank. The king-patriarch took his coffee and set it on the edge of the sand table to cool, the sun's rays illuminating the steam rising in the morning air.

"Also, we will be up against troll-bats, which is why we

had to wait for the kimjii root. Also humans in impressively large numbers, about which no one seems terribly concerned. Count Braley, what did you find out about their weapons and armor?''

Braley lowered his cup of coffee. ''Their archery is first rate. As for edged weapons, well, the workmanship is crude, but don't let that fool you. The saber I tested holds its edge as well as all but our very best swords.''

''What about the armor?''

''About the same as ours. The stuff made with dragonskin is tough and slippery, and if you don't cut accurately, it could turn your blade.''

Wizenbeak nodded and referred back to his diptych. ''Our information is that the infantry uses pikes, in part because they have to fight dragons. The enemy outnumbers us no more than five to four, if we discount the rather large number of support troops who are expected to remain in the vicinity of the base.'' A little official optimism there—two to one with dragons was a little hard to take.

He paused for a swallow of coffee. ''You will have heard that we are opposed by women and eunuchs. This appears to be true, but bear in mind that these enemy warriors are battle-hardened veterans.''

''What about the line of march?'' Braley asked, bringing up a question that had provoked considerable discussion.

''After meditation and prayer, we have decided to go the long way,'' Wizenbeak replied. He pointed to the sand table. ''Crossing the Jidderswash, we march up the east bank, which is the high side, rather than following Jidderswash Road, which meanders with the streambed it follows. We then turn west on Harmony Church Road. Here.'' He stabbed a gnarled finger at the place on the sand table, creating a great crater. ''Which brings us directly to the Goldentrive camp. The extra miles will be well worth it, enabling us to march on the high ground, free from ambush at places like Dardjao Bluff.''

''What about the baggage train?'' Murado asked.

''Leave it in Damuso,'' the king-patriarch replied. ''See to it that the men carry three days' rations.''

"Yes, sir. What I meant was, will we leave three companies to guard it?"

Wizenbeak took a sip of coffee. Here was the point where the bridges started burning. "No," he said at last. "The men on sick call, the halt, the lame, those not fully up to hard marching. How many would you say there were, Pardus?"

"Altogether? Half a company, if that. Maybe fifty or sixty tops."

"Fine. Pull the three or four—" He hesitated, having been about to say "worst." "—least able men from each company and pick the worst of them to guard Damuso. Sixty, you said? Don't go much above it. Put them under that ensign who took an arrow in the leg." What else? He consulted his diptych once more. "The order of battle will be the Green, Red, and Blue regiments. That's it, gentlemen. Let's get moving!"

He was putting his armor on when Count Braley came in with one of the cavalry pickets. "We have news of the enemy," he said urgently, and led the picket forward. "Tell his Majesty what you saw."

The picket was dusty and unshaven, a local volunteer from the look of him. "Yes, sir. A few miles north of here there's this great bloody army advancing on Damuso."

Wizenbeak held up his arms so his orderly could tie the breastplate properly. "How many men?"

The man shrugged. "Three regiments, packed in closer order than our own. Archers and pikemen. No horse, though."

"Did you see any dragons?"

"None flying. There were maybe a dozen on each flank."

The king-patriarch took his swords as they were handed to him and thrust them into his sash of scarlet silk. Why hadn't he ever learned to use the damn things? "How soon will they be here?"

"Half an hour, your Majesty," the picket said, rubbing his stubble. "An hour at the most."

"Well," Wizenbeak said, as his helmet was tied under his chin. "The sons of bitches made a night march, seemingly, something we had been seriously considering. The battle is upon us. The only question is, How are we going to fight it?"

"Yes, sir," Braley said politely. "In the circumstances, however, we may not have a choice."

"There are always choices," the wizard growled. "Jankura?"

"Yes, sir," she replied.

"I'm taking Bythanastros, after all!"

18

The Battle of Damuso: Morning

THE Tarelian Order formed up just north of their camp, left flank touching Old Damujao Road, right flank a few hundred yards beyond the ditch surrounding Damuso. Fully armored, King-Patriarch Wizenbeak sat on his big blue mule, with Bythanastros on his shoulder. Behind him the banners of Guhland, the Tarelian Order, and Darji-Damuso were fluttering gently in the morning breeze.

"Does the smell of kimjii root bother you?" the wizard asked.

Bythanastros shook his ears. "As one Honorable Kivu to another, I have to tell you that it does."

"Oh?" We're depending on you for I don't know what-all. How bad is it?

"It hovers at the threshold of distraction," the troll-bat replied. "If it doesn't get worse, there shouldn't be any problem."

A dragon appeared just over the horizon, flashing green and gold as it circled lazily in the early morning sunlight. Then there was another, followed by two more. The enemy was in sight.

"All right, Bythanastros," the wizard said softly. "These are your people. Why would they be making a night march?"

Citron shifted to vinegar. "Goldentrive seeks a decisive victory here," the troll-bat said. "If they anticipate needing dragons on the field the whole day, then humans have to march at night."

More dragons appeared, slowly gaining altitude, and now they became aware of the rumble of a distant drum.

Wizenbeak sighed. "A decisive victory, eh. How would they

try to win it?" Going over familiar ground was easier than standing silent.

"We are an army without dragons," the troll-bat said. "The classical stategy in this case would be for Goldentrive to run the dragons back and forth above your lines, showering your infantry with arrows until they were rotten ripe for the pikes."

"The gingals have improved their shooting somewhat," the wizard said. "It may be that there will be a discrepancy between theory and practice."

"Maybe." The troll-bat sounded skeptical. "They already know that you have something that will bring down a dragon. If I were directing that attack, my stategy would be to throw the full force of dragons at the enemy commander, simultaneously with a push of the pikes against the enemy infantry."

Wizenbeak shifted his weight on the mule and thought about Count Darji-Damuso mounting a cavalry attack after he had reported that cavalry was useless. "It is not unreasonable to hope that Goldentrive's generals will follow the classical strategy, Bythanastros." It was, after all, what they had planned to defend against.

Count Braley rode over and saluted. "The battle platform is set up, your Majesty." The battle platform was three wagons arranged in a triangle, the apex pointing away from the enemy. A small shield pavilion had been arranged over the center wagon, with the flags displayed from the wagons on either side. Under the shield pavilion were camp stools. "Unless, of course, you prefer to watch the battle mounted."

And me sitting on this poor, skittish mule, the wizard mused. Well, best not to improvise without good reason. They were improvising enough the way it was. "No, thank you, Braley. When the dragons attack, we'd as soon not be on a mule."

"Yes, sir." Braley dismounted and saluted. "I'll join you there very shortly," he said as an orderly led away his mare.

Wizenbeak dismounted and took the middle place, with Pardus Murado on his right and Braley's stool on his left. Behind him sat Dr. Raskidenji, holding Branka, and Jankura with Mischka. Jankura, he noted with mild amusement, was wearing a brightly colored garland of flowers cascading in gay profusion upon the plain black robes of a lay preacher that she wore over her unadorned hauberk of black and tan.

Goldentrive's infantry came into view—long lines of heavy pike supported by archers. "What sort of count do you make, Pardus?"

His captain-general stood up for a better view. "Maybe seventy-five hundred or eight thousand, your Majesty. Plus about thirty dragons." The Tarelians stood at three regiments of nineteen hundred each, fifty-seven hundred men, less about sixty who were detailed to Damuso to guard the baggage train.

"Thirty-two dragons," Bythanastros said coolly. "Four groups of four on each flank. Look. The ones on the right will be overflying us."

"Sir," Murado said. "What are those sheds they have flanking each of their regiments?"

Bythanastros?

Those would be what you people call the siege train, I guess. The shed is the housing to protect the dragon within from whatever the castle throws at it while they chew through the rock to open it up.

"Dragon sheds," the wizard said.

"Oh?" The Tarelian blinked. The reality of fighting dragons was disconcerting. "What are they for?"

"The dragons inside are too big to fly, Pardus, but they bite through stone pretty well."

There was a long pause. "Your Majesty?"

"Think of them as siege engines, all right?" Just then one of the dragons stuck out its huge head, displaying its incongruous rodent teeth. It looked around and withdrew into the shed.

"Merciful God," Murado whispered, sitting down on his camp stool.

Shaking himself free from the distraction, Wizenbeak turned his attention to the dragons, which were now flying high overhead. I see them, Bythanastros, he thought urgently. What the hell are they doing?

Bythanastros scratched himself vigorously with a hind leg. "They'll swing around and hit us from behind."

"Hunh." Well, do what you can while you have time. "Pardus."

"Yes, sir?"

"Those dragons going overhead, you see them?" Murado looked up and nodded mutely. "They're going to swing around and come at us from the rear. Can you have some of the gingals track them?''

Murado nodded and stood up. ''Odd-numbered gingals!'' he shouted. The sergeants repeated the cry, and after a moment came the echoing response. ''Odd numbers here.''

''Odd numbers, track those dragons that will be coming at us from behind!'' The command was repeated. Then the dragons formed up into two lines, the ones in front flying west and the ones in the rear flying east as their riders whistled orders back and forth.

''What is that damned noise?'' the wizard asked.

''The riders are talking to each other,'' Bythanastros replied. ''The whistle carries for miles, and they talk and whistle at the same time. After a while you can understand.''

The dragons made two or three leisurely circuits at an altitude of about five hundred yards, getting themselves lined up with the battlefield, selecting their targets. Then, as if at a given command, they simultaneously dropped down to about one hundred yards and began to shower the Tarelians with deadly arrows.

''Classical,'' Bythanastros said. ''Absolutely classical. You were right, Wizenbeak. Goldentrive isn't listening to their field commanders; they're following the book right down to the last little letter!''

They heard the command ''Gingals, lead your target!'' and a moment later, ''Shoot!'' There was a clatter of nearly simultaneous snaps, and then the quarrels took their toll. One dragon reared and looped before spiraling down onto the ground for a soft landing. Another fell like a stone, splitting like a ripe melon when it hit the ground. A third headed back, its archer swinging lifeless from her safety line. Others were holding their places, even though hit.

The ratcheting sound of rewinding gingals stopped, and again: ''Gingals, lead your target!'' The carousel of dragons seemed a little bloodied, a little shaken, but they continued their dance of death. The Goldentrive archers were lethally accurate, and Wizenbeak heard arrows hitting the shield pavilion from the rear, a curiously unsettling sound. Then, ''Shoot!''

The second volley brought down another dragon, and two more headed north, abandoning the battle, followed more slowly by a third that was losing altitude and blood as it went to ground somewhere behind Goldentrive's army.

"That's three down and four withdrawn," the troll-bat said, jittering on the king-patriarch's armor. "And there are five or six hurt! Maybe thirteen out of thirty-two; they've lost nearly half their dragons! Pull back, Goldentrive, withdraw!"

Instead, the dragons began to climb, seeking safety in altitude at the cost of accuracy in loosing their arrows. The gingals fell silent, and across Damuso Field the lines of pike formed up and began to advance.

"Archers, string your bows!" came the command.

How is it possible that sitting still could be such hard work? the king-patriarch wondered, trying without success to recall a mantra, any mantra for calmness.

Gently, gently, Bythanastros thought, a webbed hand touching the side of the wizard's face. The terrible urgency that Wizenbeak had been feeling, the need to empty his bowels NOW, faded a little.

"Where the hell is Braley?" he asked.

The Tarelian tactic against pikes was this: One company in each regiment was assigned the point, the leader of that company taking his men into the face of the enemy in three ranks. At the last possible moment the leader would throw his spear at the enemy pikemen, and the whole first line would try to throw their spears where he had thrown his. Not an easy assignment. Throw too soon, the pikes recover; throw too late, one is impaled on them. Done properly, a gap appears, into which the leader charges. The first line then follows, cutting its way into the gap, widening it. The second line, still holding seven-foot spears, rolls the enemy pikemen up to the left, while the third rolls them up to the right. The rest of the regiment then pours into the breach to roll up the enemy line in both directions. At that moment the missing Count Braley was leading the point company from Red Regiment to break the Goldentrive line of pike in the center.

Overhead, to the left of center, four dragons grouped themselves in a tight formation, circling in a tight spiral and gaining altitude as they withdrew from the carousel. Then two of them dropped out of formation and dived for the shield pavilion where Wizenbeak was sitting. They were fast, but not fast enough. On the command "Shoot!" every gingal in the Tarelian Order snapped, and the sky was filled with Tarelian arrows. One dragon fell from the air onto the spears of the Tarelian reserve. The second dragon, crewless and gushing blood from mortal wounds, flew by the wagons with a high-pitched scream, snatching off the staff and flag of Guhland before bouncing off Damuso bailey and coming to rest in the ditch.

As the gingals shot off their quarrels, the second pair of dragons dived. The ratcheting sound of gingals being rewound sounded suddenly like an embarrassing proclamation of impotence. A few hastily sped arrows rose to challenge dragons three and four without effect. The company detailed to guard the battle platform closed ranks and raised their spears to protect the king-patriarch. Roaring, the third dragon impaled itself upon massed Tarelian spears in front of Wizenbeak, thrashing furiously about and snapping right and left with its great jaws as the fourth dragon slid over its back.

The driver, an arrow protruding from her leg armor, thrust at Wizenbeak with her lance, striking a shower of sparks from his helmet, a shower of stars from his eyes. Then the dragon, bleeding from a plethora of inconsequential wounds, reared up a full ten feet above the bed of the wagon to seize the dazed king-patriarch in its terrible jaws. Jankura stepped between them.

"Get out of here, you silly son of a bitch!" was what she said, but there was an almost palpable aura about her, the smell of thunderstorms just before lightning strikes. Wizenbeak cringed, but it wasn't directed at him. The dragon, to the astonishment of its rider and perhaps Jankura as well, shot straight into the air and headed north.

From the dying third dragon, the troll-bat that had driven it launched himself toward Wizenbeak with a terrible single-mindedness of purpose. As if in a dream, the wizard feinted at it with his right hand and caught it with his left, crunching the delicate bones as he slammed both hands together and hurled the broken troll-bat to the ground. A jolt of something paralyzed his left arm up to the shoulder, sending lightning flashes of sensation so intense that they weren't felt until shocked nerves reprised the insult in the afterimage.

"Look out!" Jankura gasped, so shaken that she could hardly speak.

There was a smell of crushed mint and hot oil. Nice try, Arvesthanas, but close doesn't count!

There was a pungent stink of dragon dung as the broken troll-bat fluttered about in a circle. Then he stopped, and the smell faded as he died.

Count Braley, arm cocked, spear in hand, ran toward the line of Goldentrive pike, screaming a falsetto ululation as he measured the distance, throwing the spear with all his force and skill at the last possible instant. He was rewarded with the sight of forty spears arching down over his head, and he pushed his way through the suddenly distracted pikes, cutting to the right and left with two-handed strokes. Blood sprayed on his armor. The company he had volunteered to lead followed hard on his heels, and the Tarelians poured into the breach.

White and shaking, Captain-General Pardus Murado climbed back onto the battle platform, boosted from behind by Dr. Raskidenji, who simply leaned on the wagon. "Excuse me, your Majesty, excuse me, excuse me . . ."

"It's all right, Pardus," Wizenbeak said, trying to rub his armored left arm. "I would have dived under the wagon myself if I could have moved." He looks as if he's going into shock. God, my arm hurts! What happened to it?

"Nothing permanent," Bythanastros said after a moment. "And your friend is tough; he'll have hold of himself before his pants dry."

Wizenbeak looked around. "Bythanastros? Where are you?"

In that muff you fixed up for me. No point in being the only troll-bat in sight, even if you are friendly.

Wizenbeak sat down, wondering how the battle was going to go while he wasn't paying attention. Jankura sat down beside him and took his left hand. Perhaps it was his imagination, but the surges of pain were becoming less intense and less frequent.

On his right Pardus Murado just sat there, gripping the hilt of his sword, white knuckles showing beneath his handguard.

Finally the king-patriarch gave him a nudge. "Hey there, Pardus, how is the damned battle going?"

Given an order, the Tarelian stood up and looked around. "Pretty good, sir," he said at last. "We broke their line on the left; we held them on the right. It looks like their center has pretty much collapsed.'' He hesitated. ''No, the sons of bitches are re-forming around those damned dragon sheds.''

Count Braley returned to the battle platform and leaped nimbly up. ''Sorry I'm late, your Majesty, but it looks as if the battle is going to be going on for some time.''

Wizenbeak looked at him. His armor battered and splashed with blood, he had clearly seen heavy fighting. ''Where were you?''

''I led the Red Regiment point company in the center, your Majesty.''

''Idiot! Imbecile! We depend on you for advice, and you run off to have a good time!'' Jankura squeezed his hand, and he could feel her rehearsing one of the mantras for serenity. Astonishingly, he could feel it bite.

Braley's handsome face looked perfectly composed. ''Sorry, sir. No excuse, sir.''

Right. What was it Murado had said? ''So advise us, already. What are we going to do about those damned dragon sheds?''

Braley had returned to the battle platform to ask Wizenbeak the exact same question. Now he pulled back from his passionate enthusiasm for mortal combat and considered the battle as a whole. Smash the sheds and one smashed the enemy. Except that one couldn't smash the sheds; the soldiers wouldn't even press close to them. So this battle was pretty much a wash. Therefore, they should press on with the original plan. ''Not much you can do about them, sir,'' he said at last. ''I saw a quarrel hit one of those monsters right between the eyes and bounce off through the damned roof. That great, ugly monster didn't even blink. You want my advice?''

The king-patriarch gave a long sigh. His arm hurt like hell, and he was going to have to make hard decisions. ''What have I been *telling* you, for God's sake!? YES!''

''Follow the plan the way we worked it out, your Majesty. At this point there's no use taking the long way around to avoid the enemy, either.''

Wizenbeak flexed his arm under the armor. Already the shoulder and elbow joints were feeling merely arthritic. Tentatively, he flexed the fingers on his left hand. They hurt, but they moved. That left the decision. ''Re-form the troops and march north?''

Count Braley nodded. ''We've already had a mean-fought fight just for the exercise, right? However, unless we lose, nothing that's going to happen here will be decisive. So we need to head for the Goldentrive camp in order to *take* those sons of bitches!''

''Right. Killing a few of Goldentrive's chattels isn't going to win the war for us.'' Wizenbeak felt an alarming lightness in his limbs, as if his arm were of no consequence. Tomorrow I will surely pay for this, he thought, if we are still alive, that is. But at this moment I shall seize the day. ''Pardus!''

Murado blinked. ''Yes, sir,'' he said.

''You heard?'' The Tarelian nodded assent. ''Disengage from the enemy. Form the regiments back up.''

''Yes, sir. Disengage and re-form.''

''You got it, Pardus!'' the king-patriarch said. ''We're back to the original plan, heading north the shortest way!''

19

The Battle of Damuso: Noon

THE gingals had been decisive. After the first half hour all dragons still able to fly had been recalled. Nevertheless, Goldentrive's humans remained formidable fighters, and the battle continued, dirty, messy, and bloody, with no quarter given on either side. There were surprises on the field; the gelded pikemen fought with totally unexpected ferocity and courage, as did the archers. Tarelians cutting their way into the ranks of Goldentrive's female archers—tough and tenacious as they were, they gave away too much weight and strength—would often encounter troll-bats or, once in a while, a grounded dragon who would rear up spitting half-chewed pieces of some bold fellow at his comrades.

The command to disengage and re-form came as a welcome relief to friend and foe alike. After they had re-formed and eaten a standing lunch, the Tarelian line of battle was bent. The Red and Blue regiments stood north to south, about a quarter mile east of Old Damuso Road; on their right the Green Regiment stood to the southeast, facing Goldentrive's broken center, which had rallied to form a pair of hedgehog formations around the dragon sheds. Goldentrive's right flank now occupied the center, while the left flank, broken and re-formed, stood as a half hedgehog with its tail extending toward the center.

Pardus Murado surveyed the field. "They fight well," he said, "but very defensively."

"That's poor generalship," Count Braley said. "They must have been depending on their damned dragons to sweep the field for them, and when it didn't happen, someone lost his nerve."

Murado took a sip from his canteen and spit. "Victory through dragonpower, eh? Depend on it that whoever they have directing the attack just got shook to his shoes."

Braley's mare lowered her head to take a mouthful of grass. "Probably," the strategist agreed. "It must have been worse than Darji-Damuso losing his cavalry."

"What are the figures on our losses, Pardus?"

"We've had some hard fighting, your Majesty," the captain-general said, opening his diptych. "We're missing five hundred thirty-seven from all ranks. Probably a couple of hundred walking wounded made it back to Damuso. The rest are on the field, dead or left for dead."

Wizenbeak shifted his weight in the saddle. "Too bad," he said at last, glancing at the sky. No dragons were in sight, at least none that were flying. That was no guarantee that they wouldn't run into them.

"The dragons have been recalled to protect the flues," Bythanastros said. "Goldentrive must now be concerned for its own survival."

The king-patriarch turned. "Jankura? What do you think?"

"Bythanastros is right. But they won't go away unless you push them."

I'm putting off the decision, Wizenbeak thought, but now is the time. If we just sit here, we've been defeated. But moving is so damned dangerous. "What do you think, Doctor Raskidenji?"

"I am a scholar, not a warrior, your Majesty. But this morning—" He hesitated a moment. "—this morning we started out to fight a decisive battle, and all we've done is scuffle in the dust of our own front yard."

He is scared, Bythanastros thought, and ashamed of being scared. He wants to go, and he wants not to go very badly. He knows going is the right thing to do, but don't expect him to make your decision for you.

I'm being bullied by my own troll-bat!?

The highest function of the trive is to decide correctly in times of crisis.

Are we really a trive? Wizenbeak thought uneasily.

Wizentrive is pretty strange, but yes, we really are a trive,

Jankura replied. And marching north is really the right thing to do.

Well, there's no help for it, then. "Pardus."

"Yes, sir?"

An inward sigh of resignation. "Let's go."

Pardus Murado gave the command, and the Tarelians marched west to Old Damujao Road, Goldentrive's infantry standing in place, letting them retreat. Then the Tarelians formed up on the road and marched north. Weary from the battle at the end of a night march, Goldentrive's army nevertheless gathered itself together and followed them.

"How much lead do we have on them?" Wizenbeak asked as they reached the top of the low hill overlooking Damuso Field.

Count Braley's mare danced off onto the grass, and Braley studied the enemy for a long slow minute. "A mile, maybe," he said at last. "*Maybe* we can stretch it to half an hour, but I wouldn't bet on it."

There was a long pause. "Half an hour *might* be enough time," Wizenbeak said after they had rejoined the march. "If we forced the pace, could we get it?"

"Alternate marching and running?" Murado asked. He shook his head. "Not if you need to fight at the end, sir."

"We need more time at the flues," Wizenbeak said. Bythanastros, I hope to hell you know what you're doing, I really do!

There was a faint smell of pickled cabbage. History is my guide, Wizenbeak. Now, to tell you the truth, for what we are trying to do, there isn't any precedent.

Come on, Bythanastros, Jankura thought. That damned tunnel you all marched through wasn't there by accident.

If the incident has been expunged from the record, came the troll-bat's reply, then there isn't any precedent. Right?

Raskidenji sniggered. If there is a precedent *event*, the outcome of which is deleted from text, trying to cite chapter and verse on it won't do us much good, will it?

"I can give you an hour, your Majesty," Count Braley said.

"What?" Wizenbeak shifted in his saddle to look at his strategist. "How will you do that?"

"Four or five miles up the road is Dardjao Bluff. The natural place for an ambush. Give me the Red Regiment, we'll jump

Goldentrive's vanguard, and we'll stop the sons of bitches for all the time you need!"

"Hunh." There was a long pause. "What sort of casualties do you expect?"

"You *will* lose the ambushing regiment," Braley replied. "Depend on it, your Majesty."

"Couldn't the regimental commander do it?" the king-patriarch protested. "You *know* we depend heavily on your advice, Count Braley."

Count Braley smiled and shook his head. "You want it done right, your Majesty."

"Count Braley is right," Jankura said, bringing her mule abreast of the king-patriarch. "Do you or don't you want to kick Goldentrive the hell out of Guhland?"

Wizenbeak shook his head. His arm was hurting again, and the scale of the sacrifice demanded appalled him. "Let me think about this," he said at last.

"Surely, your Majesty." Braley laughed. "Take your time. Dardjao Bluff will come in sight soon enough."

What should we do? For God's sake, what should we do?

If you don't do it, what then? Bythanastros asked. There was a smell of leaf mold and something floral. You'll mount a half-assed attack on the flues and scamper home, having done nothing.

Men will die no matter what, Raskidenji thought. It is your Majesty's first duty to drive the invaders from the soil of Guhland.

You're worried about the Reds, aren't you? Jankura's thought came, fragrant with the garland of flowers she was wearing. They can buy the time you need without fighting to the death.

Wizenbeak flexed the fingers on his left hand. The memory of the pain lingered, tiny ripples shimmering up his arm, and his decision was suddenly taken. "All right, Braley, you have your ambush."

His strategist smiled. "Thank you, sir."

He really is too pretty to take seriously, Wizenbeak thought, though that battered armor distracts you from his too, too beautiful face. What a pity they put a dent in his skull instead of breaking his nose. "This is the way the thing is going to be done. Now listen up, you hear?"

"Yes, sir."

"First the gingals. Goldentrive will have all sorts of dragons defending the damn flues, and the infantry coming up the road after us doesn't have any except the ones in the siege sheds."

"Yes, sir. Red Regiment has twelve gingals. How many do you want?"

Wizenbeak pulled at his mustache. "How many do you think, Pardus?"

"We could use them all, probably."

Wizenbeak gave a shiver and a sigh. "We'll take ten. That will leave the Reds two for emergencies. You understand, Braley?"

"Yes, sir."

"Second, the time. We don't need to squeeze out every last second, but we *will* need warning when the enemy is on the road again. We have maybe a dozen mounted scouts with us. You get six of them."

Count Braley nodded. "Yes, sir, six couriers. Two sent off when we spring the ambush. Two sent off when they break through. Two in reserve."

Wizenbeak shifted his weight in the saddle. "Third, we don't want the Reds fighting to the last man. You make the ambush, the enemy stops and regroups, that's an easy half hour. Right, Pardus?"

"They aren't well led," Murado said thoughtfully. "It might take even longer."

"Take what they give, Braley, but don't wait around for the sons of bitches to land on you. Head east with the regiment and take up a position on Jidderswash Road."

"Up around Harmony Church?"

Wizenbeak tried to remember the sand table they had been using, and Raskidenji floated the image up for him. "No, no. That's too far north."

Count Braley smiled and shook his head. "I disagree, your Majesty. The sooner the Reds rejoin the order, the better for everyone. East to Jidderswash Road and north to Harmony Church, and we'll wait for you there."

"You don't think Goldentrive's army will come after you?" Raskidenji asked.

"Not if we're headed east," Braley said with a shrug. "If

they do, we'll turn south for Damuso and you'll have all the time in the world."

"That's how it will be done, then," Wizenbeak said. "Pardus, Count Braley is detailed over to Colonel Janzhi of the Reds to set up the ambush. See to it."

The Tarelians marched north without opposition, without even seeing any high-flying dragons until well after midday. Then the Blues crested a low rise and encountered the Goldentrive reserves formed up across Old Damujao Road about a half mile south of the flues. In the near distance Goldentrive's flues gleamed in the afternoon sunlight, three inverted funnels woven of rope and glass, covering most of the south slope with cleanly designed elegance. The other structures, tents of various sizes serving assorted purposes, had a ramshackle and improvised appearance.

"What count do you make, Pardus?"

The captain-general shook his head. "No pikes, sir. For the rest, maybe five or six thousand with some sort of reserve behind them. And dragons, of course. I can't tell how many."

"More than two score," Bythanastros said, resting in the crook of the wizard's arm. The reek of kimjii root was cumulative, and he was making a real effort to stay awake. "Depend on it, all the dragons they have left will be fighting on the ground." He shook his ears and crawled into his soft wool pouch. Close support of the infantry is standard practice when you've lost control of the air, came the musky thought. Roust me out if you need anything.

"You heard that, Pardus?" Wizenbeak asked.

"Yes, sir. But it is unnatural, *extremely* unnatural, to take advice from a troll-bat, if you don't mind my saying so."

The wizard shook his head. Bythanastros sleeping was less of a distraction, to be sure; on the other hand, he needed all the help he could get. "Being invaded by dragons is unnatural, too. Afterward we will have to devise some appropriate penance for our sins."

"Yes, sir. How shall we order the attack?"

Where is Braley when we need him, Wizenbeak thought.

Running an ambush to buy us the time we need, came Jankura's thought, fragrant with the flowers she was wearing. We already got word that he sprung it, so do something.

All unbidden, a thought floated up in the wizard's mind. Sometimes finesse won't do a thing. Sometimes you have to rely on brute force. And then Braley's voice came, from one of the strategy sessions back at Damuso: "Keep the right flank strong."

"Extend the Green Regiment to cover the left and center," Wizenbeak said, sitting straighter in the saddle to display confidence he didn't feel. "Have the Blue Regiment attack on the right. We're trying to get to the center of those three glass flues over there. You understand?"

"Yes, sir." Murado looked over at the battle platform, the three wagons displaying the flags. "Where do you want to view the battle?"

The wizard followed his glance. "We've been thinking about that all the way up here, Pardus. Sitting on that battle platform with dragons flying around doesn't seem awfully bright."

Murado nodded, recalling his own experience that morning. "Yes, sir. One does feel a bit of a sitting duck as they come in at you."

Sometimes finesse won't do a thing, but give your opponent a chance to make mistakes. Especially if it doesn't cost anything. "Put the battle platform in the center," Wizenbeak said, pulling at his mustache. "And man it with volunteers. Tell them to sit there until those damn dragons start to come at them and then get off in a tearing hurry." He paused briefly. "Put the ten gingals we got from the Reds alongside it, five on each side."

"Yes, sir. And where will you be?"

He gave a sigh. "We'll go on foot with the Blues. An orderly can walk my mule for me, but until we clear out some of those dragons, starting the battle on foot looks like the way to go."

The opposition had learned from experience. Goldentrive's dragons did not form a nice line of targets, waiting to be shot out of the sky, but instead gathered on the ground behind the lines. They were close enough so that the Tarelian push lost impetus as they caught sight of the crouching monsters. Once the battle was fairly joined, two groups of eight dragons sprang into the air, followed by a third group of eight—all of them driving at the battle platform where the shadow commanders sat. Gingals snapped furiously, rearming themselves in a frenzy of ratcheting. When the dust cleared, the battle platform had been smashed, the three wagons had been knocked into kindling wood, and four of the gingals had been demolished. Of the attacking dragons, seventeen lay dead on the field and at least two others trailed blood back to their own lines.

Then Wizenbeak mounted his big blue mule behind the Blue Regiment, and the battle proper was joined, a dusty, chaotic scuffle punctuated by some of the few remaining dragons rearing up over the line to spit out the fragments of some luckless warrior. Slowly the line of battle rotated, Goldentrive's left advancing against the Greens as the Blues were pushing back the enemy's right. The right flank of the Blue Regiment was about eight hundred yards from the throat of the center flue when a courier rode up to the king-patriarch.

"Sir," he said, saluting, "the Reds have withdrawn to the east, and the main Goldentrive army is coming up Old Damujao Road."

Time is running out. Time HAS run out. Well, what we do is give it our best shot, Wizenbeak thought. He turned to his captain-general. "The extra gingals from the Reds. Bring them in from the center to the end of the right flank over there. And pick up the gingals along the Blue line that are still working. MOVE!"

As the dusty crews wheeled the hastily assembled battery of gingals into position, Wizenbeak rode over to the gingals and dismounted. "You see the shadow in the throat of the flue?" he asked the sergeant in charge of the battery.

"Yessir," the sergeant said, looking where the wizard had pointed. "You want us to put a few quarrels through it?"

Wizenbeak nodded. It had been a long day, and the end was not yet in sight. "Yes." The shadow was the pendant, the physical location of the troll-bats who made up Goldentrive. "We want you to unload on those sons of bitches."

The battery of gingals lined up, wheel to wheel: six from the Reds, seven and an extra crossbow from the Blues. The master sergeant took a ranging shot. It fell short, but the quarrel made a little hole in the skirt of the glass flue, and the hole was in line. He increased the elevation to the final notch, wound the gingal full pull, and let fly. Glass shattered in the flue, exposing the wooden pendant underneath.

"All the way, boys!" he shouted, and fourteen quarrels sped toward the pendant, followed by the single quarrel from the odd crossbow and another volley of fourteen. A few troll-bats fluttered out. Then a third volley of quarrels hit the pendant, and a cloud of troll-bats suddenly poured out of their shattered station in a panic.

"Good, good!" Wizenbeak said with satisfaction. "Now the pendant on the right!"

"Look to the south," Jankura said.

Wizenbeak turned his mule around halfway, putting a hand to his ear. "What did you say?"

"Look to the south," she said, pointing. Two horsemen were coming up Old Damujao Road, and as they watched, the riders left the road to gallop behind Tarelian lines.

"What?" The king-patriarch tried to think and came up blank.

"Those are Count Braley's last two couriers," she said. "They must be riding just ahead of Goldentrive's main army."

"All right," Wizenbeak said. "We've done what we set out to do. Pardus!" Nothing. "MISTER MURADO!"

The captain-general of the Tarelian Order rode over, pushing his way through the press. "Did you call, sir?"

"Yes! Let's get out of here. Head east, and we'll rejoin Braley and the Reds around Harmony Church."

20

The Battle of Damuso: Night

THE disengagement was initially straightforward. After stubbornly contesting every foot of ground, the Green Regiment had been pushed to the east. When their front fell back about two hundred yards, Goldentrive's infantry cheered but did not follow. The Greens then swung north, reassuming normal regimental formation, and marched east, followed by the Blues, as Goldentrive's reserves stood to their arms and watched them depart. By the time Goldentrive's main army had entered the valley on the south, the Tarelians were leaving to the east.

Goldentrive's army marched to the north of the valley, halting to re-form, a delay made necessary by their long march after the ambush at Dardjao Bluff. Goldentrive sent a line of archers out to maintain contact with the rear of the withdrawing Tarelians, following in their regular order of battle a short time later. It had been a long, hard day for everyone, and the pursuit was tenacious if not swift. At Harmony Church the sun was low in the sky when Greens and Blues rejoined the Red Regiment, what was left of the Red Regiment, and paused for a standing supper.

Goldentrive's line of skirmishers halted and waited for their main force to come up.

Wizenbeak and his officers rode slowly over to where the regimental standard was displayed. "Who's in command here?" Pardus Murado asked.

A young man with a battle-ragged hauberk and red hair stepped forward. "Corporal Engshar, sir," he said, saluting with a bandaged hand.

''No, no, son,'' Murado said gently, returning the salute. ''Who's in command of the regiment?''

''I'm the senior officer, sir. The regimental commander is me.''

''Merciful God,'' Murado whispered. ''What strength have you?''

Corporal Engshar looked around and shook his head. ''We have less than a hundred men fit to fight, a couple of hundred walking wounded, and maybe another hundred that can make it back to Damuso with help.'' He hesitated, looking very, very young. ''We have a problem.''

Wizenbeak leaned forward in his saddle. ''What is it, Engshar?''

''Some enemy archers laid down their arms, sir. We wanted to kill them, but Count Braley said no, wait and see what you wanted done.''

Stiffly and very slowly, Captain Braley came over on foot, arm in a sling, head bandaged. Behind him were perhaps a hundred prisoners, mostly eunichs with a few women, sitting on the ground with hands tied behind their backs.

My God, the wizard thought, appalled. This morning they stood 1,900 strong. ''What happened to Colonel . . .'' He couldn't think of the name to save himself and rehearsed the short mantra to restore memory. The name floated up like a little bubble. ''Colonel Janzhi?''

There was a hesitation as Braley tried to frame his answer. ''Janzhi fell leading the counterattack. All the line officers are gone.'' He coughed into his hand and spit. ''Excuse me. We have corporals heading up the companies, and we're short a corporal.'' He gave a cautious shake of the head. ''We're short some companies, too. How did the attack at the flues go?''

''Hard fighting with the reserves, but we shot the hell out of Goldentrive.'' The objective we decided on beforehand. For whatever the hell good it will do. ''We couldn't have done it without the time you bought us.''

''Good. I'm glad to hear it.'' Wearily, Braley turned and gestured with his good arm. ''We took some prisoners. What should we do with them?''

We ought to kill them, the king-patriarch thought. And then, not wanting to make that decision, he leaned forward in the saddle and asked, "What?"

"The men wanted to kill them on the spot. Nobody has been taking prisoners in this war, it's worse than the civil war that way, but I said no, we'd ask you. So I'm asking you. What should we do with them?"

"They can carry stretchers back to Damuso," Jankura said.

"For stretchers we have spears and shields," Murado said. "We can't trust the enemy with weapons in their hands."

"You're in charge," Braley said faintly. Using his sheathed sword as a cane, he lowered himself onto the ground and sat with his head on his knees.

Jankura rode over to the bound prisoners. "I am Lady Eilena Jankura," she said in Ursprach. "If you will carry our wounded back to Damuso on stretchers, we will release you unharmed. Will you do this?"

"We haven't eaten since daybreak," one said. "I don't know if we can."

We marched out with three days' rations, Jankura remembered. The food is there. "You will be fed first."

"All right," the tentative answer came. "We'll carry your wounded."

Jankura turned. Wizenbeak, Murado, Braley, and Raskidenji were all staring at her. Corporal Engshar was just standing there looking weary. "They have agreed to carry the wounded," she said, "if we release them unharmed. But they need to be fed."

"We should kill them," Murado said.

Raskidenji shook his head but said nothing.

"Whatever your majesty decides," Braley said.

Wizenbeak? There was no response. "Your Majesty," Jankura said, "killing these prisoners is the wrong thing to do."

I don't want to kill them. There has been too much killing. But I don't know how to stop it.

Mischka climbed drowsily out of his pouch and crawled onto the garland of wildflowers which Jankura still wore. Jankura nudged her mule and rode over to Wizenbeak and his officers. "Let me remind your Majesty," she said softly, "that the purpose, the essential point of today's battle was to engage Goldentrive in negotiation, to persuade them to leave Guhland."

The king-patriarch shook his head, unable to make the

connection. "We were going to use the two dragonriders we captured to carry our message. We don't need these people."

So you're going to kill them because you lack imagination? Jankura's thought was edged with a cold rage that would have cut stone. If you lack the will to do the right thing because it is right, find me a political argument for doing it!

Wizenbeak pushed his emerald spectacles back on his nose and blinked. An argument for whom? For Murado, of course, for Braley, and for the Tarelians who had been dying for him and for their country. "These are humans fighting humans for troll-bats," he said at last. "Goldentrive might find the return of the prisoners more disagreeable than their execution."

"Or they might not," Pardus Murado said grimly. "Besides, we can't trust them. What oath could they give us that might possibly be honored?"

"They scare you, do they?" Jankura asked.

Murado flushed and dropped his hand to the hilt of his sword. "Half the order is dead fighting these sons of bitches and their damn dragons. They gave no quarter, and they'll get none!"

"Do you want Goldentrive to go home or don't you?" Jankura snapped. "Now is the time to stop fighting and start talking!"

Murado turned to the king-patriarch. "We should kill the prisoners, your Majesty."

"No," Wizenbeak said. "Feed them and let them help carry our wounded back to Damuso. Then we release them with the two dragonriders who will carry our message to Goldentrive. You understand?"

"Yes, sir," Count Braley said. "A good decision, that, combining diplomacy with war."

"Pardus?"

There was a long silence. "Yes. Sir. But they must swear an oath."

Jankura adjusted her garland of flowers and resettled Mischka against her side as her mule ambled over to the prisoners. "Will you take an oath to obey me until you are released?"

There was a stir among the bound prisoners. "We will obey Lady Jankura of the Flowers," a woman said.

"What? I can't hear you."

"We will obey Lady Jankura of the Flowers!"

"Louder! I want that fool of a general to hear you!"

"WE WILL OBEY LADY JANKURA OF THE FLOWERS!"

"That's better," she said, dismounting. Drawing the knife from her belt, she began to cut the ropes that bound them.

After the Tarelians resumed their march, turning south on Old Jidderswash Road, Goldentrive's army followed them for two or three miles, until the sun went down. They then grounded their arms and stood watching along the crest of a low hill until the enemy vanished from sight.

"Where are we going to make camp tonight?" Dr. Raskidenji asked as the last streaks of color faded from the sunset and the first stars appeared in the evening sky.

"Damuso," Wizenbeak replied. He unhooked his left leg from the horn of the side saddle to sit momentarily astride, then shifted his right leg around the horn, changing sides in a futile effort to make himself more comfortable. It had been a long day and it wasn't yet over.

Since food could be made to substitute for sleep to some extent, the Tarelians stopped for a meal of flatbread around midnight.

"Why aren't those men eating?" Raskidenji asked.

Pardus Murado glanced over at him and shook his head. "They're standing guard," he said. "Half eat sitting while the rest stand guard is the way you do it in the field. Afterward they trade places."

"Right," Raskidenji said, covering a yawn. "I should have remembered that. How much farther to Damuso?"

"Don't worry about it," Murado said. "We'll be there before the black cock of night crows."

In due time they arrived back at Damuso, skirting the edge of the battlefield to arrive at the camp. The wounded were made as comfortable as possible, and the doctor and his assistants, weary from a long day's work patching up the casualties of the morning's battle, started all over again.

"All right, Lily," Jankura said to the leader of the Goldentrive prisoners. "You and your people have fulfilled your obligation. You can either get some sleep in one of the empty tents and take off in the morning, or you can go now."

"We'll go now, I think," Lily said. "It isn't that we don't trust you, but your soldiery . . ." She stopped, at a loss for words.

"What, they make you uneasy? I could see that."

"No, no." Lily shook her head. "Well, yes, uneasy, but not the way you mean. They smell wrong, somehow, and it's very disturbing."

Jankura turned to Wizenbeak, who was standing beside the two dragonriders. "They want to go now. Are Yosie and Julia ready to go with them?"

"They're here, anyway," the king-patriarch said. "They only need to receive our message." He paused and yawned. "It's been a long day. What message are we going to send?"

Jankura shrugged. Bythanastros?

What I told you before, came the sleep-fogged answer.

Wake up, Honorable Kivu Bythanastros, we need to talk with you. Jankura was gentle but insistent.

The troll-bat crawled out of his warm pouch and slowly climbed on Wizenbeak's shoulder. He looked around, then opened his eyes and shook his ears vigorously. The smell of mist in a pine forest suggested bleakness. "What is it?" he asked.

"What message do we send to Goldentrive to bring them to the conference table?" Wizenbeak repeated.

"Tell them that Wizentrive wants to talk to them," the troll-bat said. "Ask them to send a representative to arrange a meeting."

"On a dragon?" Jankura asked.

"Dragons are traditional," Bythanastros said. "If they come, it will be on a dragon."

"Right. We need to know not to shoot them with gingals. Can you carry a white flag of truce?"

Bythanastros hesitated. "Yosie, could you display a white flag on a dragon?"

"Ah, maybe," Yosie said, rubbing her head. "How fast are we going with how big a flag?"

"Something visible at a thousand yards," Jankura replied, "and you don't have to be going fast at all. Just wave it until someone on the ground waves back so you know it's all right to land."

"This big?" Yosie asked, spreading her hands.

"That should do," Wizenbeak said, yawning again. "Tell your people that maybe we can work something out."

"All right," Yosie said. "Wizentrive wants to talk. Set up a meeting. Wave a white flag to show you come in peace. Is that it?"

He nodded. "That will do for a start, anyway. Good night, and God bless you."

The prisoners formed up around Yosie and Julia and walked over to Old Damujao Road. There they turned north and began singing, the song lingering long after they had vanished into the darkness.

21

Diplomacy with Barn Burners

THE first day after the battle the Tarelians buried their dead who had fallen on the field of Damuso. On the second day a strong party went up to the Dardjao Bluff and buried the dead of the Red Regiment that had fallen in the ambush. On both days dragons were seen flying high above, observing but making no attempt to interfere. On the third day General Lasco Genzari marched into Damuso with 3,000 heavy infantry, 2,100 archers, and 50 gingals.

Wizenbeak embraced his old friend in front of the Tarelian camp. "You must have marched like the wind to get here so soon, Lasco."

Genzari smiled and shook his close-cropped head. "Nothing of the sort, your Majesty. We rode most of the way, courtesy of Duke Viluji, who provided us with mounts. We rode until we saw the first dragon, anyway."

"Oh? Where was that?"

"An easy day's march to the south of here, your Majesty. Whereupon Viluji's men took back their horses and scampered off to Cymdulock."

"What about your baggage train?" Count Braley asked.

"Oxen are slow,' Genzari replied. "The baggage train will be here in a few days with another seven hundred men."

"Archers or heavy infantry?"

Genzari laughed. "A mix. That seven hundred is the men who can't ride horses."

The Royal Army settled themselves into the Tarelian camp,

which was now mostly vacant, and Wizenbeak moved into the Royal Pavilion with his officers.

"Rather than all of us talking at once," the king-patriarch said, "suppose Pardus and Count Braley here give you an account of our recent battle. Then we'll answer any questions you have, and then you can tell us how things are at home."

"Yes, sir." Genzari fingered his closely trimmed mustache. "So tell me about this great, murdering battle, Mister Murado."

"What was the last dispatch you had from us?"

"You were waiting for a shipment of kimjii root," Genzari replied, "and wondering if you could depend on the information obtained from prisoners."

The Tarelian walked over to the sand table. "Right. We found out early on that the Goldentrive army has troll-bats, something we mentioned in the dispatches. The Royal Army has kimjii root?"

"Oh, yes. Vilujii sold it to us at extortionate prices. Go on."

Murado nodded. "The bastard! We were delayed maybe four or five days until we got ours. When it arrived, it was issued, and we fell out after breakfast, prepared to march north." He pointed to the sand table. "Here we were. Anyway, Goldentrive had made a night march, and here *they* were." When he and Braley finished, Murado asked if Genzari had any questions.

"You left Cymdulock with fifty-seven hundred men," Genzari said. "How many could you field today?"

Murado frowned. "Fit to march with the Royal Army?" He opened his diptych. "I make it sixteen hundred nine, but that includes five hundred eleven LDOs."

"Light duty only." Genzari nodded. "All right, they can stand in reserve if we need them. What about the wounded?"

"This morning we buried another twenty-one, so the wounded are down from eleven-sixty-three to eleven-forty-two. The critical list is down to—what?" He looked over the diptych. "Fifty-eight, but some of those will recover."

"You've been doing some hard fighting," Genzari conceded. "How many gingals have you left?"

Murado snapped the diptych shut and slipped it back in his pocket. "Twenty-six, with three extra crossbows. We're low on quarrels."

"We have quarrels," Genzari said. "Your Majesty also has a quarrel at home."

Wizenbeak pushed his emerald spectacles back on his nose. "My child bride is playing footsie with Duke Bedirny?"

"Say rather that your queen is flaunting her paramour before all the city, your Majesty."

There was a long exhalation of breath. "You know, Lasco, you have a touch of the poet in you," Wizenbeak said at last. "That was very nicely put. 'Flaunting her paramour before all the city' suggests that we may have a major problem."

Genzari almost smiled. "Your Majesty retains his gift for wry understatement," he said gently. "These reinforcements are probably the last in Guhland that are loyal to you. We had them holding down Syncretist hot spots like Rosano. The queen ordered us up north, partly to help you fight dragons but mostly to get us out of the way of the Syncretist counterrevolution."

"You think the Syncretists are trying to snatch back the crown?" Murado asked.

"Some of them, anyway," Genzari said, looking at the Tarelian with speculative eyes. "Ah, Mister Murado, times are hard when you have to ponder on who owns your loyalty."

"What are they saying, Lasco?" Jankura asked.

"The same old scurrils," he replied. "The most dangerous of which is the report that Queen Marjia is going to have her marriage annulled because it was never consummated."

"Hunh," Wizenbeak grunted. "That was going around before we left Cymdulock. Anything new?"

Genzari rubbed his head. "Well, just before we left some lay preachers were saying that God sent Wizenbeak to scourge the Church for its sins, and the dragons to punish Wizenbeak for his unseemly enthusiasm. It seems that once the dragons eat you, your Majesty, they will disappear."

"Hunh." A slow shake of the head. "It might be worth it to get them out of the country."

Jankura traced a finger lightly over Bythanastros' ears. "And if the dragons don't disappear?"

"It will be my fault, of course," Wizenbeak said. "Well, then, we have to take care of the dragons first." He pushed his glasses up on his forehead and rubbed his eyes. "Never mind how the monsters were conjured up; the thing to do is get them the hell out of Guhland!''

From outside the Royal Pavilion there was a shout and the ratcheting sound of gingals being wound. Wizenbeak and his officers went outside, and high overhead a dragon was circling, a white flag fluttering from behind its head.

''All right! All right!'' Wizenbeak shouted. ''The son of a bitch is come to parley! No gingals!''

The dragon continued to circle. ''Hell,'' the king-patriarch growled, ''how do we get him to come down?''

Jankura went into the Royal Pavilion and came out with a bed sheet, which she folded in quarters. ''This way,'' she said. ''Follow me.'' She waved the white sheet and walked out to Old Damujao Road. There she turned to the king-patriarch and his officers. ''Wait here,'' Lady Jankura of the Flowers said, and walked out into the field on the western side of the road, letting the white sheet flutter in the breeze.

The dragon spiraled down, landing safely outside gingal range. The driver thrust the staff of her white flag into the ground beside the dragon's head, and the woman in the archer's seat unhooked her safety belt and slid off onto the ground. Jankura walked halfway from the road into the meadow, and the dragonrider walked over to meet her.

''Well, well,'' the dragonrider said, looking her over. ''You do indeed look somewhat like the statue of Lady Alanji of the Flowers. Do you claim to be an avatar of Lady Alanji?''

''I am Lady Eilena Jankura,'' was the cool reply, ''and I am, among other things, an Honorable Kachka of Wizentrive. If you need an avatar, find someone else.''

''My apologies, Lady Jankura. I am Heatherfields-Hsven, and I must tell you that your presence on the battlefield was noted by more than a few of us.''

Bythanastros climbed out of his pouch and up onto Jankura's shoulder. ''Heather, darling,'' he said, ''how does it happen that a delicate diplomatic mission like this gets entrusted to a barn-burning radical like you?''

Heather did a double take. ''Bythanastros?! What are *you* doing here?''

''That's Honorable Kivu Bythanastros to you, darling. The Lady Jankura and I are part of Wizentrive.''

"My daughter, Yosie, thought you were dead," Heather said. "I should have known better than the witness."

This is rather strange, Wizenbeak, Jankura thought, and probably it will take awhile. Why don't you get out of the sun and wait in the Royal Pavilion?

Back at the road, the king-patriarch and his officers returned to the Tarelian camp.

"The rumors of our demise were greatly exaggerated," the troll-bat said. "What's all this about Lady Jankura being an avatar of the long-dead Lady Alanji?"

"Well, Julia is an idiot, but Yosie thought so, too," Heather said, "and Serafina was of the same opinion. Serafina was driving the dragon that was about to chew up your commander when you stepped forth and dismissed them both. That impressed the hell out of a lot of people."

"I see," Jankura said, who didn't see at all.

"Not to mention those prisoners whose lives you saved."

How very interesting. I wonder if Queen Shaia might have been an avatar of Lady Alanji of the Flowers. Might *also* have been an avatar? It would explain why we looked alike, anyway. "Your arguments defy refutation, Heather," Jankura said at last. "All I can tell you is that I make no claim to be anyone else, but no doubt the avatar is the last to know."

"The will to believe, the *need* to believe, is very strong, Lady Jankura. Are you truly an Honorable Kachka?"

Jankura spread her hands. "We are standing here conversing in Ursprach, a language which I do not speak, because other members of Wizentrive speak it."

"What? What is your native tongue, then?"

Jankura shifted out of Ursprach. "We are standing here conversing in Guhlish, a language which you do not speak, because Guhlish is my native tongue."

"Which of you speaks Ursprach?" Heather asked, and answered her own question. "Oh, Bythanastros, of course."

"Never mind," Jankura said, not wishing to mention Raskidenji. "Incidentally, Heather, how *did* you get this diplomatic assignment?"

"The humans took a vote to see who would go. A lot of us believed that Lady Jankura of the Flowers was the Lady Alanji come back to us in our hour of need, and there were quite a few who said absolutely not. My open-minded skepticism eventually won the day."

"My congratulations." Jankura smiled faintly. "As you might suspect, we have troubles of our own, the most notable being what to do with Goldentrive. Did you bring us an offer?"

"Of course." Heather nodded. "We buried your dead near the flues, but we numbered them and marked the grave site. You can send up one of your holy men to bless the ground if you wish."

"That's very kind of you," Jankura said cautiously. "Do you have any prisoners to return?"

"Alas, no. We are in your debt."

"No prisoners at all?"

Heather shook her head. "If we had thought to take prisoners, we would have returned them after you very graciously returned our people."

"How about talking directly with Goldentrive, then?" Bythanastros asked.

"I'm afraid not," Heatherfields-Hsven said. "When you shot up the pendant, a lot of Honorable Kachkas were killed. They can't really talk to you until they get reorganized."

"Oh?" Jankura fingered her garland of flowers. "And how long might that be?"

There was a faint smell of urine and vinegar. "Six months to a year," Bythanastros said, spreading his long webbed fingers. "If we were a regular trive, we'd march on the flue and demand their surrender, and they'd have to make terms with us."

Hey, Bythanastros, I can find out what you know any time. I'm trying to find out what *she* knows, all right? "Heather?"

"The troll-bat has it, Lady Jankura."

Jankura gave a sigh. "What sort of terms?"

"Basically?" Heather scratched her head. "The big deal is which of the losers are going to be incorporated into the victor's trive." From the dragon, her driver whistled something at her. "We have to get on home, Bythanastros, Lady Jankura. Are you going to send a holy man?"

"Probably. If he has a white flag, he might even be bringing a message."

22

Diplomacy with Troll-Bats

THE next morning Goldentrive awoke to find that Guhland's Royal Army, reinforced with the Tarelian Order, had made a night march and was now encamped on Harmony Church Road, almost within sight of their three flues. The Guhlish Army, formed in neatly ordered ranks, stood in place, awaiting the order to advance. Goldentrive's army, shocked awake, scurried about whistling orders as they formed a hastily improvised line of defense at the eastern edge of the valley, about a thousand yards from the enemy.

After it was clear that they were pretty much in place, Lady Eilena Jankura, wearing a garland of flowers and carrying a white flag, rode out at the head of a company of Tarelians. Jankura stopped about halfway between the two armies and grounded the white flag. The soldiers with her quickly raised a small shield pavilion, setting up a table and chairs underneath it. A linen tablecloth was draped over the table, and on it was set a cut-glass decanter with matching goblets and bowl, a gift from Count Darji-Damuso, presented in a tooled leather traveling case. Water from a canteen filled the decanter, and army ration flatbread was placed in the bowl. Lady Jankura of the Flowers dismissed the company of soldiers and sat down with her troll-bat to wait.

As the sun rose in the morning sky, the flues began to draw, and a single dragon of green and gold rose into the sky and circled over the valley a few times. After a short time the dragon landed about a hundred yards from where Jankura was waiting,

Heatherfields-Hsven slid off the archer's saddle and walked over to the shield pavilion.

"Good morning, Lady," she said, shading her eyes against the morning sun. "What is it that you want?"

"And a good morning to you, Heather," Jankura replied. "How did a barn burner like yourself get the job of herald?"

Heather grinned. "They just asked who went last time, and I put up my hand. What do you want?"

"I want to talk to Goldentrive."

"Oh, dear. I'm afraid that's out of the question."

Jankura stroked the fur on Bythanastros' back with a gentle finger. "If they aren't here by noon, my army will come to them. Humans will die because troll-bats can't make up their minds."

"Lady Jankura, the Honorable Kachkas of Goldentrive can't decide on which of them should come to see you, nor on what to say, nor on anything."

Bythanastros flexed his long webbed fingers in a curious gesture that Jankura had not seen before. "We don't doubt it," he said. "Nevertheless they must come."

"But I just told you that they can't."

"Goldentrive will come," Bythanastros said. "The whole sadly confused lot of them will come and meet with the whole of Wizentrive. Here. Before noon."

Heather nodded. "I'll give the Honorable Kachkas your message, but they'll doubtless want to know about Wizentrive. What should I tell them?"

"Tell them it consists of three humans and three troll-bats," Jankura said. "The troll-bats are Bythanastros here and two male juveniles named Mischka and Branka. The humans are the learned Doctor Raskidenji, Guhland's King-Patriarch Wizenbeak, and myself."

"A distinguished company, for humans," Heather said. "But a trive with juvenile males? Goldentrive will scoff."

"A trive camped on your doorstep with an army," Bythanastros said. "Goldentrive will come."

"Goldentrive *may* come," Heather replied. "Just possibly. Perhaps. I can't speak for them, of course, but I shall relay your message."

Jankura sighed and composed her hands in an attitude of prayer. "Thank you, Heather, but . . ." There was a long pause.

" 'May come' isn't good enough. I want them here! How can we make them come?"

"Only Lady Alanji of the Flowers could make them come," Heather said softly. "Who are you to bid Honorable Kachkas to come and go at your pleasure?"

Jankura poured herself a goblet of water and took a slow, careful swallow. "If I say that I am the avatar of Lady Alanji, I have committed myself to your people forever."

"Things have not been going well with us, Lady," Heather said, shading her eyes against the morning sun. "We could use your help."

Jankura felt Bythanastros' hackles rise under her finger, and a moment later she felt her own rising. She listened to her own voice saying "When I awoke this morning, I realized that I am, in fact, the avatar of Lady Alanji of the Flowers."

"Myself, I wouldn't be hard to convince," Heather said. "I'll take your message to Goldentrive at once." She walked into the shield pavilion, took Jankura's hands, and kissed her on the cheek. "Forgive me, I could never do this once I acknowledged you as the Lady of the Flowers!" Then she was on her dragon, the dragon climbing back into the sky.

The dragon made two or three slow turns and flew down the length of Goldentrive's line as Heather put her fingers in her mouth and shrilled out the news. "Lady Alanji of the Flowers has returned! Lady Alanji of the Flowers has returned!"

Goldentrive didn't meet the noon deadline. However, a portable pendant had been improvised by then, immediately in front of the shield pavilion, and the Honorable Kachkas began arriving shortly afterward. First came dragons carrying scores, and then the more important Honorable Kachkas arrived by dozens and tens and even fives.

When the last dragon had departed and all the Honorable Kachkas were in place, the Honorable Kivu of Wizentrive presented themselves. Wizenbeak with Branka, Raskidenji with Mischka, they rode over from the lines of the Royal Army and took their place at the table under the shield pavilion.

After much twittering and the generation of complex and not entirely pleasant odors, three Honorable Kachkas of impressive size and seniority fluttered gently to the table.

"We were part of the Sisulia Trive," the one with notched

ears said, "coming into Goldentrive in the furtherance of our mutual interests."

"We were part of Imperial Trive," the one with silver back fur said, "coming into Goldentrive in the furtherance of our mutual interests."

"We were part of Goldentrive," the one with a blind eye said, "working and rising within Bythanna Group until our gifts were marked for advancement. Together, with the consent of the trive which listens, we will speak for Goldentrive." The use of Ursprach in trival matters is an appalling breach of manners!

"The invasion of our country and the laying waste of our land is *not* appalling?" Wizenbeak said politely. "We are Wizentrive. I, myself, am simultaneously king of Guhland and patriarch of the Syncretist Church, King-Patriarch William Wizenbeak." There was an excited twitter among the onlooking troll-bats. "Why this commotion, gentles?"

"Your name is one that appeared to us in a dream," the Honorable Kachka with silver back fur said.

Should I pursue this? Wizenbeak wondered. No, no. Probably it is merely weird rather than important. "We see," he said, pushing his spectacles back up on his nose. "And this is little Branka." Branka looked around, fascinated and scared, and said nothing.

"We are Wizentrive," Dr. Raskidenji said, following the formula they had agreed upon. "I, myself, am Doctor Raskhim Raskidenji, and this is little Mischka."

"We are Wizentrive," Mischka said, quite unexpectedly, "and I am Mischka, an Honorable Kivu."

"We are Wizentrive," Bythanastros said, "and I myself am the Honorable Kivu Bythanastros, lately come from the Bythanna Group of Goldentrive."

"We are Wizentrive," Jankura said, "and I, myself, am Lady Eilena Jankura, the avatar of Lady Alanji of the Flowers." There was a sigh from the assembled troll-bats and a mélange of complex odors. "It is our intention to incorporate the whole of Goldentrive into Wizentrive, pruning and removing those of you whom we consider unsuitable for our trival modality, the perfect harmony which we seek. It is also our intention to depart at once from Guhland, passing under the mountain and sealing the hole behind us as it was sealed in antiquity by Lady Alanji. How say you all?"

The notched-ear Kachka looked around. The incorporation of the trive as a whole, even with pruning, was a generous offer. Even so . . . "We cannot go back defeated. Goldentrive faced a coalition of trives in a war which was resolved by a compromise. This compromise involved the invasion of your country through an ancient path, remembered. If we return defeated, the coalition will fall upon us, even Sisulia Trive, our own beloved mother, and destroy us. We cannot go back."

"Goldentrive isn't going anywhere," Dr. Raskidenji said softly. "Goldentrive is going to become Wizentrive, an entirely different entity."

"Wizentrive will return to your blessed land beyond the mountains," Wizenbeak said, "and there will be no war. Why will there be no war? Because we will win any war in which the enemy depends upon dragons. The Royal Army of Guhland will give us fifty gingals, training your warriors how to use them, your artificers how to build them."

"Wizentrive will return to your blessed land beyond the mountains," Jankura said, "and there will be no war. Why will there be no war? Because we will win any war in which the enemy depends on humans. I am Lady Jankura of the Flowers, and you, the troll-bats of what once was Goldentrive, are here because Goldentrive's own humans have hailed me as an avatar of Lady Alanji of the Flowers."

"Wizentrive will return to our blessed land beyond the mountains," Bythanastros said, "and there will be no war. Why will there be no war? Because Wizentrive will *win* any war. Not by virtue of superior strength but because of the strength of superior virtue. I am Bythanastros, the first Honorable Kivu in more than six centuries, and our enemies, Hashma Trive, Imperial Trive, and all the others, must bend with the winds of change which are blowing or be broken. Who says that we shall not return?"

"We say it," the three troll-bats said, crouching on the table. "There is no return."

Bythanastros hopped from Jankura's shoulder onto the table, and there was an audible gasp from the gallery of troll-bats and an agitated smell of musk with spice highlights. He extended his long fingers and began what Jankura suddenly realized was a courtship dance, moving slowly around the three Honorable Kachkas, who huddled together facing outward.

Bythanastros' hair stood on end, and he was now walking around the three on the tips of his fingers, crooning a song of great antiquity. The Honorable Kachka with one eye was the first to present herself, then the Honorable Kachka with silver fur, and finally the one with the notched ear.

Bythanastros mounted them one after another, and the room filled with a roiling boil of dense and complex aromas. There was no protest, no outcry. The only sound was the patter of fewmets on the grass under the pendant supporting the Honorable Kachkas newly incorporated into Wizentrive.

"We are Wizentrive," Bythanastros said. Who are you?

"We are Wizentrive," came back the scattered answer, "We are Wizentrive, we are Wizentrive, we are Wizentrive."

"Good," Jankura said. "Strike your camp and let's get moving."

23

The Last Breakfast

THE march to Saint Arvo's Hall, an abandoned monastery nearest the hole in the mountains from which Goldentrive's army had invaded Guhland, was smooth and without incident. The weather was beautiful, and both armies easily marched thirty miles a day while keeping a respectful distance from each other's picket lines at night. Nevertheless, it was the most stressful time Wizenbeak could recall. During the day he was immersed in the organization and logistics of the newly struck Wizentrive, a task requiring his entire concentration. In the evenings he had to resolve as best he might the terrible problems he would be leaving as a legacy to Guhland. He found little time for sleep and none at all for dreaming, but such was the nature of the wizardly mind that he would often discover solutions to the problems of one group when he had immersed himself in the problems of the other, scribbling notes to himself in the diptych he always carried.

On sundown of the last day of the joint march the two armies camped outside the ruined monastery. Wizentrive camped to the north, a few hundred yards from the mouth of the subterranean passage under the mountain, a giant sinkhole, the collapsed roof of a great limestone cavern, out of which had been built a wooden ramp to reach the surface. The Royal Army of Guhland camped a quarter mile to the south. The order of march under the mountain would be first the dragons, then the vanguard, then the baggage train, now augmented with gingals, then the van, then Wizenbeak with his Wizentrive bodyguard, and finally the rear guard, leaving behind him Guhland with its beaten but intransigent witchfinders and smoldering civil war.

The next morning, as Wizentrive's army marched down the ramp, Wizenbeak gathered the Guhlish officer corps into the Royal Pavilion for his farewell breakfast. When they had eaten, he stood up and took his final turn as king-patriarch.

"Well, then, gentlemen." He looked around the pavilion. "When a man takes his final leave from his friends, it is customary to distribute those goods and chattels which he must leave behind. It is also customary for him to seek to impose such order as he thinks best upon the matters to which he had set his hand." The king-patriarch coughed nervously and addressed his senior officers directly.

"General Genzari, Captain-General Murado, Count Braley, gentlemen of the Royal Army of Guhland, Tarelians . . ." He paused and recovered his voice. "My beloved Tarelians. Those before me now and those who have fallen . . . too many . . . those who have fallen under my command, I will remember and love you forever." Wizenbeak stopped and wiped his eyes, then, replacing his emerald glasses on his long nose, opened his diptych.

"Let me rehearse one last time the arguments which have so embroiled us these evenings past. First, that since I am master of Wizentrive, we should march south, an army with dragons, and restore us by *force majeure* to the throne of Guhland. To this my reply is first that one man cannot possibly be king, patriarch, and Lord of the Troll-Bats all at the same time. To do justice to you would injure or destroy them. To do justice to these creatures which are now the flesh of my flesh would entail such turmoil as to roil secular and sacred alike, violating all the oaths which we are sworn to uphold." He cleared his throat and slowly shook his head. Doing justice to troll-bats would be bad enough, but doing justice to *their* livestock would be impossible. "A second consideration is that we are not that firmly seated in control of this strange and curious army. One of the reasons for which we are obeyed is that we promise to lead them . . ." He hesitated, weighing his words against his audience. ". . . where they want to go, home."

He pushed his spectacles up on his nose and again looked over his officers. There was a third consideration, thoroughly ventilated during his daytime discussions: that Goldentrive might not be the only dragon army to come swarming out from under the mountain. That Guhland, beset by civil war, might also be overrun with dragons seemed too awful to contemplate. If possible, he intended to close the hole behind him, but the intrigues of troll-bats, trival politics, and wizardly good intentions for the future could hardly interest these brave men he was leaving behind. "The third consideration? As king of Guhland and as patriarch of the Syncretist Church, I would have given anything to rid my land of this plague of dragons which has afflicted it. As Lord of the Troll-Bats, I can joyfully lead the dragons and their supporting army home again while honoring all my oaths to church and state."

He adjusted the scrolls lined up on the table beside the dais and looked over his emerald spectacles at the audience. "By the grace of God the dragons have been sent home. What remains for me to do now is to serve the cause of peace to the best of my poor ability." Whatever doubts he had felt in the passionate debate that had racked his evenings were now quiescent. "Will Pardus Murado please step forward." The simplest steps sometimes proved the hardest to take. Murado had wanted nothing for himself but passionately desired the survival of the Tarelian Order. Wizenbeak watched his captain-general approach the improvised dais. In many ways Pardus, wanting the least, had been the most difficult to accommodate. He had been a rock against the dissolution of his beloved order, to which he had, after all, devoted life and honor. In the end it must have been the sum of many small considerations which had moved him. Probably giving land to the survivors of the order weighed more in his balance than being seized of a county in his own name. Certainly he had been touched by the ennobling of his officers, and he had been touched if not persuaded by their unanimous vote to accept the dissolution of the order on the terms offered.

The argument that the Tarelian Order might be used as the seed of an army for a Kahunista counterrevolution hadn't moved him at all. What had he said? "It is right that the Tarelian Order be in the thick of things." Contrariwise, the argument that dissolving the Tarelian Order might prevent the resumption of the civil war was one which he could honor and understand. Perhaps because that was why Wizenbeak wanted what he wanted,

Murado seemed not to hold dissolving the order against him. But probably that was no more than a rationalization he used afterward to justify the decision he was now taking.

What had brought him around? The best guess was that it was Braley saying that Syncretisty Hall was going to use the order to restore themselves to power, which was unlikely but just barely possible, and then put in their own officer corps, an act which would require removing the current leadership in disgrace. This was conjecture piled upon pure speculation, albeit rooted in the recent past. In the end he must have accepted the notion that his Tarelian Order was marching into glory with banners held high and honor fully restored as a sop to his conscience. Just as he had chosen to obey the man he had, after all, chosen to make his leader. Why was it so hard to understand such a simple man?

Wizenbeak returned Murado's crisp salute. "Captain-General Murado, we have been in some hard fights together, but this is the hardest command I have ever given and surely the hardest you will ever have to obey." He picked up one scroll from the table and held it like a marshal's baton. "This decree abolishes the Tarelian Order. Will you faithfully perform this service for your king, your patriarch, and your country?"

Murado took the scroll. "I will," he said in a firm voice. That was the final validation of the rest of the deal, which was already in the hands of the clerks. The distribution of the Church lands supporting the Tarelian Order to the survivors of the order would give each man thirty-six fertile and well-watered acres. The charter to organize a mutual assistance society would ensure that they could survive the casual aggression of powerful neighbors. His surviving officers would be rewarded with larger holdings and patents of nobility even as Murado would now secure the plum of Shemwick Abbey.

"Congratulations, Pardus Murado. Count of Shemwick," Wizenbeak said, leaning over the table to embrace him.

Count Shemwick returned to his seat, a single tear streaking unheeded down each cheek as he bore the unwelcome order which he would faithfully execute.

"Front and center, Count Braley." The count limped forward, assisted by a young aide, and Wizenbeak returned his left-handed salute. "Count Braley, our fates have been intertwined for a long, long time." He removed the two swords from his sash and held them out. "Accept these swords that I wore as Guhland's king as a mark of my high esteem."

Braley removed his own two swords and handed them to his aide, then accepted the royal swords in his good hand and awkwardly thrust them into his sash. Wizenbeak picked up a couple of battered, mismatched scroll cases and waited until the swords were secured. "These are my diaries for the past couple of years. Accept them as a mark of my deep and abiding affection." Count Braley took the diaries and handed them to his aide.

The king-patriarch then picked up a large scroll and a small one. "As an utterly inadequate recompense for your heroic services, please accept this ninety-nine-year lease to the Czajka Palace in Cymdulock. A device which my lawyers assure me will be far more difficult to repudiate than any outright transfer of title." Count Braley accepted the scroll, handing it also to his aide.

"You are, you know, inviting the most awful trouble upon yourself with this," Wizenbeak said, holding the small scroll in both hands, "but if what you want is a fencing academy, here is your royal warrant to establish the Cymdulock Institute of Strategic Studies." Braley smiled and thrust it into his bosom.

"Thank you, your Majesty. Not all of us look forward to the delights of peace and tranquillity. Through your skill and wisdom this war may at last be ending, but as long as I draw breath, I shall be a thorn in the side of our enemies." There was a standing ovation from the officer corps. Then Wizenbeak came around from behind the table to embrace him, being careful not to press the arm carried in a sling, and after Count Braley had returned to his place, the king-patriarch called for General Lasco Genzari.

In contrast to dismantling the Tarelian Order, the disposition of Yssemer Latifunda had seemed utterly intractable. The choices initially had been framed as either install the formidable Count Braley as duke, to face the immediate resumption of the civil war, or permit Marjia to choose whom she would. In that case, the land reform in the mediplano would almost certainly be undone and the civil war would resume at a time of the enemy's choosing. The solution had, in fact, been conceptually elegant if not immediately obvious.

When the question had at last been taken up for discussion, Count Braley, serving as the royal strategist, had pointed out that while he was the natural choice if they were going to continue the civil war, it might be possible to select someone less partisan in the hope that he would be acceptable to the other side. He suggested Lasco Genzari, who, as a mercenary commander being rewarded for loyal service, could be seen as a respected and traditional figure whom Mambrinistas, Kahunistas, and radical Syncretists alike should be willing to let live in peace. They might regret the loss of the late Duke Yssemer's land while also accepting Duke Genzari when Duke Braley would have been intolerable.

Genzari had demurred, voicing the consensus opinion that civil war was inevitable anyway since Queen Marjia and Duke Bedirny could not afford to let the Yssemer holdings slip through their fingers. The reason that they could not endure the loss of the Yssemer land was that they had such a tenuous hold on the throne. The truth was bitter, but self-deception was poisonous, and Wizenbeak had reluctantly accepted the analysis of his generals.

That particular problem had resolved itself the next day amid a pungent swirl of troll-bat debate rehashing some passionately disputed point of trival politics. What could Genzari give the queen and her ducal lover that would at once affirm their hold on Guhland's throne while securing his own position? The question, once asked, had answered itself. As patriarch, Wizenbeak could annul his marriage to Marjia on the grounds that it had not been consummated, thereby freeing her to marry Bedirny. Then, as king, he had only to abdicate in her favor, naming her queen without a regent to make the marriage not only possible but mandatory. His enemies had used the royal infatuation to pry him from Guhland's throne? Very well, he would use that same lever to secure the peace. Besides, for all her brattish ways, he rather liked Marjia and was not unhappy to do her one last favor.

Genzari understood at once. With the Royal Army still at his command, he could install himself as Duke of Yssemer de facto, and with the two documents as leverage, he could persuade the queen to accept him as the de jure duke as well. By embracing him, she would achieve her heart's desire, which was to wed Bedirny. Simultaneously, and quite unintentionally, she would be ending the civil war in the most pallid of victories for the rebellious Syncretists.

Their faction would indeed have regained the throne of Guhland, but one so crippled that it could not wage war and now compromised by making a separate peace with their enemies. Besides, Duke Bedirny, so seemingly desirable when they were looking for anyone who would destroy the hated Wizenbeak, was not at all the one they would have freely chosen, being hopelessly moderate and, except for his affair with Queen Marjia, an otherwise loyal supporter of the detestable wizard Wizenbeak. By freely renouncing a throne which was already lost and beyond hope of redemption, Wizenbeak's faction would be able to change sides by loyally supporting the new king and queen, who would be legitimized and strengthened thereby. Which meant that the opposition could neither continue to prosecute the civil war nor restore the status quo ante.

Wizenbeak returned Genzari's salute. "For you, old friend, we have three things. Use them wisely and bring peace to Guhland." Lasco Genzari nodded stiffly. "The first invests you with title to the Yssemer Latifunda." The king-patriarch took the scroll in his left hand.

"The second is the patriarch's decree divorcing my beloved wife, Marjia." Wizenbeak took the second scroll in his left hand and picked up the third. Then he paused.

Now that matters had come to the point, a wholly unexpected pang of grief stabbed at his heart. The corners of his mouth turned down, and he mumbled something inaudible. "What did you say, sir?" Genzari asked, leaning forward.

"I will be king of Guhland no more forever," the wizard whispered in a choked voice. Then he recovered a measure of composure and continued. "This is my abdication as king of Guhland, naming Princess Marjia as queen in her own right. Good luck and may God be with you." He handed over the three scrolls to Genzari, who took them in his left hand and saluted with his right, a point they had discussed at some length. If Duke Genzari was to make peace with their enemies, it would be well to seem distanced from his departing master.

After he returned to his seat, Wizenbeak picked up the final scroll. "I have abdicated as king of Guhland. As Patriarch, I now ratify the decision of the Council of Deacons urging the abolition of that office and that title and also abolition of the Congregation of Clerisiarchs." He smiled and handed the scroll to one of his clerks. "It is so ordered. Make copies and see that they are widely distributed." Then he removed the patriarchal signet ring from his forefinger. "The tokens of my reign as your king—crowns, sigils, scepters, and the like—have all been returned to the Royal Treasury whence most of them came. This, however . . ." He held it up for all to see and closed it in his fist. "After all this trouble a man is entitled to a souvenir, so since Guhland will also have patriarchs no more, this ring will be mine." He opened his fist, displaying the empty palm, and received a standing ovation for what was, after all, a very simple bit of sleight of hand.

And that was the end of it. As Wizenbeak and Jankura were waiting for Wizentrive's bodyguard to form up, Pardus Murado asked him a last question. "Your M— ah . . . Doctor Wizenbeak, how could you ever bring yourself to give up all that pomp and power?"

The wizard, his mind elsewhere, answered without thinking. "I did it for love."

"Oh?" Murado blinked. "Of Guhland?"

Oh, hell, the wizard thought, did I say love? Wizenbeak pulled his attention back to the question at hand. How do I slide out of this? Love of Jankura, who has so much of what I loved in Shaia? Love of Marjia, my child bride who held Shaia's spirit? I can't tell Pardus that; he'd think I was bedding the lot of them. Love of Bythanastros, in many ways so much better than my little Gruchka, and so much more? God knows what he'd think I was doing with the troll-bat. "Of course," he said without missing a beat. "For Guhland, of course. What else? Good-bye, old comrade."

They embraced one final time, and Wizenbeak, seeing that the procession was ready to move, went to join Jankura, Raskidenji, and Bythanastros.

24

At the Ending, Nice and Tidy

WIZENTRIVE. It is reasonable to believe that they lived in interesting times ever after, but the archives of Guhland make no further mention of Wizenbeak, Jankura, Raskidenji, and their several troll-bats.

In Cymdulock, Queen Marjia married Duke Bedirny. Duke Genzari, Count Braley, and Pardus Murado all prospered after their fashion, for while Guhland was not at war, neither was it at peace, and they lived in times that were sufficiently interesting for any reasonable man.

Epilogue

WIZENBEAK and company, although gone, were not forgotten. The Cymdulock Institute of Strategic Studies eventually issued a small volume, *Wizenbeak's Campaigns*, which became a military classic, and a large volume, *The Annotated Diaries*, which was put on the burn-before-reading list by both the Orthodox and Syncretist churches.

On the seventh anniversary of his passage under the mountain the Orthodox Church made Wizenbeak a saint. The Syncretist Church, which could hardly utter his name except as an imprecation, did just the opposite, naming him as the Lord of the Troll-Bats, a lesser demon now promoted to the first rank. While acknowledging in theory that he had been sent as a scourge of God to cleanse the unnamed wickedness of the now abolished clerisy, they canonized Patriarch Gorabani and wrote Patriarch Wizenbeak out of ecclesiastical history by the simple expedient of ending patriarchy and the Congregation of Clerisiarchs at Gorabani's resignation.

Lady Jankura fared rather differently. The Orthodox hardly mentioned her at all, even as Saint Wizenbeak's faithful assistant. In contrast, the Syncretists embraced her as the avatar of Saint Posalanji, giving her full credit for the divine intervention which had removed the dragons from the land, thereby using the heavenly radiance emanating from her presence to obscure the existence of her master. Even Shaia, the late and much hated Witch-Queen, was now understood to fill the honorable role of failed avatar whose necessary failure made possible the glorious success of Lady Jankura.